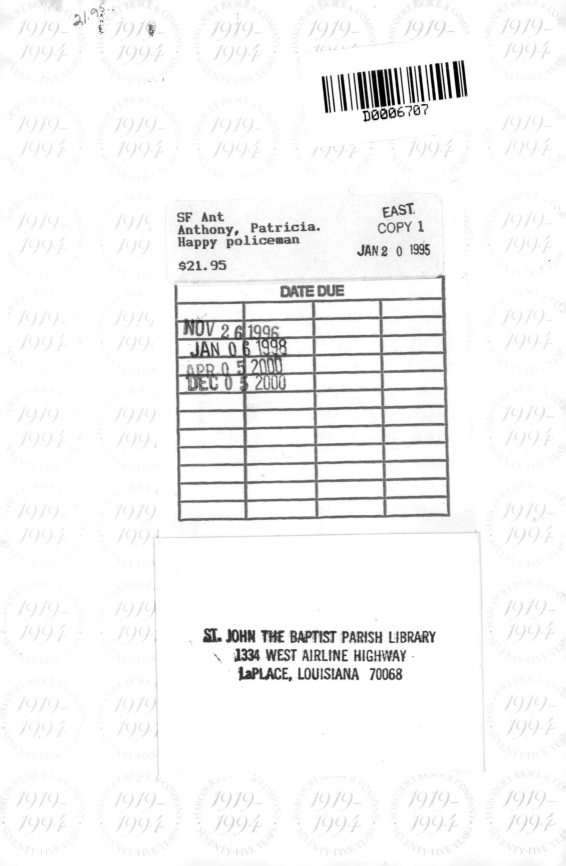

HAPPY
POLICEMAN

PATRICIA ANTHONY

HAPPY POLICEMAN

HARCOURT BRACE & COMPANY

New York San Diego London

Requests for permission to make copies
of any part of the work should be mailed to:
Permissions Department, Harcourt Brace & Company,
6277 Sea Harbor Drive, Orlando, Florida 32887-6777.

Library of Congress Cataloging-in-Publication Data
Anthony, Patricia.
Happy policeman/Patricia Anthony. — 1st ed.
p.   cm.
ISBN 0-15-138478-9
1. City and town life — Texas — Fiction.
2. Police — Texas — Fiction.   I. Title.
PS3551.N727H36   1994
813'.54 — dc20   93-42949

Designed by Linda Lockowitz
Printed in the United States of America
First edition
A B C D E

A good editorial job is,
by its very nature, invisible;
only poor jobs attract notice.
Unfortunately for him — very fortunately
for me — you cannot see the work
of my co-conspirator,
Michael Kandel.

1

ON HIS WAY to see B.J.'s alleged body, Police Chief DeWitt Dawson noticed that the window of Coomey Hardware was broken. Since B.J. had also once reported a prowler whose "scary white face" turned out to be Hereford, DeWitt reined in his mare.

The early morning shopper had swept the glass into a pile, using one of the store's brooms. It lay propped in the bright fall sun against the front door, price tag dangling. A telltale trickle of chicken feed led down the sidewalk and stopped at the point where the shopper — Etta Wilson? Gene Selby? — had noticed the hole in the bag.

DeWitt dutifully marked the broken window in his book, then dismounted, and on the back of a traffic violation slip wrote a note which he stuck in the empty frame: *Harlan. I'm getting tired of this. From now on, leave your store unlocked.*

Monday morning, downtown was deserted. The head-in parking spaces were empty, the meters all showing their red EXPIRED. The only car in sight was Webster Riley's Pontiac, and it sat abandoned in the intersection of Main and Poteet.

DeWitt rode on. A half block away, at the Mobil station, Webster was trying to milk a few drops from the pump. Before the man could lift his accusing gaze from the red-and-yellow gas can, DeWitt kicked the bay into a trot.

He skirted Guadalupe, riding three blocks out of his way. Cars or not, Bo would be lurking in wait at the town's single red light. DeWitt didn't want to see him. He suspected that his junior officer lived in a state of constant expectation where every speeder was hauling dope and every runner of a red light was a DWI. The idea of a dead body might get him overheated.

At the bend of the road, a lone UPS van sat in the gravel parking lot of the Biblical Truth Church. Through the open doorway DeWitt caught sight of full pews. No gas, but the true believers had walked. Pastor Jimmy's voice drifted from the church, cold as the breeze, brash as the sunlight. Damn him. Preaching about demons. With that UPS van parked there.

DeWitt, now in a mood, kicked his horse harder than he meant to. She bolted into a dead run. He let her have her head until he turned off at an old logging road. Until branches along the brush-choked trail slapped the fury out of him. He hauled back on the reins. The mare pulled up short, lathered and blowing hard.

Something big had come down the rutted clay road. And recently. There were fresh tire tracks, broken saplings. Feeling the first thrill of unease, DeWitt dismounted. He and the mare climbed the slope together. By the time they reached the balding crest of Sparrow Point, they had both cooled off.

The hill was quiet but for a grackle whistling atonally in the brush. To the east lay the Line. Paisley today, like a bad 60's tie.

DeWitt dropped the reins. Sticking out from a bush was a pair of shoeless feet. He walked closer: legs. Copious naked torso. Shocking casaba-melon breasts. And a face—Loretta Harper's.

The Mary Kay rep had been dead for hours, and her skin was the color of old newspaper.

Oh crap, DeWitt thought.

Leaf-filtered sun threw spotlights across the nude body as though some puckish god had chosen to grant Loretta a belated fame. Her thunder thighs were spread as wide as a picture in a cheap beaver magazine. One blue eye was staring with idiot interest at a brown oak leaf near her nose. The other eye was missing. The flesh of her cheek and the skin at her neck had burst apart, exposing the tough, pale tube of the larynx.

Swallowing hard, DeWitt reached into his pocket for a cigarette, his mind fallen back six years to the forbidden habit. Encountering only his ballpoint Bic, he pulled off the blue plastic top, slipped it into his mouth, and looked around.

Between the chalky caliche outcroppings were more tire tracks. And scuff marks, evidence that something Loretta-sized, Loretta-heavy, had been dragged.

The shade by the body was cold. The air held the sour smell of autumn. DeWitt knelt by the body, wondering how he could make the death look like an accident.

The deep-throated purr of a car engine brought his head up fast. A red Bronco was inching up the gravel trail. It stopped, and Doc and Purdy climbed out. B.J. had been on the phone again.

"Y'all been hoarding gas." DeWitt walked down the incline to greet the pair.

"Got to hoard a little, the way you been laying down on the job." Doc ran trembling morning-after fingers through his Van Dyke. The wind whipped his overcoat about his legs. A little taller, and the diminutive physician would have been a ringer for Lenin.

"I told them about it. They're just slow."

"You're missing your cigarettes, ain't ya?" Doc peered closely

3

at the pen top. "Had an ex-wife went through the menopause easier than that."

Purdy Phifer emitted a whinnying giggle. A flat black look from DeWitt shut him up. DeWitt was anxious. There was a cramp of nicotine hunger in his chest that the pen top couldn't quell. If his pistol hadn't been confiscated, he might have shot Purdy just because he hated that laugh.

"Well, what's going on?" Doc asked. "Bo had his shorts in a wad. Told Purdy to get his camera and me and come on up here. But you know how Bo is."

Glum now, DeWitt nodded.

"Anal-retentive, like," Doc went on.

Purdy pointed. "Is that a foot?"

DeWitt tracked the plumb line of Purdy's finger.

"That *is!*" Purdy crowed. "It's a *foot!*"

Doc and DeWitt followed the tubby photographer to the glade. They stood and looked at the corpse for a while.

"Jesus." Purdy's voice was high-pitched with excitement. "She been murdered?"

"No, Purdy," Doc said. "She come out here, took off all her clothes, spread-eagled herself and gouged out her eye. DeWitt, damn it. Why don't you cover her up?"

"Can't," Purdy told them. "Bo said to take lots of black and white stills."

The pen top gave as DeWitt angrily bit down.

As Purdy bent with fat difficulty in order to snap a crotch shot, the roar of a motorcycle split the silence. DeWitt hurriedly took the pen top from his mouth and tossed it away.

"You got mud obscuring your license plate, Doc." Bo set his kickstand and walked up the hill toward them. His uniform was spick and span; his motorcycle boots spotless. "I'll let you go this

4

time, but get it cleaned off before I have to cite you. Well, well. DeWitt. What tears you away from your vandalism lists?"

DeWitt planted himself between his junior officer and the corpse. He stared hard into the man's mirror sunglasses and then dropped his gaze to the Dudley Do-Right chin. "Better get back into town, Bo. Folks'll start running that red light."

Bo's words were strung like birds on a wire, like clothespins on a line, linked by thin contempt. "You weren't going to tell me about the murder, were you." In a sad half-whisper he repeated, "Were you."

Bo knelt by the body, snapped on a pair of surgeon's gloves, and picked up the pen top. "Evidence," he said with triumph.

"Mine," DeWitt said.

Bo's smile faded. "Well. No blood. Must have been killed somewhere else and dragged here. You can see the marks in the weeds."

Killed. DeWitt tested the flavor of the word and found it bitter.

Now Bo was playing This Little Piggy with Loretta's stiff fingers. "Rigor's set in. It misted rain about five this morning. Ground's dry under her. Purdy. There's a clear bit of tread mark in that soft spot. Make sure you get a picture of that."

Maybe we could say Loretta drowned, DeWitt thought. It had rained harder than Bo imagined. The force of the flood tore Loretta's clothes from her back. Her neck was ripped open on the rocks. And the rising waters deposited her here. Right here, he thought in faltering hope, some fifty yards up the rise.

"This wound's been busted out, like it was exploded from underneath," Bo said. "There's no murder weapon I know of that could do this. You know what it looks like. I'll bet—"

"Just shut your goddamned mouth!" DeWitt shouted.

5

Purdy circumspectly stepped back.

"Don't you see?" DeWitt said. "We have to keep quiet. We have to goddamned *think!* All right, we have a body, but anything could have happened. No telling what—"

"When's the last time any of y'all seen her alive?" Bo asked.

DeWitt looked to Doc for help, but Doc was contemplating Loretta.

"When?" Bo asked.

Purdy scratched his ass. "I'm thinking. I'm thinking."

"She probably went to church last night," Doc said. "Loretta never misses church. All them church folks are addicted to that talk about demons."

The dawn of conclusion broke over Bo's face. "Demons. There. That's the motive."

DeWitt shoved Bo aside. "Let's get her into town. Who all's gonna help me?"

Purdy made a few sounds suggestive of gagging.

"Wait a minute." Bo dusted his hands. "Curtis needs to see the homicide scene first. It's Texas law."

"Fuck Texas law." DeWitt grabbed one of Loretta's arms. The body was cold and clammy, the touch of it between fish and flesh. DeWitt pulled, not getting far.

"Damn it, DeWitt," Doc said. "Your back won't take much of that. Help him, for Christ's sake, Purdy. Be useful for once."

Purdy picked up an ankle as though he were a decorator forced by his clients to consider a knotty pine lamp. At the count of three, Purdy let the ankle slip from his grasp.

"She's too heavy," Purdy said.

DeWitt said, "She'll get to stinking if we don't do something soon."

"All right, all right." Doc bent to seize Loretta's calf at the five-o'clock shadow. It took the efforts of Purdy and Doc and

DeWitt to carry her. Still grumbling, Bo followed them down the rise.

They shoved her into the back of the Bronco. Her torso slid in easily. Her legs didn't. They were spread too wide, and no amount of coaxing could unspread them.

They turned her sideways, but her toes caught on the roof. By mutual consent, the three gave up and stood by the tailgate of the Bronco, panting. DeWitt stared blankly at Loretta's open crotch and then looked quickly away. "Check for semen, Doc."

"Come on, DeWitt. Nobody would have raped—" Bo began.

"Doc," DeWitt growled. "Check for semen."

Doc gave DeWitt a just-between-us look. Around his eyes the skin was sickroom gray; his cheeks were a festive, alcoholic red. Doc was a man of contrasts. "Chief. You'll want to inform Billy."

"I'll take care of that," Bo said.

Doc winced.

"No need, Bo. I will." DeWitt took off his leather jacket and covered the strategic parts of the body. There was a lot to cover, and he had to arrange carefully.

Watching DeWitt fuss with the naked corpse, Purdy snickered. DeWitt cast one baleful glance at the doctor, then all three men convulsed into helpless guffaws. And Bo's lips tightened into a disapproving scowl.

2

NOBODY WAS AT LORETTA'S, so DeWitt rode the four miles to Billy's place. The remodeling was nearly finished: the roof was on; the siding nailed up. From inside the new game room came the screech of a saw.

DeWitt dismounted and walked the planks to the rectangular hole where the new front door would be. In the yard a few islands of spiky grass rose from an ocean of ankle-deep mud.

Inside, he paused. The house smelled of moist concrete, latex paint, and solvent. The ear-splitting whine of the saw ended abruptly.

DeWitt made his way down the hall and into the barren kitchen. Loretta's whipcord-thin estranged husband, pencil in hand, was measuring a two-by-four laid across a pair of sawhorses.

"Billy."

The man whirled. "Chief. You scared me."

A forelock of lank hair fell into Billy's eyes. He flicked it away like a girl. At his neck was a ponytail caught by a pink rubber band. Despite that, there was nothing feminine about Billy.

Nothing masculine about him, either. He reminded DeWitt of his traumatic childhood glimpse of a weasel, gutted and skinned, its ropy muscles still oozing blood and its lips pulled back in a snarl from its needle teeth.

"Where's your kids?" DeWitt's question echoed across the unfinished concrete floor. The sheetrock was primed for paper, but the paper hadn't been applied yet. The only color in the room was the red of Billy's shirt and the faded blue of his jeans.

"Might ask Loretta."

"Loretta's dead."

Billy's hand froze reaching for a planer. He turned, fists clenched, veins and muscles standing out in relief along his forearms. Under his open shirt, his board-flat stomach rose and fell in a slow, regular rhythm. Either the news hadn't sunk in yet, or the death wasn't news at all.

DeWitt waited for Billy to speak. He'd never had a murder to solve, but over the years he'd had heart attacks and car wrecks to announce. The family always asked how; and then they asked where the person was, as though DeWitt could direct traffic to the afterlife.

Billy kept his mouth shut, and DeWitt, suspicions aroused, made the decision not to speak first. They waited, the silence getting bigger and bigger until it filled the raw corners of the room. Outside the unglazed windows, a bluejay squalled.

The black eyes shifted. "Dead?"

"That's right."

They played the waiting game some more; then, "Y'all want me to come identify the body or something?"

"We already identified it. Just wanted you to know."

Billy nodded.

"Where were you last night?"

"Was asleep."

"From when to when?"

"Soon as it was dark I went to sleep. Woke up at dawn."

"You got any witnesses?"

"Nope."

"Where's your kids?"

"Don't have no idea."

"Aren't you interested in how she died?"

Beneath the waterfall of greasy hair, Billy's eyes shone with reflected light. "Already know. Sometimes I know stuff like that. Dream about it and all. Loretta done wrapped that titty-pink Regal of hers around a tree. Your fault, damn you, for letting her drive like a maniac. Should of let Bo put her in jail for speeding."

Billy sounded so sure that DeWitt wondered, briefly, if he should go back to the crime scene and dig around in the dirt for the Buick.

Then he took a breath and actually said it: "She was murdered."

There was no motion in the face, no lift of an eyebrow, no frown. The planer dropped to the concrete with a clang. "Who done it?"

"Don't know that."

"How'd they do it?"

"Don't know that, either. Yet." Nothing in Billy's array of tools could have made that unique and puzzling wound; and if Billy were going to kill someone, he'd shoot a staple into the cranium. He'd shove a screwdriver into the eye. Billy was a practical sort of man.

"You best have a talk with Hubert Foster."

"Why Foster?" DeWitt asked.

"Overheard her discussing him during one of her phone-in hen parties. She was whispering, so I couldn't pick out more'n his name. You best talk to him. If I question that horny bastard, I'll start out by molly-bolting his balls to a door."

"Who was on the receiving end of that conversation?"

"Don't have no idea. Could have been any of them Mary Kay church biddies she gossiped with. Don't think about not telling me what you find out, now. Goddamn it, I'm holding you accountable. And if you know what's good for you, you better see what Foster done with my kids."

DeWitt started out the door, eerily aware of the man's presence at his back. At bad news some people cried; and some became angry at the messenger. DeWitt thought of the planer on the floor, the nail gun on the bench. If it wouldn't have looked ridiculous, he might have run for his life.

3

KICKING THE MARE INTO A GALLOP, DeWitt rode to the lake. At the Drop On By Bait House the screen door was standing open, the wooden porch empty.

Across the water, its surface smooth as glossy olive paper, rose a stand of pines. Beyond that was the Line, its paisley clashing with the sky's powder-blue horizon.

DeWitt walked inside the convenience store and stopped. A yellow dog had dragged a family-sized bag of Lay's potato chips from a shelf, had torn it open and was feasting. Golden flecks were stuck to the dog's pink nose. The retriever looked up, still domesticated enough for guilt.

"Get!" DeWitt hissed.

The dog slunk out the door.

DeWitt walked the center aisle and picked up a pack of Twinkies. "Curtis?"

The counter was empty, the cash register open. "Curtis? You in back?" Down the next aisle DeWitt pulled a can of Coke from the cooler. He popped the top and took a long, burning gulp. The Coke was so cold, it made his sinuses ache. He tore open the edge of the Twinkies package with his teeth and took a bite of greasy cake. "Curtis?"

No one answered. DeWitt put down the Twinkie and walked across the yard to the house.

Curtis answered his knock. The mayor's round face was puffy with sleep, and his receding hair stuck up in brown explosions. He was still in his bedclothes. Fighting a smile, DeWitt studied the pajamas. They were cotton and had faded blue sheep on them.

"Dog was in the stock. You got a mess back there."

"Dog can have it." Curtis walked into the kitchen.

DeWitt followed. "You seen Loretta's kids today?"

"Nope."

In Curtis's sink dirty plates sprouted like Melmac fungus. Creature-from-the-Black-Lagoon dishwater made a high-tide line on the stainless steel. "When's the last time you seen 'em?"

"Why?"

"Well, they hang around here a lot, don't they? Fishing and all? You know of anything Hubert Foster could have had against Loretta?"

Curtis plucked a cracked mug from the sink and poured himself some coffee from a dented pot. "No. Want a cup?"

DeWitt's mouth twitched. "Nuh-uh."

"Why the third degree?"

This time the words came easier. "Loretta's been murdered."

Curtis spasmed, spilling coffee. "Jesus H. Christ on a crutch." His eyes were so wide that the whites haloed the brown irises. He looked at DeWitt and then at the floor. It was hard to distinguish the new coffee stain from the historical. "You say murdered? Who the hell done it?"

"Don't know yet."

"Shit's gonna hit the fan, DeWitt. Man. Oh, man. I need some." Curtis looked up fast. "You want a little?"

The shit *was* going to hit the fan. And there was nothing DeWitt could do about it. "Hell, why not?" He slugged down the rest of his Coke and tagged after Curtis.

In the cramped bathroom, weak sunlight struggled to penetrate a high, dirty window. As Curtis locked the door, DeWitt perched in the meager glow at the edge of the tub.

Curtis dug his hand into a cracked ginger jar. "How'd they do it?"

"Huh?"

"How'd they kill her?"

"Don't know that exactly, either. But she was naked. It was terrible."

Curtis laughed, then clapped a censorious hand over his mouth. "Sorry. Poor Loretta was just butt-ugly."

"Yeah, well . . . it was awful that way, too."

Rolling a scrap of corn husk into a cylinder, Curtis picked up a greasy box of kitchen matches, lit the joint, and took a toke before passing it.

DeWitt sucked smoke; hitched it deep. "You have the right to remain silent . . ."

It was an old joke, and Curtis ignored it. He lowered the seat of the commode and sat. The bathroom was so small that the two men's knees touched. When they got to the end of the joint, Curtis lit another and handed it to DeWitt.

"How come you don't know how they killed her?"

DeWitt inhaled the reply. "Weapon."

Curtis studied the burning end of the joint critically before taking another drag. "I mean, was she stabbed or strangled or what?"

"Her throat was torn apart."

Curtis nodded sagely. "Werewolves."

A whoop of laughter. DeWitt slipped off the tub and onto the damp floor, where he got tangled in Curtis's feet.

"Think about it, boy. That dog you seen in the store could have been one."

The tile at DeWitt's back felt clammy and chill. "No blood left in her body, either." He pinched the dwindling roach from the mayor's fingers.

"You just think about it, DeWitt. Do you know what these people around here do when the moon's full?"

Upside down, Curtis's face seemed less comical and more menacing. "You always like to scare me when I'm high."

"I want you to think werewolves, DeWitt. I want you to think vampires. See, werewolves you can lock up in jail, but vampires—"

Tap.

At the soft knock, both men turned, DeWitt having to roll around on the littered floor.

Tap.

DeWitt and Curtis looked at each other. The joint was tweezered between Curtis's thumb and middle fingernail. Suddenly his eyes widened. "Wittie? Did you order me a delivery?"

"Shit!"

Raising the commode lid, Curtis dropped the joint inside the bowl and flushed. DeWitt clambered to his feet and threw open the bathroom window. A fresh breeze and an anthem of sunlight burst through the close, hot room.

"Just a minute!" Curtis shouted. "I'll be with you in just a minute!"

DeWitt waved his arms. Curtis flapped a towel.

"I'm fucking wasted," Curtis said in a low, pained voice. "God, I'm so fucking wasted."

Tap.

"Just a sec! Jesus Christ, Wittie. I look okay?"

DeWitt looked at the blue sheep and bit his lip to curb a laugh. Curtis unlocked the bathroom door and slipped into the hall. There was a muffled conversation.

"DeWitt." The voice was Curtis's.

DeWitt stood, shoulders against the peeling wood.

"DeWitt. They know you're here, and they want to talk."

Opening the door, DeWitt eased around the jamb. Kol Seresen's bulbous eyes, the hue of shrimp jelly on a blue plate, were trained on DeWitt's face. The Torku leader's hands swelled like balloons, then slowly deflated. His skin, a living mood ring, changed from mottled brown to beige.

DeWitt tried to straighten his uniform. Curtis stood next to him, his bare toes twitching on the hardwood floor.

The Torku gave silence as good as Billy did. Maybe better.

"How are you, Seresen?" DeWitt asked when he couldn't take the tension anymore.

"There is gas." The small alien pivoted and walked out the front door, his Banana Republic shirt flapping around him.

"He knows!" Curtis whispered urgently as the screen door banged shut. "He's figured it out and he's going after my stash!"

Padding hurriedly into the bathroom, slipping a little on the wet tiles, Curtis grabbed the ginger jar. He fled into the bedroom.

DeWitt trailed after. The mayor's king-size waterbed was in magnificent disarray. The mayor himself was standing knee-deep in clutter, the jar clutched to his belly. "You're a cop. What should I do?"

"Don't act suspicious."

Curtis dropped to the bed and, bobbing on its agitated, vinyl waves, curled himself around the jar. "I won't let this go extinct the way cigarettes and booze did. I'm telling you right now, DeWitt, they'll have to kill me."

"You think somebody told them about the murder?"

"Look out the window!" Curtis hissed. "See if they're in the garden."

DeWitt peeked through the dusty blinds. No Torku were roaming the privacy-fenced rows of green plants. "Nope."

"Go and talk to them, DeWitt. Make sure they're not planning nothing. I got these thoughts of them with aerosol cans of Agent Orange."

DeWitt walked outside. Four Torku were taking boxes from a brown UPS van and carrying them into the store, giving DeWitt's grazing bay mare a wide berth.

Behind the wall of video machines, DeWitt found Seresen. The Kol had turned his normal brown again and was loading six packs of Cokes into the cooler.

"You may go fill your car now," the alien said. "There is gas, as I told you."

"Thanks."

Seresen finished with the Cokes and began stacking Jimmy Dean sausage biscuits, the hot first and then the mild. Around the other end of the aisle, a Torku had found a broom and was sweeping up the remains of the dog's impromptu snack.

"Is that all you wanted to talk to me about, Seresen? To tell me about the gas? There's nothing else on your mind?"

The disorienting eyes, more a murky pink in the gloom than blue, stared holes through DeWitt. Suddenly Seresen lowered his gaze and continued stacking. "The gas seems important to you. You complain about it."

Reaching past Seresen into the cool depths of the cardboard box, DeWitt took out a tuna fish sandwich. He stripped the plastic wrap from the end, extracted the soggy bread, took a bite and winced. The Torku imitations were exact: Nothing was ever worse; and, certainly, nothing was ever better.

"The Bo is upset," Seresen said.

Bread stuck in DeWitt's throat. He choked. Seresen absently handed him a diet Dr Pepper.

"I don't understand why. I thought you might explain it."

The Dr Pepper was warm. When it hit DeWitt's stomach, nerves nearly made it come up again. He belched wetly.

"Oh. Somebody died. He tell you that?"

The pink eyes dropped to a carton of Sara Lee brownies. "Yes."

"Well. That's all there is to it. Somebody died."

The boneless fingers fondled the boxes in what the humans called "Torku foreplay." DeWitt thought that perhaps Torku skin was different. It looked softer and thinner somehow, as though the nerves were exposed. When the Torku shook hands with humans, which they sometimes did, the hand would swell and the skin harden as if to protect themselves from the touch. DeWitt imagined that the aliens could sense more through their skin than other creatures could; that they could taste through it, and even smell out lies.

Seresen didn't bother to look up from his unloading. "There is no use being upset about such things. It is harmful. You must warn the Bo about that."

4

Police business demanded DeWitt's return to town. A mellow high drew him the opposite direction.

Leaving his horse in Hattie's show barn so the mare couldn't be seen from the road, he hurried across the yard, an anticipatory swelling in his pants.

Hattie was in the kitchen staring at a wastebasket so ugly that it had to have come from Granger's workshop. DeWitt thrust his pelvis forward, a surprise gift.

"All yours."

She ignored him. "Granger's doing things with wooden trash cans and dried flowers and gold paint. It's sort of his spray paint and environmental period."

Unzipping his pants, DeWitt shoved her hand into the front of his shorts. "Come on, come on, Hattie. Have a Torku handshake."

She grabbed him, fingernails first. It was like being nipped by an annoyed dog. At the unexpected pain, he moved away, a wilting, a deflated man. "You could have just *told* me you didn't want to."

"How would you know what I want, DeWitt? You never ask."

DeWitt needed Hattie in an intense but simple way, as an itch needs a scratch. "Are you in one of your moods? If you want me to leave, Hattie, just goddamned *tell* me."

Putting the wastebasket down, Hattie walked to the hall. Still hopeful, he followed. It was in the bedroom, with the door closed and locked behind them, that he was sure he would have what he came for.

They undressed and got into bed. DeWitt didn't waste time exploring Hattie's familiar territory. He assumed the missionary position and, with one ear, listened for the sound of her teenaged sons' return.

The instant before climax he pictured Janet beneath him; and after he came, he rolled away—a distance without promises.

"If you're mad about Bo taking charge of the case, why aren't you out looking for the murderer?" Hattie asked when he told her about Loretta.

DeWitt put a hand on her breast and replied, "I'm working on it," before realizing the evident fallacy in what he had said.

"Any suspects?"

He cleared his throat. "Well, Billy implicated Hubert Foster, but I have the feeling he's just trying to avoid suspicion himself."

From their tumble in bed, Hattie's brown curly hair had gone nappy. The glow from the window highlighted the furrows of encroaching age on her cheeks. "It's such a cliché to suspect the next of kin."

That stung. "So where were you last night?"

"Asleep. You want to bring my boys in as witnesses?"

"I'm making a point. Billy is an estranged spouse. Police build cases on opportunity *and* motive. You don't have a motive that I know of."

"I suppose if Janet died under suspicious circumstances, I'd be the first one you'd interrogate."

Tight-lipped, he sat up. It scared him when Hattie mentioned his wife. It sounded like she expected something from him, as if she were an honest-to-God mistress. "Who do *you* think did it?"

"The Torku."

An abrupt intake of air made him cough. Hattie pounded him on the back. She had hard hands and strong, mannish arms. The pummeling nearly knocked him out of bed.

"Think about it, DeWitt. From what you told me of the fatal wound—"

"You don't know shit about police work, Hattie. And I don't want to talk about this."

"The kids are missing. Bo's right, the Torku had to have done it. A man isn't going to kill his own kids."

"Before Bomb Day it used to happen all the time, remember? Remember how the real world used to be?" His tone was sharp.

Hers wasn't. She was careful: a cultured bull in a china shop relationship. "Yes. But we don't have the same pressures we used to have. I think a good deal of those murders were economic. The—"

He swiveled, put his feet on the floor. His angry words came out as if shot from a cannon. "What kneejerk liberal shit!"

The bed bounced. He turned to see her sitting ramrod straight, her small breasts still jiggling. "Don't patronize me!"

The tears in her eyes startled him. "Hattie? What's the—"

"Jesus God! I don't know why the Torku bothered with us. Why didn't they save innocent people? There must have been lots of innocents to choose from: folks in Norway or Spain or Poland."

"Maybe they did. Maybe . . ."

21

"Don't you get it yet? There *is* no one left out there. Reagan dropped the bomb. He dropped the damned bomb, Wittie. You thought Mondale and Carter were pussies. Well, was nuclear war macho enough, DeWitt?"

A vein in his neck throbbed. "Goddamn it. This city council thing's gone to your head. Why do you always bring politics into everything? You're not running for reelection. Besides, the Russians attacked us."

"How could they? Chernenko was dying. Who was left to push the button? Reagan figured he'd catch the Soviets with their pants down."

Crises magnetized beliefs; they created polarities. If Pastor Jimmy divided the world into sinners and believers, Hattie divided it into those who had voted Republican and those who had not. Still, what she said made uncomfortable sense. The responsibility for the war was so compelling a question, in fact, that DeWitt refused to think about it.

"Why are you getting upset? You should like the Torku. Big Brother dole. A chicken in every pot."

"God! I hate when you do this." She floundered among the sea of covers, raising whitecaps of sheet and waves of comforter.

"Do what? What am I doing?"

"Making me angry. Evading the question by starting an argument."

"I didn't start this." DeWitt lurched to his feet and began furiously pulling on his clothes. Hattie was standing, facing him, stark naked. She was thinner than Janet. And older. At the fold beneath her stomach was a line of tired, sagging skin. Her pelvic bones poked at her hips. She was sad and pensive suddenly, a homely orphan watching a prospective set of parents leave the shelter without her.

"It must be time to go, right? That's why you're pushing me away."

"Don't exaggerate, Hattie, I—"

"Fighting with me makes it easy for you to go home to Janet."

Tottering on one leg, DeWitt tried to pull on his boot. His foot stuck halfway in. "We set up rules two years ago, remember? My home life is none of your business."

"What *do* you want to talk about?" She grabbed him by the arm, tried to force him to look at her. He steadied himself on her dresser and averted his eyes. "The murder has changed everything, don't you see that? God. If Bo wasn't around, you'd go on doing what you always do, wouldn't you. You'd drive around drinking coffee and writing up what the Torku need to get done. You're Seresen's gofer!"

DeWitt wrenched from her grip and lumbered off, buttoning his shirt. His left boot hit the floor with a solid tap; his right boot, still only halfway on, made a double clunk. He bent and, grasping the sides of the boot, jerked upward. The sudden, clumsy move toppled him, and he landed on the throw rug, a pile of embarrassed fury.

Hattie's lips twitched. She snickered.

"Shut up! Just shut the hell up! You're not my goddamned wife!" DeWitt tugged on the boot and rose.

A whispered, "I love you."

He ducked as though the whisper had been a hard object thrown at him.

"I can't help it, Wittie. I love you."

He couldn't give her the reply she wanted, and he couldn't help that, either. He squeezed his eyes shut. Hattie was a strong woman, a self-reliant woman. DeWitt was her only vice. "Don't make this more than it is. It's not even an affair, it's a goddamned friendship. Besides, Hattie, if you really loved me, you wouldn't keep pushing me away. Jesus. I don't know why I come back."

"You like Torku handshake."

He laughed. When he opened his eyes, he was surprised to see she was crying.

5

Pastor Jimmy Schoen could smell sin. He smelled it through his telescope when he caught sight of the adulterer leading his mare into Hattie Nichols's barn. He could smell it lingering like sulphurous aftershave on the godless doctor. He could smell it in the pharmacy, too. Sin stank of brimstone and burning insulation.

He could smell it around the condom rack and on the black teenager who was surreptitiously studying the stock. And when Purdy Phifer came in, the stench of homosexuality nearly overpowered him.

"Hey, pastor!" Purdy called.

Schoen riveted his gaze to the shelves of analgesics. Picking out the store brand of aspirin, he walked to the rear counter.

"Hey!"

Turning down an aisle, Schoen left the little man between the cold remedies and the laxatives. Reaching the back counter, he rang for the pharmacist. When no one came to check him out, he dug into his pocket and got a folded Bible verse.

It wasn't right not to pay for things, Schoen thought as he laid the small slip of paper next to the register. Handouts made life too easy, like the smooth, well-traveled road to damnation.

God was testing Coomey for idle hands. The Lord probably had some divine nitrate test which He could paint on your fingers. *You,* God would thunder when the solution turned color, *you have been idle.*

But Schoen had laboriously written his verses, an exchange of sweat for goods. Schoen knew the price of salvation was vigilance. He'd watched. He waited. He memorized sin, and counted the sinners, as any good watchman should.

"Hey." Purdy rounded a pyramid of Diet Coke. "There you are, pastor. You ain't never gonna guess what happened. Loretta Harper's been murdered."

Startled, Schoen whirled to stare into the beaming face of Purdy Phifer. Then his eyes fell to the Bible verse he had exchanged for the aspirin. The quote was the shortest. The most pithy.

Jesus wept.

6

DeWitt, DEPRESSED AND FRUSTRATED, turned his mare away from town instead of toward it. On the road that had once led to Longview, by the sign that announced the speed limit dropped from fifty to thirty, DeWitt reined his mare. He stopped because he could go no farther—the Line straddled the highway, an insurmountable paisley wall.

The white 30 MPH sign was a pale glimmer in the dusk. The bare spot in the ground where Bo used to lurk had grown to high weeds, a crumbling monument to the speed trap.

Dismounting, DeWitt walked over and stood by the gathering of mementos washed in the Line's glow. FOR JASON WALSH, a card wired to the laces of a football read. The plastic seal around the card had split; the ink was six years bleached. The football, waiting playless, had long ago deflated.

A rain-warped book lay for the hands of TAMORA ADAMS, BELOVED SISTER to reach through the Line and pick up. For JENNIFER WASHINGTON, ADORED GRANDCHILD, there was a multicolored plastic necklace, its facets shiny, colors still bright.

DeWitt's eyes marched the graveyard of keepsakes: a fishing

pole for BOBBY FLETCHER, FATHER; a vase of plastic flowers for NANA, BEST GRANDMOTHER. His eyes settled on a police chief's badge: TO DAD.

Quickly he lifted his gaze. The Line was almost transparent. Sometimes DeWitt, after standing for a while, was certain he saw the gray ribbon of the road as it curved up the hill on the other side. Sometimes, if he stood there long enough, he thought he heard sounds behind it: the rushing of the wind, the call of a bird—patterns built of hope and incomplete data.

The eye, the brain, were cheats. DeWitt had read somewhere that the first astronomer to map Mars had fallen victim to delusion—the same delusion to which Hattie, in loving, had succumbed. She charted meaning in DeWitt's every careless act and drew sentimental canals.

Putting his palm forward, DeWitt watched his hand sink into the glow before resistance halted it. The light was as warm as blood. A tingle of energy thrilled up his arm and settled into the joint of his shoulder.

DeWitt gave up trying to look through the light and stood back. As Hattie should. His eyes focused on the Line itself and not what might lie beyond it.

Dusk settled slow and blue around him. A cold night wind breathed down his neck. He stood looking until his eyes watered.

"You do not want the gas?"

Seresen was standing a few yards away from the tethered horse as though he had materialized there.

"You complain that we do not deliver, and then when it comes, you ignore it."

"I'm not ignoring it." DeWitt wondered how long Seresen had stood watching him.

"Perhaps it would be better now for you to go into town and

get gas for your car. It is growing dark. Can the horse make its way in the dark?"

"Sure."

The Torku seemed neither interested nor uninterested in the reply. But DeWitt had learned to read subtleties. The aliens hardly ever demanded; they dropped hints. Seresen wanted him out of there.

DeWitt walked to his horse and paused in indecision. Under the safari shirt, the Kol's legs were hinged wide over his pelvis. Seresen had the shape of a twin popsicle.

DeWitt's shoulder ached, as if the energy of the Line had jittered his socket bones together. "Can anyone get through there?"

"Do you wish to try?"

"No." DeWitt thought of his father. It was best to picture him vaporizing in a superheated flash. Harder to think of his life draining in crimson, watery stools. But the idea that he might still be alive caused DeWitt the most pain—the sort of helpless, purblind agony left in the wake of the missing. "Yes," he said. "Sometimes."

DeWitt imagined the Line as he saw it in his dreams: the end of the world, the place on maps marked "Here Be Monsters." In those nightmares he was always wasted on Curtis's dope. Searching for his father, he would climb over the barrier only to fall down a starry well.

Staring hard at the glow of the Line, he imagined he saw headlights. He looked away quickly, a sick feeling in his gut.

"Where were you last night?" he asked Seresen. "What were you doing?"

Seresen didn't reply.

"I need to know."

The alien looked up at the spangled sky. "The questions are contradictory, and I do not understand why they are important. To know where I am makes me less aware of what I am doing. And in knowing what I am doing, I lose awareness of location."

"Hazard a guess."

A pause. "It is probable I was in the center."

"Did anyone see you? Can anyone verify your whereabouts?"

"I cannot be certain of either."

"Okay. So it's probable you were in the center. What about the rest of your people? Were they with you?"

"This is important?"

"I told you this morning: someone's dead. And we don't know who or what caused it. Is it possible that a Torku went crazy or something?"

A bat flittered out of the gloom, approached the empty space above the Line, then darted back toward the trees, not as though it had run into a barrier but as though it had sensed something evil.

"You ask the wrong questions." With that, Seresen turned away and disappeared into the darkening woods.

7

FULL NIGHT HAD FALLEN by the time DeWitt reached the poor neighborhood of the Hollows. Streetlights cast golden pools on the asphalt. Frame houses crowded near the road like cattle gathering to fences.

In each brightly windowed living room was a VCR and a big-screen Sony. Every refrigerator was stocked, the result of the Torku's largesse. DeWitt hadn't admitted his contentment to Hattie, for fear of being misunderstood. It pleased him that the hard-scrabble poor had come into their own, not for justice, but for the sleepy satiation it brought.

No more burglaries. No more holdups. Glutted by consumerism, Coomey, Texas, napped.

But in the wealthier neighborhood on the other side of Guadalupe Road, vandals had painted a stop sign yield-yellow. Someone, uncharmed by the Torku's magnanimity, had sprayed EAT SHIT on the side of the volunteer fire station.

By the time DeWitt reached Foster's well-kept Victorian house, he had lost his smile. Propping his notebook against the saddle horn, he made a note of the vandals' damage; then he dismounted and climbed the stairs to the wraparound porch. Windchimes, nudged by the breeze, plinked like three-year-olds on xylophones.

As DeWitt knocked, his gaze snagged on Foster's '68 Corvette gleaming on the concrete drive. The classic car might have been used to transport the children's bodies, but Loretta was too large to fit in that trunk.

Foster jerked open the door, his bearded face in a grin. The white-haired banker might have looked snappy in his suit had the tie-dyed shirt under the vest not been such a hideous orange.

"Hey." His hand lifted, the index and middle fingers spread into a V. "Peace."

Without waiting for an invitation, DeWitt eased around the banker and into the warm living room. Arranged on the wall, fronted by scented candles, was the pictorial altar of Foster's past: a young naked Foster, one of the many nude and beflowered disciples surrounding Timothy Leary; a clothed Foster smiling and shaking the hand of a thankfully-clothed Phil Gramm. Next to that was Foster's framed college diploma and the photo taken the night of the Coomey High School Senior Prom: Foster's possessive arm around a beaming, sixteen-year-old Janet. Janet's blond hair was in a French twist, flowers tucked into its gleaming plaits. She looked different—younger, of course. She also looked happier than she had in years.

DeWitt wrenched his eyes away. The dining-room door was shut, but behind it DeWitt could hear quiet activity. A rattle. The clack of something small and hard hitting a firm surface. What woman did Foster have in there this time?

"Don't mean to disturb you," DeWitt told him, his eyes still on the door.

The back of Foster's hand collided with DeWitt's chest.

DeWitt staggered back a half-step in surprise and saw that the banker was holding a swatch of pale yellow fabric to his uniform.

"Spring, I think." Foster frowned at the piece of cloth and then at DeWitt's face. The banker was so close that DeWitt could see the subtle brick color of his eyeshadow, the touch of blush on his cheeks.

"You're a Spring. Should wear more bright colors. Your hair's highlights are toward the blond. Yellow would make that brighter. Eyes—what are they? More blue? More green? And the skin, warm peach. Yeah. Spring." Foster stepped back and opened his vest to flash more of his shirt. The necklace of beads and bells he wore jingled. "I'm an Autumn, myself."

"What about Loretta?"

Foster stroked his beard. From the other room came a rattle. A series of sharp taps. Foster seemed to be fighting an urge to glance toward the closed door. "Loretta thought I was a Winter. She never could do colors well. She didn't understand the vibratory resonance."

"Was? Have you heard she was murdered?" DeWitt hoped to catch him off guard, but the banker's expression was as empty in its own way as Billy's had been.

"Do you meditate?"

"I—"

"You're a Spring. Full of life. A hair-trigger temper that you regret later. Summers are impulsive, busy-work people who hurt without ever realizing it. Winters never forget a slight, but they possess psychic powers. Autumns are the most spiritual. I knew Loretta was headed for murder. Definitely a Summer. The quintessential victim. Summers never know revenge is about to fall until it hits them in the face."

"Who'd she hurt?" DeWitt tried to picture Loretta as one of

Foster's conquests and failed. Then he pictured Janet waiting in Foster's dining room. The vision stuck in his mind like an annoying snatch of melody.

"A Winter, obviously." Foster tossed the swatch of fabric onto a turquoise-and-burnt-umber couch. "They're brooders."

"You got anything to drink?" DeWitt parked himself on the sofa next to the square of fabric.

Foster looked toward the dining room. "Lemon verbena tea? Peppermint? Maybe some Red Zinger?"

"Mint sounds great." DeWitt relaxed into the cushions.

After a hesitation, Foster left. When DeWitt heard water running in the kitchen, he got up and crept over the hardwood planks to the closed door. The glass knob turned in his hand.

DeWitt froze, the image of Janet returning. What would he do if he found her? he wondered. But he had no choice. If she left him for Foster, DeWitt would place his love at the Line of their estrangement: JANET, FOREVER AND ALWAYS, CHERISHED WIFE.

He pulled the door open and peeked around the jamb. Jealousy assaulted him from an unexpected direction, impaling him so quickly, so painfully, that he found it difficult to breathe. On Foster's dining room table a Monopoly board was set up. Sitting across from each other, wordlessly intent on their game, were a pair of Torku.

DeWitt eased the door to. Confused, he made his way back to the sofa. Foster walked in, toting two mugs. A shell-and-bead necklace was entwined in the banker's hand like a rosary.

"Sorry I took so long." The edges of Foster's smile twitched.

DeWitt met the man's suspicion with a studied lack of guile. Taking the mug, he asked, "Loretta ever hurt you?"

"Hurt me?" Foster put his mug down on the glass-topped table and offered the necklace to DeWitt. "Start wearing this. It helps the vibrations. Ties are out now. Phallic symbols, you know. We have to get in touch with our feminine sides after that game of nuclear hardball."

DeWitt put the necklace into his pocket.

"Hurt me?" Foster asked again, plunking himself into a worn Laz-E-Boy. "Nothing can hurt me anymore, DeWitt, now that I've set my priorities in order." The chair reclined with a thump and a groan of springs. DeWitt found himself staring at the bottom of the banker's sandals.

"They did us a favor." Foster spread his feet to peer at DeWitt. "The Russians. The Torku. You know, in college I thought the trick was revolution. Then later, when I followed my father and became a Republican, I imagined money was the answer. But there aren't any answers. When you get right down to it, nothing's meaningful. Nothing at all."

Foster was talking a notch too loudly, and DeWitt began to wonder if the speech was meant for the Torku in the next room. The rattle of dice, the clack of the pieces along the board, fell silent.

DeWitt sipped at his tea. It was watery, and Foster had put no sugar in it. "Loretta thought you were a sinner."

"Loretta thought a great many things that weren't true. She was the wrong season to be perceptive, remember?"

DeWitt put his cup down.

"Loretta was a Thou Shalt Not," Foster told him. "Consider me a Thou Canst. When the bombs hit, I lost a lot of money in the stock market, but you don't see me crying over it, do you?"

No, DeWitt thought. *But I see a pair of Torku in the next room learning all about acquisitions and mergers.* He wondered what Kol Seresen, what Pastor Jimmy, might think of that.

"So you hated Loretta."

The chair returned to sitting position with a startled bang.

Foster leaned forward, his face too pink, too Summery, against the strident orange of his shirt. "Why would you think that?"

"Pastor Jimmy's people prayed God would take the sinners. Seems to me that when you have a congregation that wants something bad enough, one of them might help God along. The law would understand if you killed Loretta in self-defense." In a kindly tone he added, "Secrets eat you up inside, Hubert. So tell me. Where were you last night?"

Foster's cheeks went a sickly shade of gray. A Winter-sky hue. "Here. At home."

"Any witnesses?"

"Jesus, DeWitt. Loretta was the town's only Mary Kay rep. And I'm completely out of skin toner. Why in the world would I kill her?"

Slowly, pointedly, DeWitt looked at the living-room door. He had thought Foster could get no more sallow, but the banker's cheeks went through a Torku transformation. He was as pale as Loretta, as white as his trimmed hair.

"What's going on between you and the Torku? Does Seresen know his people are here? And what did Loretta find out?"

Irate, Foster shot to his feet, then appeared to be amazed to find himself standing. "The Torku and I have a lot in common. There's no crime in that, is there?"

Putting his hand into his pocket, DeWitt was surprised to feel the cold beads tucked away like a secret.

"Well? Is there?"

"Let me handle the Torku, Hubert. It's better if they talk to one person. It keeps things from getting confused. I don't want the Torku confused."

"Oh, I understand. You're jealous. That's what all this is about. Well, you don't *own* the Torku. Envy is a pre-holocaust

36

idea, DeWitt, and you'd better learn to get rid of it. The whole town had better learn to get rid of a lot of things. Outmoded ideas of demons. The Judgment Day holding tank that Pastor Jimmy thinks we're in."

DeWitt looked at the piles of tie-dye, the beads, the canny little incense holders scattered about the room. An old paisley tie just the pattern of today's Line. Foster was an ingenious man. He could have devised an ingenious murder weapon.

"So you're telling me life is meaningless."

Foster laughed. "I'm the one who should know. I campaigned for McGovern and then turned around and campaigned for Reagan. Find meaning in that."

"Funny thing." DeWitt's fingers slipped over the beads one by one. "There's never any vandalism in the Hollow. It happens over here, right on the good side of town."

"So?"

"So it makes me wonder about rich kids. Remember when you were in high school, Hubert? And my daddy arrested you for DWI? And how the circuit court judge just seemed to drop the case?"

Foster's jaw muscles tightened. "You drove drunk, too. You were just never caught."

"Well, your daddy can't bribe you out of trouble this time."

The banker swallowed hard.

"Isn't it ironic?" DeWitt asked. "We get everything we want, and rich kids tear it up. They break street lights, they spraypaint graffiti on walls. All those people starving on the other side of the Line, and here you are, telling the Torku that life is meaningless."

"Of course I tell them!" Foster's voice was strident, a voice to carry though closed doors. "I'm a teacher now. I'm not a wild teenager or a corporate pirate anymore. I've studied the arrogance of power dressing. The male Anglo-Saxon mind-set it creates. And if I could get through the Line, I'd teach those people the truth."

DeWitt pushed himself off the sofa and turned as though to leave. He whirled. Foster was planted, feet apart, pose defensive. "Did you borrow anyone's car last night?"

"No."

"I'll find out if you did, Hubert. Don't bother lying. I keep thinking that only murderers would believe life's worthless."

Foster's eyes wavered, dropped. "I never said that."

8

"WITHOUT FAITH," Jimmy Schoen thundered, "good works are meaningless!"

He stopped, trapped by the eyes of the demons. *Meaningless*, he thought, his hand still upraised.

The demons' eyes were a murky pink, with undertones of blue and hints of saffron: the color of chaos. Down one side of the small church they sat, shapeless hands in laps, their expressions intent.

Quickly, Schoen looked at the human half of his congregation. Dee Dee sat in the front row, prim and stiff and smiling, her gaze adrift. Daydreaming again, even though Schoen, by Biblical right, should be the appointed focus of her world.

At the unexpected silence, the others became restless. A few shifted in their seats. The Minister of Youth quietly, discreetly, coughed.

"Won't you pick up that cross and follow?" Schoen pleaded.

At the rear of the church a child paged noisily through a hymnal while his mother checked the status of her nails.

"Won't you follow?"

Why wouldn't they listen? The head of the building committee was staring out the window into the parking lot. One of the Washed in the Blood Cake Sale members seemed to be counting ceiling tiles. If they didn't follow his lead, he would never attain Glory. When Schoen entered Heaven, God expected him to bring his lambs along.

Glancing down at his sermon notes, Schoen realized he had lost his place.

He had been silent so long that an elderly deacon was now snoring. Schoen, too, was bone-weary, tired of it all. He could feel, as he could feel the boredom of his congregation, the succor of Heaven just out of reach.

In sudden impotent rage he sent his notes flying. The papers fluttered to the carpet, a flight of wan moths.

"AMEN!" the demons cried.

Startled, Schoen looked at the left side of the church. The demons were on their feet, caught in a tide of ecstasy.

The Minister of Music, obviously perplexed by his pastor's cues, hit an E-flat chord on the piano and the choir slid into the first verse of "Just As I Am."

No, Schoen thought in horror. But wishing couldn't stop the inevitable. Prayer had not helped, either. As they did each and every evening service, the demons were lining up to be saved.

9

Doc's CLINIC DOOR WAS UNLOCKED. DeWitt fumbled through the dark offices to a back examining room. There, on a gurney, he found Loretta, her body positioned under a surgical lamp like an actress in a tedious play.

The edges of the wound were dry and the torn skin sat up in frays. The laceration was so deep that he could have put his hand inside. There was not a drop of blood anywhere.

DeWitt tried but failed to imagine what weapon could have caused that destruction. Around the eye socket the soft tissues had been gouged out, laying the bone bare. The other eye was open and focused in surprise at something behind DeWitt's back. He fought an urge to glance over his shoulder.

A soft belch from a shadowed corner made him flinch. Doc was sitting alone in the dark, sipping Granger's moonshine from a Mason jar. There was a gold wastepaper basket next to him.

"Scare ya?"

DeWitt walked over and, still shaken, poured the cold contents of a coffee mug into the sink. Picking up a red-and-yellow gas can, he served himself some liquor. The batch, like the gold trash baskets, was one of Granger's least successful attempts.

"Jesus," DeWitt gasped. "What'd he use?"

"Canned peaches."

DeWitt sniffed at the cup.

Doc was sitting on a swivel stool, his legs stretched in front of him. "You find Loretta's kids?"

"No."

"I finally remembered when I seen Loretta's kids last. Funny thing. I kept trying to picture them running around like they always do. They had to be the worst pair of boys I ever knowed." Doc held the Mason jar to the light. From where DeWitt was standing, he could see the murky impurities in the liquor. "Just flat-out mean kids."

"So?"

Doc's eyes were unfocused, myopic. He was drunk—on schedule.

"But when I seen them last, they wasn't messing around like they usually do. I seen them professionally, DeWitt. They was sick."

"When?"

"Couple of days ago, near as I can remember."

"Where were they?"

"At the house. Loretta was with them, fussing over them like she usually done. Always was a poor mother. Ain't like she hated her kids or nothing. Just loved them too damned much. Never made them mind, and they grew up spoiled. Not like Hattie and her boys. Not like Janet."

DeWitt was glad the corner of the room was dark. He felt prickly warmth cross his face, and knew he was blushing.

"Get to the point."

"Them boys was bad sick." Doc's eyes glittered in the over-

42

flow from Loretta's spotlight. "Nausea, fever. I thought it was the flu. Now I ain't so sure."

"So?"

"They had cramps, a lot of pain. Maybe it was something they ate, I thought, but Loretta's always careful about her food. Cleanest kitchen I ever seen. But you know that. You know all them Homemaker-of-the-Month awards she won from the ladies." He took another sip of his drink, grimaced. "If it wasn't Loretta's cooking, maybe the Torku supplies ain't as good an imitation as we think."

"Yeah?"

Doc put his Mason jar down. "Maybe the Torku poisoned them."

Air came into DeWitt's lungs in an aborted hiccup.

"Think about it, DeWitt. Could be that they made a mistake somewhere and didn't want the rest of us to get panicky. Big corporations used to hide mistakes just as careful, just as thorough."

"Sounds like a stupid idea." DeWitt's voice held a reedy note of horror. "The Torku have taken care of us so far. There's no reason to believe they'd hurt us. I mean, I'll consider it. I even interrogated Seresen because I've got to talk to everyone, but—"

"I'll give you another scenario, then."

DeWitt fell silent. Anxiety settled in, tickling the hairs at the back of his neck. Next to him, Doc was a lumpy blur in the dark. The room was hushed but for the whispery sounds of their breathing, the quiet slurp as Doc took another drink.

"Let me start by asking you a question," Doc said.

"Okay."

"When's the last time you been sick? I don't mean the bursitis in your knee. I mean sick, like with the flu or a cold?"

DeWitt felt his forehead knot. He couldn't remember.

"Not after Bomb Day. I been checking my records. We been hurt in accidents, yes, but nobody's been sick after Bomb Day. It's been six years, DeWitt. Most of our antibodies are gone, if we're living in a clean environment. I think we're bubble babies."

"So?"

"So, thinking back on it now, them kids was real febrile. Hundred and two, hundred and three fever. What if it wasn't salmonella? What if it was cholera, instead?"

The silence became so heavy, so complete, that DeWitt could feel its press on his shoulders. "Cholera?"

"Think of where the house is. Right near the Line. What if there's a civilization dying on the other side? Cholera's the disease of disasters, and maybe the Line ain't as good a filter as the Torku think. Maybe Loretta's well got tainted. And if the boys was sick with cholera, the Torku would have to protect the rest of us, wouldn't they?"

When DeWitt didn't answer, Doc's voice rose. "Wouldn't they, DeWitt? The Torku take the kids away, only Loretta fights them. They kill her and then hide her body so it looks like one of us might have done it. Now they get two birds with one stone, Wittie."

At the use of his childhood name, DeWitt felt his stomach twist. He wanted to be eleven again. He wanted to forget Hattie and his wife and the murder and go hide at the top of his favorite tree. From the tree all the adults had looked tiny; and all his problems small.

"They get to study how we deal with it," Doc said.

10

THE HOUSE SMELLED OF BAKED CHICKEN. Janet, her back to the door, was seated at the kitchen table, reading. When DeWitt stopped at her side, she didn't turn. She didn't say hello, how's your day, didn't utter any of the banal but comforting marital welcomes. DeWitt hesitated to touch her. His hand traced the air, following the indentation of her back to her waist, like someone longing to comfort a burn victim. When he bent to kiss her cheek, she pulled away.

"You're late. You stink of Granger's moonshine." She slapped the book closed. *Auto Mechanics Made Easy*, the cover read.

His eyes followed her as she rose and went to the stove. With vicious jabs she spooned potatoes from a pan into a bowl.

"Something wrong with the Suburban?" he asked.

The counters were too tall for her. When she worked in the kitchen, she stood tiptoe. Janet was delicate, tiny, a woman of child-clothes and doll-shoes. DeWitt's hands could span her waist.

"Janet? Did you hear me? Is the Suburban driving bad or something?"

Without taking her eyes from the pan, she said, "Needs a tune-up."

"I'll get Seresen . . ."

"I want to do it."

"The Torku won't mind. That's what they're there for. Why bother getting your hands dirty?"

"Why do you bother going to the police station? Why do you bother going to work, DeWitt? Why bother doing anything?"

In the back of the house the children were playing. DeWitt could hear Denny's squeal; Linda's fuss-budget tirade. A door slammed with a forty-five-caliber clap.

"It's funny," Janet said into the ensuing silence. "In an engine, everything means something, everything makes sense. You can fix what's wrong. Completely. Not like housework, where . . ."

"Don't worry about it, hon. I'll take care of it. I'll drive the Suburban down to the Mobil station next week and see what I can do."

She whirled. "What are you, some kind of expert? All you know is how to change the oil, and you never do that anymore."

He should have changed the oil. Now she would punish him for his inattention. There were traps in his marriage: land mines and pungee-stake snares. He stood in the warmth of the kitchen, not knowing which path to take.

"Tomorrow," he said, desperate to make amends. "I'll do it tomorrow. Is that soon enough? I'll take the Suburban over, change the oil, and have Granger help me with a tune-up. We'll lube it and check all the belts . . ."

The spoon made a plopping sound in the potatos, a clink as it hit the glass of the bowl. "I already changed the oil. I lubed the car. That was Chapters One and Two."

It was suddenly difficult to breathe. DeWitt noticed the curl of Janet's blond hair around her narrow shoulders. Caught a heart-breaking sight of the small bones of her wrists. Her hands were perfect, like those of a porcelain figurine. "You *lubed* the *car*? What do you mean, you *lubed* the *car*? Christ almighty, Janet. What'd you do, jack it up in the driveway and crawl underneath?"

"I took it to the Mobil station. I put it on that thingy that goes up and down . . ."

DeWitt felt frantic, as if even now he were seeing her beneath the hydraulic lift, tons of metal above her fragile shoulders. "Don't ever do that again! What if something went wrong? I didn't know the oil needed changing. Why didn't you tell me?"

"I want to learn how."

"Why don't you stick to your hobbies? Isn't it enough to pretend to sell makeup? And have people pretend to pay you? I had Seresen get you a knitting machine and you never use it. All that candle-making stuff is collecting dust."

She faced him, spoon in hand. "You're the one who thought I should have a knitting machine! *You* decided what hobbies I would like. That's the problem with this marriage: you never listen. I tell you I want a Celica, and one Saturday you come home with a grin on your face driving that fat-assed Chevrolet!"

The profanity surprised him so much, he stepped back, banging his hip on the corner of the table. "I'll tune the Suburban, Janet. I really want to do that for you. Won't you let me tune your goddamned car?"

Her lips tightened. She started spooning again, her movements jerky and awkward. The bowl toppled, fell with a crash. A shard of milk-colored glass pirouetted across the linoleum and came to rest by his boot.

Janet bent over the counter with a reedy note of anguish. Her body shook with sobs.

DeWitt stood unmanned and inept, desperate to contain the storm; realizing he couldn't. He didn't know from which direction the gale had come.

"Janet." He picked his way to her through the broken glass, the spilled food. "It's okay. It's all right, honey. I'll clean it up."

She pivoted from under his calming hand. In the charged air of the kitchen, DeWitt felt the wind shift. The tears left abruptly as they had come. Not a hurricane, then. A passing thunderhead. "Get ready for dinner."

He went into the living room, unbuttoning his shirt.

"Where's your jacket?" she called after him.

He paused at the phone on the end table and dialed 911.

A Torku answered: "Emergency."

"This is DeWitt Dawson. I left my jacket at the clinic. It's a leather jacket with sheepskin lining. Make me another one."

"The other is broken?"

"Don't argue with me. Just make me a new one."

Putting down the receiver, he continued his strip-and-walk, draping his shirt and wide leather belt on his arm. He showered and pulled on a pair of jeans and a sweater.

Janet and her book. What were Chapters Eight and Nine? Replacing the Transmission? Rebuilding the Engine?

By the time he returned, the children were already seated around the kitchen table. Denny, face bright from a pre-dinner scrubbing, was playing war games with his utensils. The clashing of silverware annoyed Linda, DeWitt's solemn middle child, and she schoolmarmishly told Denny to stop. Tammy, her lips a faint Avon pink, was seated next to Janet, a detail-perfect miniature of his miniature wife.

"Hi, Daddy," Tammy said. "Is it true Mrs. Harper got murdered?"

"You see her?" Denny lay his silverware soldiers down.

"Of *course* he saw her." Linda rolled her eyes. "Daddy's the Chief of Police. That's part of his job, looking at dead bodies and everything."

Denny bounced on his chair. "Was she all gooshy? Did she have ants crawling out her eyes?"

"Not while we're eating," Linda said.

DeWitt sat. The roast chicken squatted spread-eagled and stiff in the middle of the table. Fighting a wave of nausea, he took a piece of bread, folded it, and filled the hollow with a buckshot load of green peas.

"Did you see Loretta at church last night?" DeWitt asked his wife.

She didn't look up. "I don't know. I got there late. We sat in the back."

"No, we didn't, Mommy," Denny said.

Janet's pink sweater matched the tender hue rising in her cheeks. A Summer. Janet would be a Summer. All shallow, point-less energy, hurting without ever realizing. Preordained to be a victim.

"You made your Avon deliveries last night," Denny said. "Don't you remember? You was going by Miss Wilson's to bring her the toothpaste? And you were late coming home 'cause she kept talking about being down in her back?"

"Oh." A strained smile. "That's right."

DeWitt took a bite of his pea sandwich, found it difficult to swallow, returned the rest to his plate. He needed to escape from his next question. Removing the napkin from his lap, he stood.

Janet got to her feet. "Where are you going?"

"Out." When he opened the door, a cool night breeze hit his face. Shivering, he made his way to his squad car.

"When will you be back?"

Janet was framed in the light of the doorway, her blond hair tangled by the wind. He had been married for twenty years, and knew her body better than he did his own: the silken skin at the inside of her elbows; the honey-brown mole on her thigh. Twenty years of sharing a bed, and he didn't know her at all.

"I'll be at Loretta's. Go on back in the house."

He climbed in his car as the kitchen door closed on the light.

DeWitt drove to the Mobil station. His hands were so unsteady, he dribbled gas on his alligator boots. When the tank was full, he drove east down Guadalupe Road.

It shouldn't have surprised him that Loretta's house was dark; but it did. He parked in the drive and trudged across the grass.

"Boys?" He stepped up on the porch. "Billy?"

The yard was aglow from the nearby Line. A fall breeze snuck through the oaks, rattling dead leaves, plucking at the collar of his sweater. "Billy?"

The door opened at his touch. Entering, he slid his hand along the inside wall. "Police." He found the switch and flicked on the lights.

Loretta's living room was uncompromisingly neat. A folded afghan lay on a striped sofa. A plate of potpourri on a gleaming end table scented the air with apples. Loretta's trophies dominated one corner of the room. Next to a crystal bowl of worthless dollar bills and uncashed checks stood a line of knitted Home-maker-of-the-Month awards.

DeWitt's house was never neat enough for the Homemaker Committee: Janet's Avon came in a distant second to Loretta's Mary Kay. The tally of dollars was a barometer not of wealth but of power. Janet, once head cheerleader, once Queen of the Senior Prom, had become an also-ran.

"Boys?"

There had been a welcome mat outside the door. Just inside

was another, a last-chance warning. He wiped his feet and walked into the kitchen.

The back door stood open. Across the surface of the no-wax blue-and-white floor, up the matching wallpaper, and over the polished cabinets were splatters of red.

DeWitt found a pot crusted with spaghetti sauce on the floor on the other side of the cooking island. Bending, he touched a finger to one of the red splatters and brought it to his nose. It stank of old garlic and oregano.

A sound made him look out the doorway into the backyard. The noise came again, the ring of metal on metal.

Crouched, he made his way through the kitchen into a bedroom. Halting, he let his eyes adjust to the darkness. It was a boy's room, he saw, a place Loretta hadn't tamed. The floor was ankle-deep in dirty clothes, and the walls were festooned with rock posters. By the bed he found an aluminum bat, its handle wrapped with black electrical tape. Hefting it, he crept into the yard.

Three Torku were capping Loretta's well in the light of the Line. The closest looked up as DeWitt emerged from the house. Instantly comprehending the threat of the bat, of DeWitt's aggressive stance, he stopped working and stepped away.

The other two, shadowy boxes with legs in the semi-dark, paused to stare.

"What do you think you're doing?"

A Torku on the other side of the well took a stick from his belt. "You will go away now."

"No, damn it. I won't go away. Where's Kol Seresen and what are you doing?"

DeWitt took another step. With a startled jerk, the Torku aimed the stick. DeWitt dropped the bat.

51

"You will go away now. It is good for all that you will be going away," the nearest Torku said in a hurried, inflectionless voice.

"Goddamn it, where's Kol Seresen?"

"Danger here. There is danger here."

"Danger? As in sickness? Is there disease in that water?"

"I do not understand." The Torku went back to his work.

DeWitt watched as the metal cap was fastened down. "I'm ordering you to stop. You're destroying evidence in a murder investigation."

"The Kol's orders. Seresen's orders. You must speak to Seresen."

"Where is he?"

"Soon," the Torku with the stick said as he turned to help his co-workers.

DeWitt sat down on a stump. In a little while a white postal truck drove up. Seresen and two other Torku climbed out. Seresen handed DeWitt a bill of lading. When the paper was initialed, he gave him the new jacket.

"You're capping the well. I wanted Doc to study the water," DeWitt said, sniffing dubiously at the jacket before he put it on.

"You should not be here," the Kol said.

"This is part of my investigation into Loretta's death." DeWitt watched the Torku unload the white truck.

"Why should the doctor study the water? He has water in town to study."

"Maybe the water here is different."

"Why should it be different?"

The Torku, working in unison, were placing canisters around the foundation of the house. "You'd know best why it'd be different. Maybe that's why you're capping the well."

"I do not understand. There is plenty of water for everyone."

"What are your workers doing?"

52

"We will erase the house."

DeWitt jumped to his feet. "Erase? You mean destroy?"

"Destroy in a clean manner, yes."

"I can't stand by and let you destroy more evidence. Something happened in there."

Seresen walked away.

DeWitt followed, close enough to see the coffee-with-curdled-milk color of the Torku's brindled skin. A Winter, he decided. The Torku were all Winters. "Are you afraid of what I'll find?"

"I am not afraid of you," Seresen said over his shoulder.

A chill wind worked its way inside DeWitt's jacket. "This is the kids' house now. You're destroying private property."

"Perhaps I will build them another in another place."

"Far from the Line?"

The alien swiveled, his expression unreadable. "Perhaps."

The Torku workers ran back for a whispered conversation with the Kol. When Seresen finished his instructions, which included gestures and a great deal of grunting Torku speech, he looked at DeWitt. "We are ready. It would be safe if you would go now. The light that is given off is harmful."

"Why destroy the house?" DeWitt asked. "You need to tell me, because right now it looks like you're covering up something. Don't do this."

"And you expect me to answer your why, because if I do not, you will suspect my silence, too?"

Startled, DeWitt said, "Yes."

"Then learn to imagine things differently. Suspicion is what comes of linear thought."

"Seresen, look," he said patiently. "There's always a why."

The Kol sighed. "It makes you unhappy, then. Not my intention. So. If I tell you what you wish to hear, you will go? The light given off at the time of erasure is strong. We have no wish to hurt you."

"I'll go. Now tell me."

"The woman is trapped in the house." Seresen's blank gaze moved to the darkened doorway.

DeWitt opened his lips to speak. Cold entered his mouth like a possessing spirit.

"You do not understand," Seresen said.

DeWitt shook his head.

"There are universes where the woman is attached to place. To what has happened. We must unattach her."

"Are you trying to tell me the house is haunted?"

"If that is how you must understand it."

Seresen walked off to the postal van, the other Torku crowding around him. He looked to where DeWitt still stood, frozen by the autumn wind and his own surprise. Then DeWitt went to his squad car, keyed the ignition, and drove off. He'd not gone a hundred yards when there was a blue-white strobe behind him and a quiet crunching sound.

He stepped on the brake and turned. Loretta's house had vanished.

11

DeWitt opened the door of his darkened house and was struck with the chest-thudding, nonsensical fear that it was vacant. Following a glowing trail of moonlight, he crept into Denny's room and studied the blanket-covered mound of sleeping child.

Denny was a silent slumberer given to gentle dreams, a child who surrendered so freely to unconsciousness that he sometimes appeared to have died without protest in his sleep.

DeWitt loved his children with the fierceness of despair. There were so many dangers: the heavy tires of school buses; the lake that could turn a tiny body into a pale, bloated sponge; traffic accidents that made unrecognizable splashes of red and splinters of white. Each time DeWitt investigated a child's death, he would imagine Denny's face, or Tammy's, or Linda's, on the small, dead body, just to see how surviving felt.

He put his hand near Denny's mouth, close enough to feel the boy's warm breath.

Realizing that he was hungry, DeWitt tiptoed to the kitchen, opened the refrigerator door, and indexed the food. He settled on the last of a Sara Lee chocolate cake, which he ate standing in the lighted V of the open refrigerator.

Licking the frosting from his fingers, he made his way to the back bedroom.

Janet was a hard lump under the bedclothes, a granite mountain range with snow cover. He sat in an armchair and pulled off his boots in the dark. The right one made a clunk as it hit the floor. Guiltily, he looked up. There was no answering creak from the mattress.

In stocking feet he rose and took off his belt, eased the top drawer of the dresser open, and by feel took out the old sweatsuit that functioned as his favorite winter pajamas. He laid his jacket, his sweater, and his jeans carefully over the back of the chair.

His wife's voice was a disembodied thing. "Who killed her?"

Was it you? Now there was a white form between DeWitt and the headboard. Janet must have sat up and pulled the covers with her.

"I don't know."

"What about the kids?"

"I haven't found them yet." He had a sudden image of Tammy or Linda missing: he pictured himself, clothes rent in Biblical mourning, wandering through the streets shouting their names.

"Do the Torku know who the murderer is?"

The question made the cake in his stomach churn. What if Janet *had* killed her? And what if the Torku had seen? DeWitt was Seresen's main liaison. If Seresen knew Janet had killed Loretta, he'd never tell.

"They're acting like they don't."

"Are you coming to bed?"

He was tired but no longer sleepy. A nerve twitched in his neck.

Tammy had been a terrible sleeper in infancy, all body jerks and small cries. Every night DeWitt and Janet had wrestled with her until terror wore her down. He was exhausted like that. "In a minute."

An angry squeak of bedsprings as Janet flung herself under the blankets. The left side of the bed, his side, was suddenly brighter. She'd taken the covers with her to make an annoyed cocoon.

Holding his keys to prevent them from jingling, he walked barefoot to the carport, flicked on the thirty-watt overhead bulb, and closed the kitchen door. By the woven mat lay Janet's sneakers, socks inside like nesting hens. Over the canvas sides was a drying scum of mud. He picked the shoes up. In the soles' ornate grooves were chips of something white. He looked quickly at the Suburban. There was a pebble in the muddy right front tire.

DeWitt put the sneakers back, and pried the pebble from the tread. White, soft caliche, like the gravel that littered Sparrow Point.

He got to his feet. A cardboard box had been partially hidden in a tumble of gardening tools. Leaning over a rake, he peeked inside: Avon packages. A Torku bill of lading, the hue of bubble gum, sat atop three boxes of toothpaste labeled ETTA WILSON.

DeWitt took his penlight from the squad car's glove compartment and went to the rear of Janet's Suburban. He faced the navy blue door in painful indecision.

Impossible. Loretta had been five inches taller, a hundred pounds heavier; Janet couldn't have killed her. But before DeWitt could sleep, he had to banish all doubt.

The come-along. That might have been enough to get the body into the Suburban. He shone the penlight into the shadowed depths of the carport. The small block and tackle, rusty with disuse, lay atop his workbench where he had left it.

DeWitt opened the rear of the Suburban and swept the pencil-thin beam over the roomy interior. Balls of fluff sat atop the beige carpet like pills on an old sweater.

Janet would have had to catch her victim by surprise. Look here, Loretta, look what I got. The snap of a garrote around Loretta's neck. No time, no air, to scream. The struggle. Loretta's shoes whipping back and forth across the carpet. Maybe Loretta didn't bleed to death. Maybe her throat had been torn out to obliterate the marks of strangulation.

But a lot of things could have caused those scuffs. Janet had carted lumber. The boards had shifted.

DeWitt crawled inside, searching on hands and knees. He found a tiny lipstick sample. A toy car. A soda straw still in its paper sheath. He ran his hands along the side, dipped his fingers under the carpet. A penny. A toothpick. A piece of foil.

He brought out the foil and studied it. Heavy grade, blue on one side, silver on the other; the circular indentation of what it had contained.

The instant DeWitt recognized what he was holding, his brain froze. His instinct was to fling it away. He couldn't. His fingers clenched the condom package as if they had seized a live wire.

He'd take this to the bedroom, wake Janet up, ask her who she was sleeping with. Ask her for God's sake why. And if she didn't tell him, he'd shake her so hard, her delicate neck would snap.

No need. He already had the answer. DeWitt always knew that one day he might lose his wife to Foster. And if he confronted her now, she would leave and take the children. He could deal with her affair if she didn't flaunt it, if only she would stay.

Besides, he had lost Janet a hundred times before: in high school, when Foster had the money to take her to the prom; in college, when he'd had the better car. An MG then. A Corvette now.

In trying to please her, DeWitt had repeatedly made the wrong choices. He sat in the Suburban that Janet hated, that he had bought with such pride; and suddenly he realized how Foster had gotten Loretta's body to Sparrow Point.

DeWitt took the foil to the rows of garbage bags and gave it an indecent burial, between an empty Doritos package and a wet mass of coffee grounds.

Faintly, far away, someone screamed. DeWitt returned to the house, and in the hall nearly collided with Janet.

"I'll get it," he snapped, his resentment still raw.

Without a word she turned and went back to bed.

The bedside lamp was on in the girls' room, and Linda was sitting up, staring at her sister. Tammy's hands were over her face. Her mouth was open, and an odd, inhuman wail was coming out of her.

"Here, baby. Daddy's here." DeWitt sat down and tugged her fingers from her face. The screams became hiccupping sobs. Settling her cheek against his chest, he crooned a worried parent's song.

From the opposite twin bed, Linda watched.

"Go to sleep, sweetheart."

She yawned. "Bathroom." Fumbling her way out of the covers, rubbing her eyes with her small knuckles, Linda padded out.

"I was watching cartoons," Tammy said.

DeWitt stroked the side of her wet face.

"The cartoons went off. It made me mad."

Down the darkened, hushed hall came the sound of a flush.

"So in my dream the sirens start and you and Mommy come and we all run out into the street."

DeWitt's soothing palm stroked as though anointing her mind with forgetfulness.

Linda came back, lay down, and pulled the bedclothes around her.

"Then we go down into Mrs. Stanley's storm cellar, only there's a bog monster there." In his cradled arms Tammy had become four again, calling the name of the bogeyman she'd known when she was younger, a more innocent form of nightmare. Something to do with dogs, DeWitt remembered, and the four-year-old Tammy had not been able to pronounce the word.

"So we scream and run away, only there's a bog monster outside, too."

DeWitt's hand paused. "What does the monster look like, honey?"

She took a breath punctuated by a shiver. "I don't know. I can't see it."

His hand continued its interrupted stroke. "That's a scary dream."

"Degenerate, Daddy. It's just a degenerate dream." In his embrace she had somehow aged ten years. *Time flies*, he thought, picturing her as she had been before Bomb Day, before the discovery of boys, before the discovery of favorite new words.

"Well, it sort of happened like that," he said. "Except there wasn't a real monster in Mrs. Stanley's cellar." Only the Stanleys, DeWitt's family, and Foster.

DeWitt has ended up in the elementary school basement with about seventy others. When he tried to leave, Bo, who DeWitt had hired despite a troubling record, forced him back at gunpoint, saving the others from the radiation they thought lurked outside.

DeWitt spent twenty-four hours wondering where his family was, listening to the frightened silence around him, and the hiss of a radio tuned to dead air. It was nice that Tammy had included him in her dream. When bog monsters come, fathers should be there.

"When we came out, we saw the Torku," DeWitt said. "They aren't monsters, are they?"

Tammy laughed, but fear clung to her. "No, Daddy. They're sort of funny."

"It's a scary dream because what happened was scary. So when you dream about it, you make up monsters."

"Uh-huh," she said. Then yawned.

He helped her lie back on the bed. She pushed her face into the pillow, and he rubbed her back the way he had when she was very small. "I love you, punkin."

"Love you too," she replied drowsily.

"Are you all right now?"

But she was already asleep.

He got up, turned off the light, and went to the front door. Opening it, he caught the cold breeze on his face. As if in protest to his act, the central heat came on with a click and a low rumble of air.

The yard was iced with moonlight. Down the street the lights were on at the Fergusons'. Maybe they, too, were afraid of the dark.

For there *had* been a monster in the elementary school base-ment. DeWitt supposed it had been in the Stanleys' cellar as well. A monster of terror, fed by darkness. Its smell was the smell of vomit, and its voice was the utter silence of seventy people.

He'd been so afraid.

There were some things about that basement he would never forget. How he ran from one huddled group to another, calling Janet's name. The disbelief he felt seeing the gun in Bo's hand, muzzle aimed at his chest. How Granger kept thumbing the black dial on the transistor radio, like a Buddhist twirling a prayer wheel. Granger searched all night for a station, as if something were wrong with the radio and not with the world.

And when they could no longer endure their own fear, they crawled out into the normal sunlight, expecting death from radiation. The Torku were waiting.

DeWitt closed the door and walked down the hall to the bedroom. He lay down and passed his palm over the covered form of his wife.

Not her fault. Not anyone's, really. He should have been beside her in that cellar. "I love you," he said. And despite everything, he meant it.

12

"JIMMY?" Dee Dee called.

Schoen disentangled himself from the covers.

"Jimmy, honey? What is it?"

He sat on the side of the bed, the carpet tickling his toes. In the cobalt rectangle of the window he could see, framed between the trees, a swatch of starry sky.

"Honey. Don't let the Torku worry you like that. Them coming up at altar call. It doesn't mean a thing."

But nothing was meaningless in God's world. *Not a sparrow falls* . . . Everything was ordered, everything preordained. The hairs on his head were as numbered as his days.

"Tonight in church you weren't looking at me. You're supposed to look at me during the sermon. Did you hear a word I said?"

"Well, honey, of course I did. I always listen, you know that. I was thinking, that's all."

"Don't think! The congregation sees you looking around like you're wondering what to make for dinner. God has called you as my helpmate. We're married for a reason. I can't save the town by myself."

A creak of bedsprings as she sat up. "Oh now, Jimmy. I help. Don't I help? I run the cake sales. I organize the visiting. I—"

"And what in God's name have you done with your hair?"

Dee Dee was a black, silent form next to him. He couldn't tell whether she was shocked wordless or simply confused.

"Oh, this?" she asked from the dark. "The frosting? Mary Dixon did it for me. She colors her hair, and she always looks so good. She said it makes me look sophisticated. Isn't that just the nicest thing you've ever heard? When I looked in the mirror, I thought I looked really sophisticated too, like I was from New York or something."

"Vanity is woman's trap. Rinse it out tomorrow. Do whatever you have to do to look like yourself again."

"Oh honey, don't you get tired of the same things over and over again? Always Grape-Nuts and dry toast for breakfast. Roast every Sunday. Steak every Saturday night. And you never want to try a new salad dressing. French. Every supper, we have to have French. I could buy creamy garlic or ranch. Wouldn't creamy garlic be fun? And I'd like to change the curtains. Get some pretty throw pillows. It'd be nice to have some bright colors—"

"Be thankful for what you have. God puts a roof over your head. Food on the table."

"Well, I get food from the store really, and of course it *does* come from the Torku, even though I figure, well, God would have to have a hand in it somehow, wouldn't He? I could make curtains. Terra cotta and turquoise, don't you think? I think turquoise and terra cotta are just the most sophisticated colors. Mary Dixon says if we don't change, we get old too quick. And it seems to me she's right. Why, all the old people I know—"

"Don't raise your voice with me." He got to his feet.

"Jimmy?"

"Be quiet. You'll wake the children."

He strode to the living room and opened the front door, for the night air to clear his mind. For the wind to tell him why, after fifteen years of marriage, his wife wouldn't obey him anymore.

Shivering, he walked across the porch to his telescope and peered through the eyepiece. Hubert Foster's bedroom window came into sharp focus. The room was dark.

Schoen straightened and sighed. Pulling a lawn chair up to the telescope, he sat down, his vigilant eyes scanning the neighborhood at the bottom of the hill.

Granger was in his workshop. Doc was drinking again in his study. The Albertsons were sitting down to a late-night snack of chocolate cake.

The night was still and hushed, most sin abed. Distance was containable. It was a soothing perspective—seeing things at arm's length, the way God sees. He felt as though the figures in the telescope lay cupped in his sheltering hand.

13

Rain was coming down in a mist. Outside Bo's cedar-shadowed cottage the garden had been mulched and bronze mums planted along the gravel drive. Bo answered DeWitt's knock. Television voices and the smell of bacon wafted from the doorway.

Without the concealing sunglasses, there was a softness about Bo's face. The round blue eyes betrayed him, displaying a vulnerability so acute that bar owners asked for proof of age, and women mothered rather than seduced.

"We need to talk," DeWitt said.

Bo opened the door wider. DeWitt wiped his feet on the mat and walked in.

The house was spare and elegant in the manner of someone accustomed to solitude. Bo's charcoal-and-salmon sofa precisely matched the drapes. The miniblinds were opened in tidy gaps to let in a precise amount of morning light. DeWitt shifted nervously on his feet. He felt more at home in Curtis's squalor; in Doc's absentminded clutter. Even in Hubert Foster's tie-dyed and beaded disarray.

On a salmon-colored TV table a plate of eggs and bacon and toast sat cooling. "What do you want?" Bo walked to the sofa, took a seat before his breakfast.

DeWitt looked at the TV. Tom Brokaw looked back.

". . . returned to the Soviet Union today," Brokaw was saying, "amid rumors that Chernenko has died."

The videotape of the final NBC Nightly News. DeWitt felt the urge to reach through the TV, through time, and hand the anchor a scrawled note: *Run for your lives.* Suddenly Brokaw fell silent, mouth open in what looked like mild astonishment. The picture on the screen jiggled, was bisected by tracking lines. Bo lowered the remote control.

Aware of the dampness of his clothes, DeWitt hesitated to take a seat on the wingback chair. "I know since Bomb Day we've worked alone, but I think now we should join forces."

Bo's smile was brief and as unattractive as a facial tic. "Why? To keep an eye on me?"

The lie was so easy. "You know better than that."

"People hate me," Bo said.

A flabbergasted pause. "You give out all those parking tickets, don't you see? If you'd loosen up, maybe they'd take more of a shine."

"I can't loosen up, DeWitt. The law's the law. It's all that separates us from the animals. I always figured society worked like a big machine, and you and I were the oil. We can't let people get away with things. We can't let them do whatever they have a mind to. First it'll be illegal parking, and before you know it, we'll have . . ."

A murder.

"I went to the clinic." Bo took a bite of his scrambled eggs. "Doc forgot that the best way to estimate the time of death is by stomach contents. Spaghetti."

DeWitt sat down in the armchair.

Bo picked up a slice of bacon. "The spaghetti had held its shape, so she ate no more than an hour before death. If I'm right about the time of onset of rigor, the spaghetti was probably ingested about five, five-thirty. Where's Loretta's car? Did you search the house yet?"

The bronze mums lining the drive were dying suns in the gloom. "The Torku destroyed the house."

A sharp clink made DeWitt turn: Bo had dropped his fork. "That about clinches it, doesn't it?"

"I'm not sure. And we have to find the kids, Bo."

"Yeah. First things first."

"So I'm going up to the school."

Bo lowered his eyes to his plate, as if he were seeing prerecorded tragedy in the remains of his breakfast. "I can't help you."

"Why not?"

Bo buttered a slice of toast. "I have the feeling you'll do anything to protect the Torku. Including casting suspicion on someone else. I'm not that kind of cop."

"And I am?" DeWitt swallowed his anger. "Look. It would be stupid to run two separate investigations, don't you think? A waste of time."

The toast crunched as Bo bit into it.

"I have to interview the people at the church. I have a bunch of kids need talking to. Come on, Bo. I hired you when no one else would. You owe me."

Bo got to his feet. "I can't believe you'd bring that up."

"This is a murder investigation. Everybody's nerves are bound to get strained. What if your temper gets out of hand again? What if—? Where are you going?"

"The bathroom."

When the officer left, DeWitt went to a nearby plant table. Incongruous clutter was piled next to a Norfolk Island pine: an incense holder and a blue bead necklace. A necklace appropriate for a Winter.

Footsteps clicked on the polished hardwood floor. DeWitt quickly sat again.

Bo was rubbing his hands together. "Okay. All right, DeWitt. I'll help you, but then the slate's clean."

"Agreed."

Bo turned off the TV. They walked out of the house and across the lawn. When they climbed into the squad car, Bo took his sunglasses from his pocket.

"Leave the glasses off. If we're going to work together, I want to see your eyes. I want to be able to tell what you're thinking."

Slowly, Bo put back the glasses.

"When we get to the school, you take half the kids." DeWitt fastened his seatbelt. "I want to know if anybody saw Billy Junior and . . . and . . ."

"Jason," Bo said in a tight voice.

"Yeah. Jason."

DeWitt accelerated up a hill. When he crested the rise, his eyes widened. Speeding head-on toward them was a huge shape. A dented grille; the round, alarmed eyes of headlights; holes where a car emblem had once been.

DeWitt wrenched the wheel right, stood on the brakes. Tires squealed as the squad car slewed and came to a stop at a ninety-degree angle to the road. The pickup nosed into a roadside ditch with a crunch of foliage. The door opened, and Curtis emerged, laughing.

Bo got out and marched across the asphalt. "License and registration!"

"Hey, Bo. How's it going?"

An icy, clipped reply: "Hands on the hood! Spread 'em!"

Curtis leaned over the Dodge's hood. Bo kicked his legs back farther and ran his palms over Curtis's jeans, groping the top of the inseam so resolutely that DeWitt, in sympathy, winced.

Curtis went tiptoe. "Whoa! Kiss me first!"

"Where'd you throw it?" Bo demanded, stepping back. "I saw you throw something down. Where'd you throw the dope?"

"I wouldn't throw no dope away," Curtis said. "Ask DeWitt if I would."

On the dotted line in the center of the road, DeWitt halted, pinned by Bo's accusing glare.

"Mr. Mayor," Bo said, "I'm arresting you for driving without a license, for reckless endangerment, and for suspicion of DWI. Chief, search the vehicle for any controlled substances."

After a moment's exasperation, DeWitt obeyed. The Dodge's rusted door shrieked as it opened. Glancing into the cab, he saw that the floorboard was awash with Bo's pink traffic violations. "Found something."

"What?" The triumph in Bo's voice was like trumpets.

"Inspection sticker's six years out of date."

"Everybody's sticker's six years out of date."

"Now you get the picture."

Bo frowned.

Curtis asked, "Where you all headed, anyways?"

"We're investigating the murder," DeWitt told him.

Curtis clapped his palm to his forehead. "Oh! That's why I was looking for you! I couldn't find Loretta's road."

"Why did you want to go to Loretta's?" Bo's voice was thick with suspicion.

But Curtis was oblivious. "Wasn't going to Loretta's, just by Loretta's. And then I seen the Torku done peeled up her road.

They already planted grass and everything. Come on and look. You ain't gonna believe it."

Curtis walked to the squad car. With stereo sighs DeWitt and Bo followed.

"I want the siren." Curtis planted his elbows on the back of the front seat.

"No siren," DeWitt said.

Curtis reached so far into the front that he nearly fell in Bo's lap. He turned on the bubble lights and sat back. A few minutes later DeWitt was stunned to smell the burning-alfalfa odor of marijuana. "Want a joint, DeWitt?"

DeWitt pointedly rolled down his window. "No."

"You, Bo?"

Bo's no was brittle.

An uncomfortable silence settled in the car. "I got a good crop this year. DeWitt? Tell the man what he's missing. DeWitt and me got stoned after the murder, didn't we, DeWitt? And I put him up a whole trash bag of dope. Primo stuff, Bo. Mellow you out some, know what I mean?"

"Shut up, Curtis." Out of the corner of his eye DeWitt saw Bo's cold appraisal.

"Passed it," Curtis said.

"Huh?"

"Passed the road, Wittie. Turn around."

DeWitt slowed the car, negotiated a three-point turn and drove back. When he found a clear spot on the shoulder, he pulled over and parked.

"I don't see anything," DeWitt said.

"'Course you don't," Curtis told him with exaggerated patience. "They done took up the road, like I told you."

Curtis started to get out, but DeWitt stopped him with a sharp look. "Get rid of that joint. The Torku might see."

"Oh yeah. Sure. I'll finish it and catch up with you."

The two officers got out and walked across the dead winter grass.

"He's stoned," Bo said. "We're wasting time here. Let's go on to the school."

DeWitt gave the ground a few experimental kicks.

"You know, DeWitt? Long-term marijuana use causes personality changes. A listlessness."

DeWitt chuckled. "That's Curtis."

There was resentment in Bo's Little-Boy-Blue eyes. "I meant you."

Curtis trotted to them. "You see it?" He darted off through the trees. "Come on. It's neat."

The two officers followed, walking in tandem.

"I remember when you first put on the badge," Bo said. "I was twelve years old, and your daddy was Little League coach then, remember? You came out to where we were playing. You looked so—" Bo paused, searching for the right word, and came up with the uncomfortable choice of "Good. You looked so good in that uniform. You're why I wanted to be a cop in the first place. You're the reason I came home when everything in Dallas turned to shit. Christ, DeWitt. What's happened to you? I used to think you were the best police officer I knew."

Before DeWitt could overcome his astonishment, Curtis shouted, "Look!"

Beyond a screen of pines was the Line, rose-trellised today, like old wallpaper. In front of the Line was a glade. In the middle of the clearing, neatly trimmed boxwoods made a square perimeter around a flat expanse of grass. Loretta's spindly redbud tree, the one she could never get to bloom, still stood near one corner.

"Ain't it something?" Curtis asked proudly. "Ain't it a hoot?"

Bo lunged forward, reaching the back corner of the boxwoods

at a run. He halted and looked around, as though he had dropped something. Then, on his long, slender legs, he paced toward the Line. After eight steps he fell to his knees, rummaged in his pocket, took out a pocketknife, and started to dig.

A lopsided smile quirked one corner of DeWitt's lips. Bo looked like a uniformed Sherlock Holmes.

The best police officer Bo had ever known. No, it was DeWitt's daddy who had been the best cop. He remembered looking up at his daddy: tall and straight, night stick and gun on his belt. Guardian of the peace.

"Goddamn it, Curtis. Don't ever talk about dope again in front of Bo. He could arrest you, you fool."

"Aw, you was there and all. He ain't gonna arrest me with you being there."

"What goes on between you and me is nobody's business. Not the town's, not Bo's. Don't ever, ever try to implicate me."

Curtis's face fell. "I didn't mean nothing."

"You nearly killed us, you airhead asshole. That's what grass does to you. A little recreational grass is one thing, but you—"

"I wasn't stoned, Wittie." Curtis sounded pathetic. "When I'm stoned I drive real slow, like fifteen miles an hour, and think I got her up to seventy."

Biting his lip, DeWitt looked away, wondering what changes the dope had made in himself.

"Got it!" Bo cried.

The pair flinched.

"I hit metal. Listen." As Curtis and DeWitt approached, Bo jabbed the blade in the hole he'd made, producing a clang. "This must have been the well." He stood, brushing dirt from his twill pants. His voice was grim, his eyes narrow. "It's the Torku, De-Witt. They killed her. Nobody destroys evidence unless they have something to hide."

14

THE LAST CHILD DeWitt had to interview was a black kid with a gimme cap and a Michael Jackson T-shirt.

"What's your name, son?" He was tired. The hard plastic backrest poked at his kidneys. His thighs ached where the Lilliputian seat ended.

"Robert." On the T-shirt was a cherry Kool-Aid stain shaped like the state of Illinois.

"Sit down, Robert. I won't bite."

The boy plopped into the opposite chair and began to swing a leg in feigned boredom. His boot tapped a water-torture rhythm against the table.

DeWitt watched the kid watch him. The library was quiet and scented with winter and children: wet woolen mittens, peanut butter, and furniture oil. Then the boy's eyes fell on DeWitt's badge with what DeWitt recognized as worry.

Most people were uncomfortable around the badge. Priests, DeWitt thought, must get the same reaction.

Forgive me, Father, for I have sinned. I coveted my neighbor's wife twice. I parked illegally five times this month.

Planting his elbows on the table, DeWitt leaned forward. The boy immediately leaned back.

"You like to fish, Robert?"

"Huh?"

"I said, you like to fish? You ever go up by the lake with the other kids?"

The kid shrugged. "Sometimes."

The conversational gambit failed, but DeWitt had others. The one thing he didn't want to do was scare the kids. He sat back again.

"What class did I get you out of?"

"Texas History."

"Um. What are you learning about this week?"

"Calvin Coolidge at the Alamo."

DeWitt wondered who was teaching the class this month. "I hated Texas History."

The kid gave him a tentative, disbelieving smile.

"When I was about your age, the government came and gave polio shots to the kids in school. I got out of English. The shot was better than the class. Yeah. The Salk vaccine. We were the first."

The memory of it came in a rush, down to the taste of the cheap cookies the school nurse gave out. There was a tray with two choices: vanilla with cream filling or chocolate with cream filling. It was only as an adult that DeWitt learned that some of the kids died from the shots. Had he known back then that they were dying, he would have said it was from those cookies.

"But I don't have a shot for you. I just want to talk."

The kid rolled his eyes. "I ain't seen them two boys."

"Well. News travels fast."

"And I don't know nothing."

DeWitt sighed, wondering how Bo had been handling the interrogations. Apparently more directly than DeWitt. The kids

75

DeWitt had talked to left the room as confused as they came in. "Maybe you do know something, only you think it's not important. Were you friends with Billy Junior and Jason?"

The gimme cap, spinach-green and printed with the words JOHN DEERE, was pulled down low over the boy's eyes. He raised his head to look at DeWitt. "Knew 'em."

The boy's tone told volumes. "Didn't like them? Why not?"

"They was mean. Lotsa kids would of killed them, I reckon. I would of killed 'em, too, if I had the chance." He made an automatic pistol of his finger and sprayed the room with rat-a-tatting fire.

DeWitt waited until the boy was finished. "We don't know they were killed."

"Bet they was killed like they mama."

DeWitt had been patting the tip of one finger against his upper lip. He stopped. "Who told you about that?"

"B.J. He my cousin."

"Uh-huh. So tell me about the Harper kids, about how they were mean."

"Threw rocks. Used to get back in them trees and throw rocks while we was walking home from school. Used to yell things at us."

"What things?"

"Nigger."

DeWitt let out a pent breath. "I see."

"Hit a Torku one time."

"Who?"

"Junior and Jason. Hit a Torku with a rock while we was standing in the road crying. This Torku come up to see what was the matter and—bang—one of them got him right upside the head."

DeWitt's mouth went dry. "What did the Torku do?"

76

"Just looked surprised. He was bleeding a funny kind of blood. Was all over him."

"He didn't go after them?"

"Nope. Just stood there. Them Harper boys run off, laughing and all. And that Torku, he walk away, his head bleeding and him not even paying no attention or nothing."

"You should have told me."

The eyes darted at DeWitt in shame. If DeWitt waited long enough, people would give their sins to him. During a casual conversation the lead-heavy truth would drop from anxious tongues. "See? So you knew something after all. Little things are what we need to build a case."

"Sir? You know their mama was gonna see that head Torku."

"Seresen? Loretta talked to Seresen?"

"Wasn't that she seen him. She just *wanted* to see him. Thursday at school I heard Justin tell another kid his mama went over there, but that head Torku, he wasn't in."

"You don't know what she wanted?"

"No, sir. He didn't say." After a fretful silence the kid told him, "I know where them boys is, Chief." His eyes and face were suddenly somber. It made him look like a pint-sized adult.

"Where?"

"Sucked up in the Line. Some of the kids seen 'em."

"Who saw them?"

"Donno. B.J. heard it from this sixth-grade white kid. They moan at night. That Line, it eat people."

"Nobody's been eaten before, Robert. There's no reason to believe the Line isn't safe."

"It eat people up. There's ghosts out there. They cry in the dark."

"That's the wind, son. Just the wind you hear. Out by the Line the wind makes strange sounds."

The kid shook his head. It was obvious from his face what this boy's nightmares were. "It eat people, Chief. And they cain't never get out of that light."

DeWitt let the kid go back to class. When he was alone with the dry scent of books and the moist smell of the rain, he rose and stretched. He walked down the scuffed linoleum hall, past a water fountain bulging urinal-level from the tile. Christmas, almost a month yet to arrive, hung in rectangles of Manila paper on the walls: tinseled trees piled high with presents; a stick-figure Santa Claus bearing gifts.

Downstairs, DeWitt found Tyler waiting. The huge black man was parked with his back against a mausoleum row of lockers, his beefy arms folded under his chest.

"You promised me you wouldn't get the kids het up." Tyler's face was a rich medicine-bottle brown, with spills of pastille freckles.

DeWitt lifted a questioning eyebrow.

"Bo's getting them riled," Tyler said in his rolling bass. "Don't want them riled before the holiday break."

Around the gaps in the closed lunchroom door the smell of macaroni and cheese wafted, carrying with it the quiet tone of Bo's voice.

". . . about the last time you saw Jason and Billy Harper."

A little girl's reticent "I don't know."

"Just think back." Distance did not cloak Bo's frustration. "Friday? Did you see them Friday?"

Tyler's clear brown eyes shifted to a crayon rendition of the angels and the shepherds. The angels in the drawing were stippled gray-brown. Torku color. "I got enough trouble without this. Three of my teachers didn't show up. Classes are all bolluxed."

From the lunchroom came the little girl's "I don't know."

DeWitt said, "Tell me about the Harper kids, Tyler."

Tyler was a huge man, and his glower was larger than life. "Bad ones. Just plain bad. I'm telling you, DeWitt, Janet and your kids aside, those folks down at the Biblical Truth Church don't teach life right."

"Well . . ." Tyler was a Catholic. Even before Bomb Day, even before he left his cornfields to take over the vacant post of school principal, the man had looked askance at the fundamentalists.

"And what worries me is, the Torku are getting awful interested in what Pastor Jimmy's saying."

DeWitt's breath hung like food caught in the gullet. "What do you mean?"

"He's converting 'em."

The lunchroom door swung open. The little girl walked out, Bo a couple of steps behind. "You remember anything, you just phone me, okay?"

The child glanced over her shoulder and hurried on.

Tyler checked his watch. "'Bout that time. Chief? You're set to teach third-grade math for a month after Christmas break. Don't you forget now. I already give Tammy your study books. You look 'em over before class. I purely hate when my teachers fail in their class preparation."

With that he was gone, hurrying back to his office.

"You ready?" Bo asked.

DeWitt stared idiotically at Tyler's retreating back.

"I said, you ready?"

"Oh, yeah. Sure."

As they climbed into the squad car, Tyler rang the bell. There was a broken-drainpipe gush of kids from the school, a few teachers caught in the flood like flotsam. DeWitt searched the tiny faces. The kids, bundled in down parkas and mufflers, looked like brightly colored Michelin men. He didn't see his son.

"Chief?" Bo prompted.

DeWitt roused himself. Keyed the ignition. And then he saw Denny, lunchbox banging his thigh as he ran in an awkward, swaddled gallop to the school bus. Relieved, DeWitt pulled away from the curb and drove down Guadalupe.

They found Doc in his spacious, threadbare office. He was talking to Granger. The men hurriedly broke off their conversation when DeWitt and Bo walked in. DeWitt could read contrition in their faces and wondered what they were hiding.

"Ah," Doc said, recovering first. "The crimefighting odd couple."

It was actually Doc and Granger who made the odd couple. Granger was a hulk of a man in a faded Farmer Brown cover-all. As though aware his height was imposing, he always stood hunched.

Granger reached into his pocket and brought out a palm-sized wooden toy. "Duckies," he explained, handing the toy to DeWitt. "See? He's got a little string that makes his beak go up and down."

"Clack-clack," said the duck as Granger demonstrated. Its voice was the sound of Torku playing Monopoly.

"Got your name on it and all."

"Thanks." The duck was white and orange with a big green ribbon on its neck. An Autumn, that duck. DeWitt slipped it into his pocket.

Doc nailed him with a look. Early afternoon, and he was sober. "You find out about them kids?"

"I found out who saw them last and when."

Bo swiveled in surprise. Evidently the officer with his direct interrogation hadn't gotten past the I-don't-knows.

"Jason spent Saturday night and all Sunday fishing with an Austin Berry. Austin saw him in school up through Thursday.

Friday, Jason was out sick. Jason was afraid of his daddy. Said his daddy came over day and night. Woke them up shouting outside the house and wanting to move back in. His mama was scared."

"You still think Billy did it?" Doc asked.

"I'm just looking for motives."

"And you?" Doc peered at Bo.

"I think it was the Torku."

Doc nodded. "I think you need to see something. Granger?"

The big man was leaning against a peeling cabinet, his hands in his pockets. "I been listening a lot." Granger's voice was a loud baritone, a voice for calling to neighbors across fences. There was a slight cast to the man's left eye that caused DeWitt's gaze to slide. He ended up staring at Granger's ear.

The farmer pulled from his pocket not another duckie but a tiny transistor radio. He turned it on. Static hissed through the room.

"Over by the window you can get better reception," Doc said.

Granger complied. He put the radio against the frame.

Music. They heard music.

It was so interspersed with white noise that you couldn't tell what sort of music it was. It might have been country. It might have been classical. But between the explosions of static DeWitt caught two notes. Then another three.

"Lock onto the station," Bo said.

"She's locked on as she'll ever be."

DeWitt tore the radio from Granger and studied the numerals at the red marker. He didn't recognize the station. Through the steam-kettle sputter, the notes were faint. Sketchy as memory.

"There's the proof civilization's back." Doc eyed them one by one. "Now the Torku got to let us go."

15

DeWitt parked by the modular building's garden, where a Torku was knee-deep at work amid a riot of autumn flowers. The rain had departed, bequeathing to the air its dank hush. In the silence, the four men got out of the car. After a little badgering, Doc convinced the gardener to call Seresen. The Kol, when he emerged from the center a few minutes later, didn't seem surprised to see them. Granger turned on his radio, and Seresen didn't seem surprised by that, either.

"It's music," Doc said.

"If you say."

"Goddamn, I do say! Don't you hear? Don't you understand what the hell this means?" Doc bounced on his heels. He was about the size of the small alien, and DeWitt was afraid Doc would take him on.

Seresen was unperturbed. "Tell me."

"We know there was a nuclear war." Doc ticked the points off on his fingers. "We know we're on Earth. We know Loretta's kids got cholera from their well, and we know you murdered her."

"Doc," DeWitt warned.

The physician was in Seresen's face, the alien staring implacably back—an imminent head-on collision. "I demand to know why you're keeping us trapped here! And where Loretta's kids are!"

"There is no nuclear war. No war. No music."

Doc said, "Play it for him again, Granger."

Granger stepped forward, towering over the tiny alien.

"What do you mean, no nuclear war?" DeWitt's throat closed, rusty-hinged, on old sorrow. "Pastor Jimmy himself told us Civil Defense called."

DeWitt remembered Schoen flying out of the fire station and into the March drizzle, translucent raincoat flapping, its folds gathering the light. The man, disheveled and unearthly, had looked like a hysterical angel.

"Thermonuclear war is impossible," the alien said.

DeWitt pushed Granger out of the way. "Why?"

"Atmospheric pressure keeps the radioactivity in the compound. Once the warhead reaches space, the neutrons are lost into the vacuum. When the warhead returns to the atmosphere, there is no radioactivity to explode."

Hope inflated DeWitt's chest like a balloon. But the next comment from Doc punctured him.

"That's bullshit."

The bulbous eyes shifted to the doctor. "We know all manner of things, and know them better than you."

"Well, I know some of the satellites were nuclear-powered. They wouldn't have worked if the radioactivity leaked out."

"They tell you they are nuclear-powered. Perhaps they lie. If you believe the emergency was war, you will perhaps believe anything. None of us have told you it was war," Seresen said with what DeWitt could have sworn was rage.

"I don't believe a damned bit of it." But Doc seemed doubtful now. "And I still want to know where the children are and why you murdered Loretta."

"It has never been my intention to discourage your questions. But I understand I have only to answer to the chief of police."

DeWitt could see where the conversation was headed. What if Seresen had witnessed Janet and Foster murdering Loretta? Suspicion was one thing; direct knowledge another. Maybe DeWitt really didn't want to know.

Bo spoke before DeWitt could. "Will you answer DeWitt's questions?"

"Yes."

Too late. The four men waited for the alien to elaborate. Seresen didn't.

"When?" Bo demanded.

"Now." Seresen turned his clumsy body and walked into the warmth of the rec center, a reluctant DeWitt at his heels.

In a corner of the large game room two middle-school girls were playing ping-pong. When DeWitt and Seresen walked in, one girl missed a return. The white ball bounced over the green indoor/outdoor carpeting like a golf shot across a fairway.

Seresen took a seat at a card table, and DeWitt sat opposite, folding his hands on the Formica. The alien was so dwarfish, DeWitt felt he was interrogating children again.

He watched the girl retrieve the ball and whack it back into play. "Where does the music come from, Seresen?"

"There is no music."

"But I hear it."

"Imagination."

"No. I don't think so."

The Kol waved his boneless hand in dismissal. "Then perhaps what you hear is a return signal. Everything that goes up must come down. This is evident. Radio signals go a long way—eight years—but they eventually fall, too."

"You want me to believe gravity affects radio waves."

"This is what I say, yes."

"Then we're on Earth."

"I did not say so."

DeWitt slipped his hand into his jacket pocket and was surprised to touch the firm edges of Granger's duck. "Six years up, six years down. You're telling me it's Earth music from the seventies." He tried to remember what had been popular then. *Disco? We're being bombarded by disco?*

The alien patted the table. The skin of his fingers puddled. "Space bends things. Things are refracted. The universe twirls like the hands of a clock. What goes up does not necessarily come down in the same place. We use this phenomenon when we travel. It is beyond your scope to comprehend."

"I'll try."

"As the stars shift, so do families," Seresen said, adroitly shifting subjects. "It is good to be concerned with the alteration of families. This has happened to one of you, but this is all that has happened. That is the reason the doctor and the Bo are upset."

DeWitt played with the duck in his pocket. "No. It was the way the mother died, Seresen. She was murdered. That's what upsets everybody."

The motion of the alien's hands on the table was so sensual that DeWitt stopped fondling the duck. He pulled his hand out of his pocket and laid it on the table.

"She made an appointment to see you. Do you know what she wanted?"

As if he had come to some decision, Seresen leaned forward and lowered his voice. "All right, then. Let us speak of this problem you imagine you have; but let us speak of it hypothetically. A man creates a car, let us say. And let us also say that perhaps the car drives into a tree and kills a family. The man is a murderer?"

"No."

"But perhaps the man does poor work on the car. He does not pay attention to the steering mechanism. Is he not a murderer, then?"

"Let me explain how it is." Next to DeWitt lay a stack of xeroxed announcements weighted by a chunk of granite. He picked up the stone. "A man bashes in the head of another man with a rock." DeWitt brought the granite down on the table harder than he intended. The crack resounded through the room, halting the ping-pong game. "That's murder. Now a man throws a rock for whatever reason. Just for the hell of it, let's say. And let's say there's a man over in the trees that the rock-thrower never saw. The rock hits and kills him. That's an accident."

Seresen turned to watch the girls. They had resumed play and were volleying easily to each other.

"One of the Harper kids hit a Torku with a rock," DeWitt said.

"Accident or murder?"

DeWitt's heart skipped a beat. "Are you saying the Torku died?"

"Never. I would never tell you such a thing. Thought is the same as act. I meant only to demonstrate the absurdity of your logic."

"Look, Seresen. A Torku was hurt. And Loretta wanted to talk to you before she died. I'm covering for you right now, but it's looking more and more like you were the one who murdered Loretta. If you killed her for revenge, that's understandable. We can work that out. I need to know the truth."

Seresen eyed him. "Your family is important to you."

It was as though the alien had slapped all breath, all warmth from his body. Numb, DeWitt watched as Seresen reached into a fold of his voluminous shirt and pulled out a small stack of photographs.

With cold hands, DeWitt took them.

Not Janet, not Foster. Three Torku. They stood at rigid attention before a mountain scene. The Torku at each end were tall; the one in the middle was shorter. The poses were so stiff that the picture seemed to have been shot with dummies.

"My family," Seresen said.

DeWitt turned the photos over. KODAK was printed across white backing. He leafed through the snapshots again. They were identical.

"We sympathize with family."

No, the pictures weren't quite the same. And the Torku in them were real. It was the lighting that was funny.

DeWitt recognized Seresen by the mottled pattern above his right eye. In the first shot the Kol had his hand draped over the younger Torku's shoulders. In the second the hand was touching what must have been the wife. In the third the wife was looking slightly to her left, away from Seresen and the child, as if something had caught her attention. In the fourth and fifth the shorter Torku had shifted his body. DeWitt leafed through them quickly, hurriedly, again. There was a pine branch above the trio. The shadows on the branch didn't match the shadows on the Torku.

"A beautiful wife, don't you agree?"

The artificiality of the pictures scared DeWitt to death. "Yes."

"And a handsome son." Seresen held his hand out. DeWitt placed the snapshots in the alien's soft palm. "So take care to speak gently. It is a dangerous thing to speak of murder. Discuss it, and acts are set in motion. Are there any other questions?"

DeWitt opened his mouth to speak, but couldn't. *Jesus God. Are you threatening me? What do you know about my wife?*

Seresen rose. "It has been nice talking with you again. And I rely on you to explain the prudence of silence to the others."

With that, Seresen walked away, disappearing through the steel door to the Torku side of the center. When DeWitt could postpone the moment no longer, he stood and walked out to the yard.

16

"WHAT'D HE SAY?" Doc asked.

DeWitt took a deep breath, readying for the burden of deception. "That, as usual, he relies on me to deal with the problem. He hopes I'll find the killer soon." DeWitt looked to Granger for support, but the canted eye lured his gaze to the man's cheek.

Doc gave an astonished chihuahua bark. "What?"

"Said he—"

"I heard what you said. Just thought if I asked again, you'd tell me the truth."

DeWitt glowered. "Get in the goddamned car. I'll drive you back to your office."

"I'd rather walk." Doc strode off. Granger hesitated as if considering the seven-block hike, then trudged after him.

Bo tapped DeWitt's arm. "I'd like to go back to the place we found the body. Maybe there's something you overlooked."

DeWitt thought of Janet's muddy sneakers, the possibility of footprints. "If you want."

They got into the squad car, and DeWitt drove slowly toward the west end of town.

"Did Seresen tell you why he destroyed the house?"

DeWitt remembered the arterial splatters of spaghetti sauce. What had upset Loretta enough to make her dirty her kitchen? What had prevented her from cleaning it? "Seresen said . . ." DeWitt cleared his throat. ". . . that she was haunting it."

A dry, "Did he really?"

DeWitt took his eyes off the road for a second and gave Bo a furious glare. "I'm not in the mood to be questioned."

"Doc's right. You're lying."

DeWitt stepped on the brake. With an angry tug at the wheel, he pulled over and parked. To their left, out past a barbed-wire fence, a small herd of Brangus steers raised their heads at the unexpected visitors. "What have you been saying behind my back?"

"Nothing. Not yet. But you're lying, DeWitt. Makes me wonder," Bo said without meeting DeWitt's challenging stare, "if you're involved with the Torku in the murder."

DeWitt hissed, "Get out of the car."

Bo didn't flinch. He was so still, he didn't seem to be breathing. "The law's the law, Wittie. If you helped them, you're an accessory."

DeWitt sat back in the seat. The car, he noticed, stank of stale marijuana smoke. "You tight-assed prick."

Bo's pupils were emotionless dots in the ice-blue of his irises. DeWitt wondered if those eyes were so cold that fatal night in Dallas.

"You asked me to join your investigation to keep tabs on me, to protect the Torku. Don't think I haven't figured it out. You don't like me, and that's fine. Nobody in this goddamned town likes me much. But listen, DeWitt. Justice isn't comfortable. The law has edges. Tell me the truth, or I'll go after you."

It was instinctive: DeWitt would always protect Janet. He would defend her against any threat: against Bo; against the truth;

90

against the law. And if it came to it, he would pay for her freedom with his own life. Or Seresen's.

Suddenly he wanted a cigarette more than he wanted a solution to the murder. If Bo hadn't been in the car, he'd have rolled himself a joint.

"All right. Okay."

While DeWitt talked, Bo sat looking at the dripping trees and the watercolor gray horizon.

"So if the Harper kid killed a Torku, we've got even more of a motive."

"If. If. We don't know the Torku is dead. I wouldn't be sure the Torku'd died if Seresen came right out and told me. He lies about everything, and not just to cover up, either."

"There's always a reason for lying."

"Is there? Maybe the aliens don't lie the same way we do. Maybe to them lying isn't wrong."

"Damn it, Wittie. I know you're a better cop than this. Why do you have to defend them?"

DeWitt punched the steering wheel. "Because the Torku are the only order we have left!"

"And you'd kiss ass to preserve order. Seresen's got you by the balls."

Seresen held DeWitt by more than that. He held him by his wife.

"I can handle the Torku." With a vicious twist of the wheel, DeWitt pulled the car off the shoulder and drove on.

"Where are you going? Sparrow Point's south of here."

"To Billy's place. Whoever killed Loretta had a truck and gas. Billy's got a portable generator. Seems to me he'd have spare gas for that."

"I made a cast of the tire treads. Dunlops," Bo said. "The Torku use Dunlops on their UPS vans."

Janet's Suburban had Dunlops.

When they arrived at the construction site, DeWitt escaped from the car and walked the planks to the open door.

"Billy?" His voice echoed back from the plastered walls.

Bo joined him. Together they walked into the garage. Against a naked sheetrock wall DeWitt found twelve gas cans. Five of them were full.

"See?" DeWitt clung to hope so desperately that his voice quavered.

"Doesn't mean much."

Next to the cans was a pile of yellowing magazines. DeWitt knelt, picked one up, and leafed through it. His gaze fell on the picture of a woman chained to a bed. "You think Billy was into stuff like this?"

"It's just a magazine, Wittie. There's all kinds of pictures in there. Let's go."

"Not yet."

DeWitt left the garage, trying doors as he went. In a shadowy corridor he stopped dead.

"This door's locked."

"Let's go ask Curtis for a search warrant."

"Involve Curtis? You've got to be kidding." Taking a penknife from his pocket, DeWitt slipped the end of it into the lock. With two fingers he gave the knife an expert twist. The mechanism clicked, the knob turned.

Billy had made himself a French whorehouse. Across the thick, red carpet stood an ornate fireplace. Smoked mirrors were suspended above a dark four-poster bed. More pornographic magazines were strewn across the tousled covers, women's under-things scattered among them. The panties were pink and white and blue and yellow.

"It's a one-handed love nest," DeWitt laughed.

Bo shot him a look. "What we're doing is illegal."

Bending over the bed, DeWitt used the penknife to sift through the undergarments. Billy hadn't been choosy. Some were big, some small, some medium-sized. Under a magazine DeWitt found a red lace see-through bra, size B half cups, with white appliquéd hearts. His chest emptied.

"Come on, Wittie. We're breaking and entering. We're violating the man's rights." Bo fumbled for his arm. DeWitt pulled away.

The bra was dotted with yellow stains and some of the hearts were rubbed off. "It's Janet's."

"It doesn't mean anything. You know that. He stole it. Remember those B&Es before Bomb Day? You remember? Nothing looked like it was stolen, but the locks were forced?"

"But that's Janet's *bra*." A tremor went through DeWitt like shockwaves in water.

Bo's voice was as soft as his eyes. "I know."

17

Schoen stormed into the living room and turned off the TV with a flourish, silencing the Roadrunner mid-beep. "I'm trying to *work*," he announced.

Dee Dee and his children, up to their elbows in color, paused in their fingerpainting. His three-year-old daughter clapped a hand over her mouth.

"Daddy's very, very busy. I have my daily sermon to write. My morning prayers. God speaks in a still, small voice. He'd have to shout to be heard over you."

Marsha dropped her hand. Around her lips was the imprint of five small green fingers.

He said, "Dee Dee, there's no sense in turning the house upside-down to keep them entertained. Can't you read them a Bible story?"

"Well, I could. But they've heard them so many times—"

"Children can't have enough of Bible instruction. And I thought you were going to do something with your hair."

She was already capping the paints, sponging clean the sheet of plastic they knelt on. "Now, you know? I've been meaning to do that. I really have. But with . . ."

The doorbell rang.

"Tomorrow, Dee Dee," he ordered as he went to answer.

Doc was standing on the porch. A whiff of agnosticism and drunkenness came off the man like the overly ripe odor of rotting food.

"Got to talk to you."

Recovering from his shock, Schoen led him to his front study, skirting the children and the dirty living room. On November 21, he had watched in his telescope as Doc played *The Exorcist* on his VCR. And when Doc taught at the high school in October, he confused the children with tales of evolution.

"Civilization's back." The physician sat in Schoen's favorite chair. "Granger's picking up music on his radio."

Schoen shut the door to childish giggles and Dee Dee's incessant prattle. His gaze fell on his bookshelves, and a collection of sermons by Jonathan Edwards. Doc read godless books full of dark anarchy, books by Dean Koontz and Stephen King.

"You listening to me?" Doc asked.

"Yes."

"The Torku killed Loretta. I'm sure of it. Killed her boys, too. Time to do something, don't you think? Ain't it time we fought back? Listen. Most of the town's pig-happy with the easy situation we got. But if they know the Torku are guilty of Loretta's murder, they'll turn against them."

Schoen's gaze slid to the Bible on the desk.

"So. You with us or against us?"

Flipping open the New Concordance at random, Schoen found he had turned to the story of Moses. Coomey had been lost in the desert for six years, thirty-four years less than the Israelites. And deserts were known for their temptations.

"What sort of music?" Schoen asked.

"What sort? Hell, I don't know. You can't hear much. A note here; a note there. The Line must be filtering most of it out."

Schoen nodded. It was obvious to him now what was happening. Granger had tuned to the choraling of Seraphim.

"Count me in." He turned, the Bible in his hand.

God was showing him the road to salvation. Schoen would loose a plague on their captors. A sign in blood must be written on each door. The tribes of Israel had been lost to chaos too, until Moses handed down the Law.

"Good. I'm glad you'll join us."

Not join you. Doc wanted a temporal solution; Schoen wanted more. From a distance there was serenity. But God's eyes, like His servant's, were keen. Schoen could see past flesh, past bone, down to the cramped burrow where the soul hid in shuddering awe of its Maker.

God had given Schoen the power to make this small man tremble. *No,* he thought. *Not join you at all.*

18

THE BRA SMOLDERED. Smoke rose from the trash can in feathery spirals until, at the mouth, a chill breeze whipped it away.

"We never had a break-in." Out of the corner of his eye DeWitt saw Bo watching with cautious sympathy.

"He might have picked it off a clothesline. He could have stolen it from the laundromat, too."

DeWitt stirred the flames with a stick.

"I'll lock the door, so he won't know we were here," Bo said.

"No. I want to throw him off-stride. If he comes to complain, we'll know he's innocent."

"You know that's not fair. He won't complain, he's got too much to hide." Shivering, Bo flapped his arms and stomped around the litter of the yard: the odd planks, flecks of dried paint, balls of concrete.

"At least we know what he was hiding," Bo said. "Why he looked guilty when you went to tell him about Loretta's murder. He probably thought you'd come to arrest him for burglary."

"I should."

Bo stood hunched, back to the wind, like a steer in rain. "No, Wittie. Just let it be."

In the trash barrel, an appliquéd heart curled like a fist.

"I'd like to talk to Loretta's neighbors," Bo told him. "Maybe we could run out there before dark."

DeWitt jabbed the stick hard into the can. The condom. Evidence that Janet's lover was a careful man. The pill gave her migraines; she couldn't tolerate IUDs. Billy wasn't careful. But Foster was.

"—think?"

DeWitt glanced up. "What?"

"I said, maybe they saw something, you think?"

"Who?"

"Loretta's neighbors. Put the stick down, Wittie. It's all burned up now."

DeWitt looked into the can, where gray ashes swirled. "All right."

"I'll drive." Bo pried the keys from his fingers.

On the way through town, DeWitt made Bo stop at the Mobil station. Bo went in and got Cokes for them both. DeWitt walked to the payphone. He jiggled the receiver, got a dial tone, called his house. The phone rang. He wasn't sure what he'd say.

The phone rang again.

Janet would be hurrying in from the yard, her golden hair down, her cheeks high-colored and Summery from her run. Her face would be pink and tender, like a flower in a field of wheat. Janet had a small face, just the size to cup in his hands.

Hi, he'd say.

And there would be a long, startled pause. DeWitt didn't call during the day unless something was very wrong.

Just thinking about you, he'd tell her, like a note on a Hallmark card. He might sleep with Hattie; but he was always think-ing of Janet.

The phone rang again.

Nothing he did, nothing he said, seemed to satisfy her any more. The bra had been an anniversary present, bought at a *Victoria's Secret* in Dallas before Bomb Day. He couldn't recall what she'd given him that year.

He'd made sure of the bra's size, had taken the time to check her dresser drawers. He'd wanted everything to be perfect. And when he saw it in the store, the red lace and tiny white hearts seemed so much like her.

She hated the gift. He saw in her face that it was too vulgar or embarrassing or something. When the kids tried to peek into the package, she hid it from them.

Only Billy had gotten use out of it.

He roused himself from his reverie and banged the receiver into the cradle. The phone had gone unanswered too long.

If Bo hadn't been with him, DeWitt would have driven to Hattie's; even though Hattie couldn't make up for the pink and gold perfection he'd lost. DeWitt had loved Janet from the time he was seventeen. Yet when he was home with her, he felt he was trapped in a cut-throat game with an invisible ball.

As he walked away, the phone rang. He walked back and picked up the receiver. "Hello?"

"Checking to see if there is damage," a Torku voice said. "You abused the phone. Damage can result if you abuse the phone."

"I'll remember that." DeWitt slammed the receiver home with such force that the cradle snapped.

19

"You all right, Wittie?"

DeWitt glanced up from his brooding scrutiny of the dash. Bo had parked in a rutted clay drive before a white clapboard house.

"You coming, or what?" Bo's door was open; one long twill-uniformed leg outside the car.

Disoriented, DeWitt looked around. Behind the house was a long chicken coop, its awning half-closed to the wind.

"Yeah." He zipped up his jacket and got out.

"Miz Wilson?" Bo called as they reached the porch.

DeWitt knocked on the chipped front door. "Police, Miz Wilson."

The house was churchyard quiet. Bo stepped back a couple of paces, his boots loud against the wood. "Etta Wilson!"

Etta Wilson: Janet's dubious alibi. "Maybe she's out at the barn." DeWitt walked to the end of the porch and peeked around the house.

"You don't think . . ." Bo began.

In the window to his right DeWitt caught a flicker of movement. He retreated, his rear colliding with the porch railing.

"What?" Bo whispered.

"I don't know."

The two men stood uncertainly. Bo's heel made a nervous staccato on the old boards. Then white lace curtains parted with a jerk and a pallid face swam out of the gloom of the parlor.

"Go away." The elderly woman's voice came faintly through the glass. The curtains closed again.

DeWitt knocked on the pane. "Miz Wilson? We got to talk to you now. Come on, Miz Wilson. It's the police."

As though forming of ectoplasm, the face reappeared. "What do you want?"

"Just want to talk, Miz Wilson. You all right?"

"Stay out there, DeWitt. We can talk just fine."

"Ma'am?" DeWitt put his ear to the window, but she rapped on the pane. Deafened, he reeled back.

"Don't get so damned close. Ain't you heard about the cholera?"

"What's she saying?" Bo asked.

DeWitt's ear still rang. "Cholera."

Bo took his place at the window. "Miz Wilson? Cholera can't spread by droplet."

"By what?"

"Through the air, Miz Wilson!" Bo was screaming. Even without the barrier of the glass, the old woman was a bit deaf. "It doesn't spread like flu! It breeds in feces!"

"In what?" She squinted.

"Feces!"

"—what?"

Bo's mouth worked in indecision. He looked to DeWitt for help.

"Bodily fluids!" DeWitt shouted.

"Oh."

"We need to ask you about the murder," Bo continued.

"I ain't killed her."

"We know that!" Bo was losing his temper. His cheeks were a furious red. "But maybe you *saw something!*"

The face vanished. The curtains slowly undulated as they came to rest. When the front door opened and the two men walked inside, Miz Wilson maced them with Lysol.

DeWitt threw his arms up, but he was too late. His eyes streamed. Bo bent double coughing.

"I ain't seen much of anything. Don't know as how I'll do you much good." The old woman sprayed a layer of disinfectant on her sofa. "Now you boys just sit down."

They collapsed on the sofa.

"Y'all want coffee?" she asked.

"No, we don't have time, thank you." Bo wiped his eyes and coughed again. "Just wanted to know if you saw anything strange Sunday."

"Nothing. You mind if I have myself a cup?"

"Go right ahead," Bo said before DeWitt had the chance to ask if she had visitors on Sunday.

Miz Wilson walked into the next room, still talking. "Loretta tore out of her place in an all-fired hurry, though."

Bo sat up as though he'd been hit with a cattle prod. "What time?"

From the kitchen came a clatter of china. "Around five-thirty."

"You sure it was Loretta?"

A cabinet door opened with a squeal and closed with a bang. "It was Loretta's car."

"Did you see it come back?"

"Didn't notice."

Bo said to DeWitt, "The car. I knew it. The car's the answer. Where'd Loretta go? And, more to the point, where's the car now?"

Miz Wilson came back, balancing a cup of coffee and a plate of homemade chocolate-chip cookies. Bo turned to her so fast that she nearly dropped her load. "You didn't see who was driving, then?"

The woman hovered above an overstuffed chair, then sat as decorously as her age allowed. "Didn't have my glasses."

"Miz Wilson?" DeWitt asked. "Were you home Sunday?"

"All day."

"Anybody come over? For a visit, maybe. Anybody who can verify your whereabouts?" He steeled himself for the answer.

"Nope. I need witnesses and all?"

DeWitt quickly changed the subject. "What do you know about Billy?"

She leaned forward. "They was having them marital problems. He never was no good. Have yourself a cookie, Bodeen."

Bo placed the platter out of DeWitt's reach. "How've you been feeling?"

She bit into a cookie. "Got the arthritis real bad in my knee. Been down in my back . . ."

"When?" Miz Wilson must have gotten her days confused. Janet had come over Sunday. They both had a laugh when Janet admitted she'd forgotten the old woman's toothpaste.

"Couple of weeks ago. Sometimes it don't even pay to get out of bed no more."

"Uh-huh," Bo said. "No stomach upset or anything?"

"Used to love that Mexican food. Can't eat it now."

"Nothing else?" Bo asked.

She considered the question; considered her cookie. "Get the palpitations sometimes."

"What about the Torku?" Bo asked.

Miz Wilson, like Seresen, was a good conversation shifter. "They put up a roadblock the other night."

DeWitt stared dejectedly at the plate of cookies.

"Roadblock?"

"Yeah. With flares and them orange traffic cones. That was the day her road up and disappeared. Oh! And I got one of them little skin cancers about three weeks ago. Doc burned it off for me." She held her arm toward Bo. There was a brown spot on the crepe skin.

"That's the only time you saw any Torku?"

Miz Wilson was delicately sucking the chocolate off her fingers. "I imagine."

"And you didn't see who was driving Loretta's car?"

"Nope."

"Could it have been a Torku?"

DeWitt tried to remember the last time Janet had made Tollhouse cookies. Six years ago. Before she began her affair.

"Might have. Did I tell you about the palpitations?"

"Pass the cookies, Bo," DeWitt said.

"No." Turning to Miz Wilson, he explained, "I'm trying to make him watch his weight."

Miz Wilson tittered and threw DeWitt an embarrassingly flirtatious glance. "Oh, now. He don't look near fat enough to me."

"Have you seen any activity at all at Loretta's?" Bo had taken a small notebook from his pocket and was scribbling.

"Just that blue flash when they up and made her house disappear."

"I see. Thank you." Bo got to his feet and stuck his notebook in his pocket. "You might want to start boiling your water, Miz Wilson. Just as a precaution."

As DeWitt rose, his gaze dropped to the cookies, and comprehension hit.

A pale hand flew to Miz Wilson's generous chest. "Oh, Lord. You think them Torku pushed them boys down in that well, don't you. And them bodily fluids is in that water."

"Just as a precaution."

She jumped up, her arthritis forgotten. "You think them bodily fluids is down there percolating around."

"There's no reason to . . ."

But with a flutter of her skirts, Miz Wilson darted out the front door.

DeWitt turned to his officer. Without the sunglasses, Bo looked no older than eighteen—as young as the boy he killed. For an instant DeWitt felt he could tell him anything. But his urge to confess broke against the granite of Bo's jaw.

"Bo? You ever wondered about the gas? Why it's the one thing the Torku don't deliver on time?"

"That's because you don't remind them. You can't see the level in the tanks, so I suppose it slips your mind."

DeWitt was irked that Bo guessed correctly. "So where did you get yours yesterday?"

"I hoard it. Like Doc. Like a few others. Anyway, the motorcycle uses less."

DeWitt nodded. Cost—the reason Curtis and the city council made Bo a motorcycle cop in the first place. "Who was out on the street yesterday?"

"B.J. But then he only uses the three-wheeler when his and his daddy's trucks are dry."

And Janet. DeWitt always made sure the Suburban had gas, even when his squad car didn't.

"Bo? I can't see Loretta hauling gas cans around."

"Shit, of course. You're right. It had to be a Torku driving."

DeWitt bit his lip. That hadn't been the conclusion DeWitt wanted Bo to reach at all.

A door banged. The two men walked onto the porch. DeWitt took a deep breath. The air outside the house smelled bland without the Lysol.

In the side yard Miz Wilson was loading chickens into her Dodge station wagon. The Rhode Island reds had been startled into nesting posture. They sat—small, neat boxes of sorrel feathers—motionless but for the deft, anxious jerks of their heads.

She plopped a pair of hens on the back seat and ran for more. When she came out, a chicken under each arm, Bo tried to stop her. She pushed past him without breaking stride. Two more trips, and she was done.

"There's no reason to panic," Bo said.

Miz Wilson got in the car and slammed it into reverse. The Dodge tore backward down the rutted drive, its windows turning rust-colored as the motion alarmed the hens into flight.

20

"Possible locations of the kids' bodies," Bo said, marking the points off in his notebook. His chestnut hair was dark with rain, and a lock of it had fallen into his eyes. DeWitt barely listened. "One, the trunk of Loretta's car . . ."

Janet might have killed Loretta, but how could she put a knife into baby fat? Strangle bright round faces to a dull gray?

DeWitt's own childhood had been so secure that it hadn't prepared him for the trouble that would come. Bo was prepared: his mother an alcoholic, his father vanished before he was six, one sister a suicide, a brother in Huntsville Prison.

". . . but Loretta's car might have been in the garage when the Torku destroyed the house," Bo was saying. "Okay. Two, the well . . ."

DeWitt's daddy had been the perfect father, active in Boy Scouts and Little League. Yet Bo, despite his childhood, had grown up more self-assured than he.

Suddenly Bo stopped scribbling. "Where are you headed?"

"You ever think about when you were a kid?" DeWitt eased the car onto the two-lane asphalt highway, but didn't accelerate.

Blue-bellied clouds were scudding south, leaving the sky a newly washed azure plate.

"Not much. Where you headed?"

"Just poking around." DeWitt pulled up behind a fire-damaged Dairy Queen and stopped.

The windows of the fast-food restaurant were boarded. Pooled rainwater pattered through a hole in the sagging eaves. He rolled down his window and heard music — as faint as that on Granger's radio. "Remember Dandy Mill? The one that burned? We used to hang out there. Did you?"

"Burned down the rest of the way before I was big enough to bike out there."

"What if the kids aren't dead?"

Bo looked up in surprise.

"Let's get out. Don't close your door."

The two men crept to the rear of the building. The back of the ruined restaurant smelled of old smoke and stale urine. Over the persistent beat of rock music came a soprano giggle; a baritone laugh.

DeWitt stepped over the sooted threshold, his boots grinding charred litter.

"Preston?" a boy's voice called.

DeWitt froze.

"Hey, Preston! You bring the stuff?"

"He's trying to scare us," someone said to someone else.

Three paces, and DeWitt was at the rear of the counter. Around a table sat five teenagers, cans of whipped cream on the grimy Formica, paper sacks in their hands.

Tammy put her can on the table with a rattling clunk. "Daddy, I can explain." Her voice shook with inappropriate glee.

Bo walked to the table. DeWitt switched off the tape player.

"Get up," Bo said.

Tammy, a small thing of pink and gold. Her face looked so much like Janet's when Janet was a girl that it brought a catch to DeWitt's throat.

Bo shouted, "On your feet!"

The three boys rose with the awkwardness of inebriation and youth.

"Empty your pockets."

The boys glanced at one another. The girls snorted laughter into cupped hands.

"Now!"

DeWitt made his way to Bo's side. Tammy wouldn't meet his gaze.

The restaurant had the sordid, littered look of all secret places. Stubs of candles squatted on the tables. A tattered mattress lay in one corner. Greasy food wrappers were scattered on the floor.

There wasn't much in the boys' pockets. Candy. Pocket knives. A condom.

The red foil package of the condom gleamed in the light from the poorly boarded windows. DeWitt stared at it, mesmerized, until Bo swept it off the table.

"Any marijuana?"

The merriment evaporated. Heads down, the boys flicked cautious glances at Bo. "No, sir," one said.

Eddie. DeWitt remembered the kid's name. A sixteen-year-old. Maybe Janet wasn't the one having an affair. Maybe sixteen-year-old Eddie had made it in the family Suburban with DeWitt's thirteen-year-old daughter.

A humming silence pressed its thumbs into DeWitt's ears. Distantly he heard Bo ask, "Glue? You boys got any glue to sniff?"

"No, sir."

"You come in here, sniff laughing gas, and then go out and

break streetlights? Do you? You spraypaint stuff on the walls in town?"

A girl tittered.

Bo whirled to her. "You think this is funny?"

Her smile died. "No, sir."

"A nitrous oxide high doesn't last for more than a minute or two. You're sober. Act like it. Get up. I said *get up!*"

The girl nearly fell getting to her feet.

A sound behind them. Preston Nix was standing in the doorway, a box of whipped cream in his hands. The carton fell with a crash. He ran.

"I could arrest you. You know that?" Bo asked.

They nodded. Tammy's graceful neck was like her mother's. Thirteen years old, and there had been a condom in the boy's pocket. Wadding leaked from the mattress like guts from a road kill. There were yellow stains on the ticking.

"There's a murderer loose around here. He probably killed two kids already. We know he killed their mother. And you kids are out sniffing laughing gas?"

They made incoherent sounds of apology.

"Y'all go home. Y'all just go on home. But I'll be watching you. Remember that."

The kids filed past. DeWitt's hand closed on Eddie's arm.

"Wittie," Bo warned. "Let him go."

DeWitt caught the front of the boy's jacket and jerked him up until they were face-to-face. The boy went rigid. DeWitt remembered the low-tide stench of sex in Billy's hideaway; he thought he could smell it here, too, like a haunting.

Bo's horrified cry of, "Wittie! No!"

DeWitt's blow was quick and hard; his fist went deep into Eddie's belly, and the force of it lifted the boy to his toes.

Something pulled on his shoulder. DeWitt reacted faster

110

than thought. His hand snapped to the side, and hit with a wet, firm smack.

Tammy stumbled backward.

Bo caught her and turned, placing his own body between Tammy and DeWitt.

DeWitt stared at his knuckles, wondering how his arm had moved without his willing it, wondering where the blood had come from. Suddenly he was aware of the boy retching at his feet, of the dust motes in the streaks of dirty sunshine from the windows. He saw Bo with his arms around Tammy, and saw the new bright red on her lips.

Eddie scurried out of the Dairy Queen.

"Honey?" DeWitt reached for his daughter. She cowered.

Bo took a hankerchief out of his pocket and daubed at her mouth. "It's okay. It's all over. It's all over now."

DeWitt watched his daughter cry. It had been easier when she was young, when she came home with no more than a skinned knee, a stubbed toe. When comfort was measured in Band-aids and ice cream.

Now his hands weren't clean enough to touch her. "Honey, daddy didn't mean it. Baby? I didn't mean to do that. Would you like some ice cream, punkin? Would you?"

Between sobs, she nodded. And DeWitt wondered, at this late and sour date, how sweet he could make the world.

21

ON THE DRIVE TO TOWN DeWitt listened to the sniffling of Tammy in the back seat, the soothing croons of Bo. Bo more than anyone knew the lure of excessive force.

His photo in the Dallas papers, the official portrait in police blue. With those disarming eyes he'd looked like a child playing dress-up; but then you noticed the ominous set of the jaw.

Did you mean to? DeWitt had asked during the preliminary interview.

Bo's expression hadn't changed; but his hand, curled on the armrest, tightened into a fist. *The grand jury no-billed.*

DeWitt was surprised at the calm, even tone of the reply. But then Bo had had practice repeating his innocence: to the press, to Internal Affairs, at the Coroner's hearing.

That wasn't what I asked you. Did you mean to kill him?

The only clue to Bo's tension was a slight tremor in his hand. *I got separated from my partner. My fault. That never should have happened. A fistfight started, and I tried to break it up.* Emotion-less. As if he had discovered that the key to indifference was repetition.

How did you feel toward Jerry Hardesty?

Feel? The round blue eyes widened. *The victim was intoxicated, belligerent. The autopsy proved his blood alcohol level was—*

He was a faggot.

The tip of Bo's tongue traced his top lip.

They were all faggots. The great Oak Lawn Halloween, everyone in drag. How did you feel about that?

Bo sat in the line of DeWitt's questioning like a frog in a gigger's light.

One of the witnesses was dressed like Marilyn Monroe, if I recall, DeWitt told him. *And Hardesty himself was in leather, like a biker, only he was wearing a strand of pearls. Did that repulse you, I guess is what I want to know. Some men feel uncomfortable around that sort of thing. Frightened of it, I suppose. How did you feel?*

At last DeWitt saw he had gotten past the recorded loop into thoughts too terrible to be voiced. *I felt the bone break.*

What?

Bo opened his fist. There were half-moon prints of fingernails in the pale skin. *When I had him in the chokehold, I thought everything was in control. Then I felt the bone break.*

It was only after Bo was hired that DeWitt learned Jerry Hardesty's death hadn't been the accident everyone, including Bo, believed it to be. The chokehold had been a symptom. It wasn't that Bo felt above the law; but that he believed himself inseparable from it.

DeWitt parked on Main. They climbed out of the car. He wanted to tell Tammy he was sorry, but she wasn't looking at him. Her head was down, her blond hair cascaded on either side of her face. A purple bruise was blossoming on her cheek.

"DeWitt," Bo called.

DeWitt stopped and turned. Bo was standing by an old station wagon. Uneven white streaks ran down the red upholstery, and white blotches marred the dash.

"Chicken shit," Bo said.

"What?"

"Miz Wilson's car."

"Let's go have ice cream," DeWitt said abruptly.

"But—"

"I don't want to think about it right now. We'll find out what she's up to later. First things first. Let's go get Tammy her ice cream." He started up the sidewalk fast, Bo and Tammy in his wake.

They passed the bank and entered the next open doorway. The drugstore aisles were empty, the front counters unmanned. Purposefully, DeWitt made his way to the soda fountain.

". . . prayed about it." Pastor Jimmy's master-of-ceremonies voice, louder than the ubiquitous Muzak, drifted over a wall of products for feminine protection. "The chief of police is an adulterer, and he has joined the forces of Satan."

Blue boxes of Stay-Free Maxi Pads at his shoulder, DeWitt stopped. *Adulterer.*

Now Doc spoke. "Bo's more used to writing up traffic tickets and killing queers than looking for a damned murderer. And ever since Bomb Day, DeWitt's been cozying up to them Torku like a newborn looking for a tit."

"Them just sitting there," a female voice put in, quavering with indignation. "Sitting there, mind, while I'm up to my ears in that poisoned coffee. Who's going to get them damned boys out of my well water, I want to know."

Adulterer. Had Tammy heard? Had she understood?

"Well, now," Doc said reasonably, "you just go on and stay with your people in town, Miz Wilson. That's the best thing. I'll

114

get a sample of your water in a few days and see just what's there."

"In the meantime . . ." Pastor Jimmy began.

"Yeah, in the meantime," Doc said, "we do what you suggested. We'll get rid of as many of the Torku as we can. Soon as the sun's down. And for God's sake, Miz Wilson, will you not say anything to DeWitt-less or that wind-up rent-a-cop?"

"After prayer service," Jimmy said. "It must happen after prayer service, so that we are sure the Lord is with us. And you must come, Doctor, to be anointed. You and all your people. Otherwise you cannot have my support. Around nine, then?"

A clunk. Someone had set a glass down on the counter hard. "Nine." Doc sounded annoyed.

Muzak was playing a lethargic "Cecilia" as the three conspirators walked down the neighboring aisle, through the antacids, and out the door.

DeWitt heard the door close, the voices fade. "What kind, Tammy?" he snapped.

"Huh?"

"Goddamn it! What flavor ice cream do you want?"

Tears welled. "You still mad at me, Daddy?"

DeWitt's legs went weak. "Oh no, baby. No." He took hold of her shoulders and pulled her close. Her hair smelled of shampoo and smoke. "Daddy's not mad."

There was no reason for his anger. The condom in Eddie's pocket was old, like the one DeWitt had aged in his wallet through four years of high school. It wasn't careful planning, but wishful thinking.

A clang startled them both. Bo was no longer in the aisle. "Bo?"

"Here." The answer came from the soda fountain. When DeWitt and Tammy walked around the end of the Kotex aisle, they found him, grim-faced, making three sundaes.

"Let's eat the damned ice cream and get out." Bo shoved one chocolate-on-chocolate sundae toward Tammy and another toward DeWitt.

DeWitt kept his head down, reluctant to meet Bo's gaze. *The police chief is an adulterer.* Even now Bo must be wondering who. He would never suspect Hattie.

"Eat," Bo said. "Then maybe we can go tell the Torku they're about to be murdered."

DeWitt pushed the sundae away, untouched. Until today he had believed himself better than Bo. That was the reason he hired him. DeWitt might have a Spring's quick temper, but he'd never injured a suspect. Never before raised a hand to a child, particularly one of his own. Had wanted, even at the cost of the law, to protect the town.

Bo finished his scoop of vanilla, rinsed the dish, and left the rest for the Torku to clean. "Come on. Let's take Tammy home."

"You drive."

With a questioning glance, Bo took the keys.

They walked to the car, Tammy licking ice cream off the swollen side of her lip. It looked as though the bruise was hurting her.

When they arrived at the house, Bo insisted on accompanying Tammy inside. Janet came in from the kitchen, wiping her hands on a dishtowel. She halted when she saw the three of them standing in the den. The towel dropped.

Denny appeared at the door behind his mother, a bag of Cheetos in his hand.

Janet rushed forward, looked at her daughter's bruise. "What happened to you, honey?"

"I fell down and hurt myself, and Daddy brought me home."

Janet turned to DeWitt, and he had the sudden urge to con-

116

fess. To tell her of his own brutality, of his own affair. And that he knew of hers.

"Tammy fell," Bo said. "She just fell down. Maybe you can put some ice on it or something."

Janet looked at Bo, lips tightening. Bo stared evenly back. Then she put out a hand to her daughter and told her to come on.

Denny, a ring of Cheeto-orange around his mouth, was the last to leave the room. He lingered at the door, disappointed that the event had been defused.

When he was gone, Bo told DeWitt, "Okay. Now we talk to the Torku."

22

THE VISITORS' LOT WAS EMPTY. DeWitt nosed the squad car to the steps of the center and parked.

Bo asked, "You sure you don't want me to come with you?"

What Bo *hadn't* asked was: "Who is she?" "When did the affair start?" Any of the expected questions.

"It's best if I go alone."

DeWitt got out and trudged up the stairs. In the rec room the lights were on, the ping-pong tables and couches empty of the usual teenagers. Feeling a tingle of unease, he walked across the indoor/outdoor carpeting.

A voice from a side room: ". . . marketing plan."

Startled, he drew back until he was hidden in the tiny kitchen. The voice was pitched low, and it oozed with salesmanship. It belonged to Hubert Foster.

"Explain marketing," Seresen said.

It was an eight-block hike from the banker's house to the center, and the weather was chilly, even for an Autumn. Foster evidently wanted to keep his visit a secret.

"Okay. Let's consider your goal. You and I know that goal visualization is the first step, right?"

DeWitt tried to imagine what sort of goal Seresen might have. He couldn't.

Foster would have continued his pitch, but Seresen became uncharacteristically garrulous. "It is the primary truth. As universes leak into each other, all things are one. All time is one. There is no here and now . . ."

"Yes, yes. That's all very interesting. And *just* what I'm talking about. Marketing means bending the universe in such a way that it works for you. Now. My suggestion is that a couple of us go to the other side and set up a program."

DeWitt was fascinated. He leaned over a coffee maker to catch Foster's every quiet word.

"Those people on the other side are probably hungry. We give them food. We talk to them a little about religion. They'll go for it. You'll see —"

"But here." The alien seemed frustrated. "We set the program here."

Religion? DeWitt didn't know what Foster meant by religion, but he knew what he was up to. And it was obvious Seresen hadn't figured out that he was being used. Foster wanted to cross the Line as some New Age CEO. DeWitt wondered if Loretta had threatened to expose the scam and that was why Foster killed her. He wondered if Seresen knew Foster was the murderer, and was protecting him anyway.

"The people here aren't receptive. That's why you haven't been able to make inroads. They're tied to outmoded ideas. Look. You start over with a clean slate. Take everything away: food, housing, safety. That's how you get a fresh market. It's simple. Over on the other —"

Seresen sounded exasperated. "Life is not simple. It is complex, yet it contains order. A leaf holds the structure of a tree. A speck of dust is a model to the boulder. These things are identical, yet distinct."

DeWitt leaned farther over, and held his breath.

"I know that, Seresen. You're preaching to the choir here. Let's go to the other side. Those people are hungry for the truth. What they need is a leader, and you know I've been preparing. How much I've worked—"

"You do *not* understand. There is no choice between one side and the other. The Monopoly players are one. The board is one with the pieces. You do *not* understand. Some think the preacher speaks of existence when he talks about this Rapture, but I suspect he does not understand, either. Six years, and you still separate the pieces from the board."

"Wait a minute! Wait a minute, Seresen! Don't leave. I brought flow charts. I've got statistics . . ."

DeWitt took a deep breath and walked around the edge of the alcove. Not five feet in front of him, Seresen came to a sudden stop. Behind the small alien, Foster went through a Torku transformation, turning pink from neck to scalp.

Childhood is hungry: it reaches out small, selfish hands. The mature DeWitt could not let go of the adolescent Janet, and Janet was snared by the teenaged Foster. The current Foster was out of shape. His gut strained the buttons of his shirt. Janet didn't see that he wasn't a teenager with a convertible anymore.

"Foster? Go home. And Seresen, I want your people in your side of the center right now. There's going to be trouble."

The obvious question came not from the Kol, but from Foster. "What kind of trouble?"

"Call them together now."

Foster stayed put. DeWitt couldn't tell whether courage kept him from leaving or if his knees had simply locked up.

"Let me handle everything, Seresen. I want you out of the way. Bo and I will need our guns."

Seresen's answer was quick and to the point. "No."

"I'm a cop. You talked a moment ago about order." Foster's blush faded to a cadaverous pallor. Now the banker knew that DeWitt had been eavesdropping. "What the badge represents is order. But I can't stand up against the whole town unarmed."

"Your type of order is ignorance. We do not need you. I will get my people into the center."

DeWitt raised his voice. "It's my *job!*"

Seresen's calm eyes were pink with threads of saffron through them. "It is your job to protect us if you must. It is my job to tell you no. Probabilities spring from this occurrence. They form a resonant pattern."

"Shit." For a while DeWitt had thought he had some idea of what the alien was talking about. Now he was totally lost.

"Look. I don't want you to do anything stupid," he said. "Bo and I will go up to the church. We'll check things out. Nothing's going to happen until around nine."

Foster shrugged. "Well, DeWitt, if nothing's going to happen until nine . . ."

"Time is arbitrary," Seresen told the banker. "And I will get my people from the church."

DeWitt checked his watch. Five to seven. "All right. Let's get moving," he said.

23

JIMMY SCHOEN CHECKED THE MIRROR that hung on the pulpit door and brushed a prodigal lock of hair into place. He straightened his tie and then straightened it again.

"You look just fine, Jimmy."

He ignored his wife. Cracking open the door, he saw that the congregation was filing in. Doc was among them. As Doc had promised, the rest of the conspirators were there as well.

Schoen would talk of Moses, of the divine right of leadership. And then he had a little surprise. He would preach of Doc's drunkenness, of Purdy's vile home movies, of specific fornication and faithlessness. Schoen knew the conspirators well, knew their lies, had kept track of every indiscretion. He had looked into their living-room windows as God looked into their souls.

The demons had already occupied their side of the aisle — but there would be no killing in his church. He would make certain of that. His people would wait until the demons were outside before the hammer of God struck them down.

"Jimmy, honey?" Dee Dee called in her syrupy voice. "Look here, Jimmy. Look who's come."

Schoen reluctantly tore his gaze from the filling church. A polite greeting died on his lips.

"Hello, Pastor," the police chief said.

24

IF THE PASTOR WAS STUNNED, his wife was beaming. "It's so good to *see* you!" Dee Dee clapped her hands in delight. "Jimmy? Isn't it good to *see* them?"

Schoen, hands trembling, straightened his tie. The knot ended up at an angle to the collar.

Dee Dee aligned it, then stood back to inspect her work. "DeWitt and Bo are looking into the murder. Isn't that *interesting*?" To DeWitt she said, "That's just the most interesting thing." Her eyes, brown and sweet, were imperceptive as fudge.

"And *you*!" she said to Bo, who had not backed up quickly enough. "You just look so *good*. Doesn't Bo look good, Jimmy? Why, I think he's a Winter. That's a really nice season to be. *Very* intuitive. And has anybody ever told you you're a Spring, De-Witt? You should wear more yellow. A light yellow, not anything too heavy. Are y'all staying to service?"

"I . . ." DeWitt began uncertainly, amazed by Dee Dee's obvious tie to Foster.

"Yes," Bo said. "At least until just before nine."

Jimmy's eyes narrowed with cunning.

"Oh. Well, you know service ends at eight," Dee Dee said doubtfully. "But then we have coffee and cookies afterwards. You can buy something from the Washed in the Blood cake sale—"

"They may not want to stay," Schoen told her.

"Well, honey, they might. Eleanor Wheeler made one of her double chocolate cakes with marshmallow frosting and—"

DeWitt's grin tightened. "'Course at nine, we got places to go, people to see."

"Y'all just stay so *busy*. Don't they, honey? Don't they stay so *busy?*"

Schoen's mouth settled into a rebuking line. "I know sin when I look it in the face."

For once Dee Dee had nothing to say.

"Murder is sin," DeWitt said.

The pastor cleared his throat with an impressive rumble. When his words emerged, they rang, as though he were already standing in the pulpit. "Murder applies to creatures with souls. These demons are godless. Make your choice, Chief: Heaven or Hell. But don't force the town into the flames with you."

"Damn it, think for once!" DeWitt said. "We depend on the Torku for everything. What would you do if they were gone?"

Schoen had his answer ready, as though he had had it ready for years. "We'll pull down the Line!"

"You can't do that."

"Heaven's over there!" Schoen's voice rose beyond his usual evangelical control. "Don't you understand? God is waiting!"

Bo put a hand on Schoen's arm. The pastor pulled away. "You listen to reason, Pastor. You do anything tonight, you'll all be cited. You don't want that. You don't want to break the law. I know you don't."

"I follow *God's* law! And you'll find out what God's law is all about if you stay, Chief. Because I'm naming names. And two

125

of the sinning names are DeWitt Dawson and Hattie Nichols."

DeWitt felt anesthetized. He wondered if this was the first symptom of a stroke.

"Don't y'all want some coffee?" Dee Dee said with hysterical cordiality. "I can get us all some coffee."

Schoen flung open the door to the pulpit. "Your wife's in her pew, Chief. The same place she sits every night. The children are with her. When I call the sinners to the altar to be forgiven, don't you want to be cleansed? When I rebuke you as Satan's messenger, don't you want to hear? After the righteous strike you down, will you dare stand before the Throne unrepentant?"

Don't, DeWitt thought. *Don't attack the Torku. Don't tell Janet.*

"You've waltzed with the demons for six years, Chief," Schoen said. "Stay. Have the last dance."

Bo stepped forward, pushing the preacher aside to glance out the door. "Seresen's getting the Torku together. Come on, Wittie. Let's go."

Bo dragged him, stumbling, outside. In the gravel parking lot Torku were climbing into their UPS vans, and Seresen was standing by the squad car, waiting.

DeWitt balked. "I'll get Janet and the kids. I'll bring them with us. She'll never have to know."

"He's going to order those people to kill you! Don't you get it?" Bo pulled him to the squad car, jerked open the passenger door, and shoved him inside. Seresen hopped into the back seat. Bo got behind the wheel and in a loud shower of gravel sent the car into wild reverse. At the road, he braked and spun. Floorboarding the accelerator, he sped toward town.

Through the rear window, the church receded until it was hidden behind a screen of winter-bare trees. DeWitt pictured Janet and his kids, hands folded in their laps, as they waited for service to begin.

25

"Seresen—What did Foster want?" DeWitt hung onto the door handle as Bo whipped around a curve. "What are you two cooking up?"

Seresen stared out his side window. "We talked of nothing."

"I was listening! I stood there and heard. Foster wanted you to take him across the Line."

"You misunderstood."

DeWitt's juggling act was in trouble, his concentration lost— Seresen, Janet, and her lover suspended in mid-air. DeWitt had always known he would have to choose. Without a pang of regret, he let Foster fall.

"I have reason to believe Hubert Foster is guilty of the murder of Loretta Harper and the disappearance of Billy Junior and Jason Harper. Are you protecting him, Seresen?"

"Foster isn't guilty," Bo said.

"Oh yes, he is. He plans to start his own little empire on the other side of the Line. Then Loretta finds out. She must have threatened to expose him."

"Foster couldn't have killed her, DeWitt. He was at my house Sunday night." But a muscle twitched in Bo's jaw.

"Oh? How long was he there?"

A pause: Bo was thinking. "He came early afternoon and didn't leave until eleven that night."

"Why did Foster tell me he was home? Was he lying?"

"I guess so."

"Why would he lie about that? What were you doing?"

"We talked." His upper lip beaded with perspiration.

"You talked, from early afternoon until eleven at night."

From the back seat Seresen piped up. "The Hubert talks a great deal."

DeWitt turned around. The car was ripe with the smell of nervous sweat, and a faint Elmer's Glue smell that must have been Seresen. "What does he talk about?"

"The Hubert is fond of two dimensions. He tries to explain things with flat graphs and charts. I find it illogical and confusing. It is also confusing why the townspeople are so angry."

"They're scared. When people are scared, they do stupid things."

Bo slowed as he entered the center's parking lot. When the headlights picked out a pink Buick Regal among the delivery trucks, he hit the brakes so hard that Seresen was flung against the rear of DeWitt's seat.

"Jesus," Bo said. "It's Loretta's car."

DeWitt jumped out as Bo sprinted to the Regal. The officer was wrapping his fingers in a handkerchief, pulling the door open, taking the keys from the ignition, and going to the trunk.

If the boys were there, the smell would hit first: the heavy green stench of a dead rat in a wall, only a hundred times worse.

Across the lot Seresen was calmly getting out of the squad car. And at the door of the center, five other Torku stood, having appeared as if by magic. They held black sticks in their hands.

Bo was breathing hard. He couldn't slot the key. A bead of sweat dislodged from his hairline and rolled down the side of his face.

The Torku were closer, only a few feet away.

"They're the murderers," Bo said in a rush. "They did it, don't you see? Maybe Loretta *did* have that meeting with Seresen. Maybe she told him something he didn't want to hear. Loretta left her house in her car that evening. Miz Wilson said so. Tore off in a hurry, she said. Wherever Loretta was headed, she didn't make it. Whoever killed her had this Regal."

"You don't have any evidence. Bo, listen to me."

The key slid home; the trunk popped open. There was a blanket-wrapped bundle over the spare tire.

"You will go now," Seresen said from the shadows at the front fender of the Regal.

Bo took the handcuffs from his belt. "Kol Seresen, I'm arresting you for the murder of Loretta Harper."

DeWitt pushed Bo aside and flipped the blankets down, exposing a pile of boxes. Loretta had never made her Mary Kay deliveries. "Seresen!" DeWitt shouted. "Hide the car."

Bo swiveled, his eyes full of rage.

DeWitt grabbed for the keys. Bo shoved him away. DeWitt shoved back with all the strength of desperation. Bo fell. The handcuffs and keys flew out of his fingers; they clinked across the asphalt.

Seresen picked up the keys and closed the trunk. Slipping into the Regal, he drove it toward the center. The garage door opened; Seresen parked Loretta's car over a hydraulic lift; and the wall rolled back in place.

Bo knocked DeWitt's offered hand away. He got to his feet and swayed, clasping the back of his head.

Seresen rushed outside. "It will be best if you come in now."

"Go on, DeWitt." Bo gestured. "Follow Seresen. Go plant a wet one on his fat, spotted ass."

"Stop it, Bo."

"You're a whore just like your daddy. You cover for Seresen just like your daddy covered for the Klan."

With an inarticulate moan, DeWitt grabbed for Bo's jacket. "You draggle-tail peckerwood white trash! Your mama was nothing but a goddamned drunk!"

Bo pushed him away.

"She crawled under the sheets with every man in town! No wonder your daddy left! And who was there to take her home when she passed out? Who made sure her kids had enough to eat? Had coats in the winter? Don't you remember? My daddy! So who was the whore?"

He charged. Bo jumped out of the way. DeWitt's momentum sent him into a postal truck. He heard a whistle behind him and knew what it meant. Before he could duck, Bo's night stick hit the back of his head.

Sharp, hot pain. DeWitt staggered away, snatching at his belt for any protection: his flashlight, night stick. His mind struggled to think, his eyes to focus. Too slow. A whistle of metal through air, and the night stick smacked his cheek.

He was on his knees now. Bo had him in a choke hold. DeWitt tried to get up. He couldn't breathe. His own baton was lying inches away, just out of reach.

DeWitt tore at Bo's arm, fingers sliding on the officer's jacket. His vision contracted, telescoped, darkened at the edges. The world lost color.

The struggle was eerily silent except for the scrape of Bo's boot soles and his rapid, grunting breaths.

The gay boy in Dallas had twitched his life out on the sidewalk, hyoid bone crushed. A prolonged death. A crowd-pleaser. The boy flailed while the drunken mob watched.

DeWitt forced himself to go limp. Instantly, Bo released him. DeWitt fell, hands outspread. He caught his night stick, and twisting onto his back, punched the end of it between Bo's legs.

Only as the stick hit did DeWitt see Bo's expression. DeWitt, who had never killed anyone, nearly didn't recognize the emotion for what it was: fear and tremendous regret.

Bo groaned and toppled, curling into a fetal ball, cupping himself.

DeWitt scrabbled to his feet.

"Get . . ." Bo said, then ran out of air.

"I didn't mean what I said about your mama. I didn't mean it."

"Get . . . out."

"But my daddy wasn't like that."

Bo didn't reply.

With the weary expediency of his father, DeWitt walked away.

26

INSIDE THE REC CENTER a battalion of Torku stood guard. Seresen ordered DeWitt to a rear meeting room. Hubert Foster was sitting there.

As DeWitt entered, the banker's eyes widened. He popped up from his seat. "What happened to you? Is this the trouble you were talking about? Who hit you?" Foster sounded not only upset but angry. He took hold of DeWitt's chin and examined his bleeding head. "Don't move, Wittie. Let me check the dilation of your pupils."

DeWitt pulled away.

"Any dizziness? Double vision?"

"Cut it out." Exhausted, DeWitt collapsed into one of the half-dozen raspberry plush chairs.

"That's right," Foster said encouragingly. "You just relax and I'll get something for that bleeding." He dashed out the door. A few moments later he was back with a Styrofoam cup of water and a handful of paper towels.

"I can't believe they'd do this to you." Foster daubed at DeWitt's wound, wincing in sympathy as he worked. "I mean, you grew up with these people. Jimmy's only lived here—what?—ten years?"

Foster's attentions were so tentative as to be ineffectual. DeWitt snatched the wet towel away and with harsh, painful strokes wiped at the blood himself. "I had a little accident, Hubert, that's all. Will you stop?"

Foster sat back like a retriever anxiously awaiting the hunter's signal. When the paper towel was in tatters, Foster wordlessly gave him another. And when the towels stopped turning red, he brought him a plastic bag of ice.

"You got a joint?" Foster asked.

Baggie pressed to his aching head, DeWitt looked up, surprised at the banker's presumption. Foster's makeup had caked. Brown shadow made arcs over his lids.

"I get mine from Curtis. He told me you toke up sometimes."

DeWitt glanced at the partially open door and the Torku outside on guard. "Smoking in here might not be a good idea."

Foster laughed. "The Torku like marijuana. They think it makes us less linear. The only reason they confiscated booze and cigarettes was that Pastor Jimmy told them to. You didn't know that? Doesn't Seresen ever talk to you about things?"

DeWitt sat up straight. "Yeah, we talk."

"Aliens as cosmic Jehovah's Witnesses. And isn't their religion weird? You notice how for the Torku time isn't really time? You know how you look at a room over on their side and it's one way? And then you look at it again and it's changed? I think the Torku are universe-challenged."

A chill droplet rolled down DeWitt's forehead and into his eye. He swiped at it in exasperation. Seresen had never invited him to the Torku side of the center. He didn't know what Foster was talking about.

"Wittie, I need a joint."

"All my dope's in the squad car."

Foster's guffaw was so loud that a Torku poked his head in the doorway. "In the squad car. God, that's priceless."

"What's funny is you and Seresen. You talk, but I bet you never told him about con artists."

Foster looked hurt. From the kitchen came a quiet rumble as the center's icemaker engaged. There was a whine of a servo-motor, then the crystalline clatter of the machine upchucking ice into its bin.

"Look, Wittie. I used to be a jerk. No wonder when we were kids you thought you were better than me. For you, goodness always came easy. But there's a whole lot of people just like me across the Line. Their beamers and condos are gone. I want to tell those people what I've learned. What Seresen's taught me about life. I want a chance to clear my karma."

"Oh, karma? So tell me, Mr. Morality, how can your karma get clear if you're screwing someone else's wife? Unless, now that you're a lapsed Catholic, you don't think fornication is immoral."

DeWitt could see, by the flush in Foster's face, that he had hit home. "You mean . . . oh, the gossip. Okay, so I know some women. What's wrong with that? Mostly we talk. Guys, you know, we really don't say what's on our minds. Women talk about their feelings. It's a whole new way of seeing the world."

DeWitt's conversations with Janet were dust on a sideboard: transitory, easily wiped away. "I know about your affair with my wife."

Foster could not have looked more surprised if during Holy Communion the celebrating priest had slapped him. "Wait. What makes you think she's having an affair?"

"Cut the crap, Hubert. I've known for some time."

"It's not—" He stopped mid-sentence and swallowed hard. "I

134

see. Did you confront her? What did she say? I just can't believe she'd . . . that she actually—"

"I figure you killed Loretta. I assume you killed her boys. And Janet helped you. The tire tracks out at Sparrow Point were left by the Suburban's Dunlops. There was caliche in the treads. Mud on her sneakers. But she couldn't have disposed of the body alone. And you had the strongest motive. Whatever happens from this point on, I don't want her implicated. And I want you to tell me why Bo's covering for you. Does he know you did it? Is he trying to shift the blame to Seresen?"

"Bo's not covering . . . God." Foster's voice shook so that DeWitt could barely understand him. "Jesus, DeWitt. You can't think your own wife murdered Loretta. That I . . . This is crazy."

"Here's your story. I want you to memorize it so no one can trip you up. You killed Loretta, but couldn't fit her in the Corvette's trunk. You said you wanted to haul firewood when you borrowed the Suburban from me. You understand? You got the Suburban from me."

DeWitt wondered how Foster made people love him. How tiny Janet could murder; how gentle Seresen could protect them both; and how the honest Bo could lie.

"Bo knows I didn't kill her. And Janet would never . . . Oh, shit. What a mess."

"Be a man about it, Hubert. Don't start pointing fingers. I promise, if you shield Janet, I'll help you. We'll go for manslaughter, if possible. Or self-defense."

It baffled DeWitt why Foster thought he was a good man. He lied to suspects just as he was lying now, because if the kids were dead, Foster would be facing capital murder. And DeWitt would try his best to hurry him to execution before he had a chance to talk.

"Stop staring at me, DeWitt. I hate when you do that. You've got your cop face on. You look at me like you'd never known me; like you don't believe a word I'm saying."

"The thing I don't understand is how you did it, Hubert. I wish you'd tell me. How did you make that wound?"

Foster didn't reply. He looked at his watch and then looked again. "It's eight-thirty already. Christ, I need a joint." His smile was off-kilter. "You want to let me in your squad car?"

DeWitt handed him the keys.

Foster came back with a handful of weed, and they smoked. DeWitt checked the time. Eight-thirty became nine, nine crawled its way to nine-thirty. At ten-thirty Foster got up and went into an unlit room, DeWitt at his heels. In the glow from the doorway, Foster walked to an L-shaped pit group and collapsed. DeWitt lay down on the other leg of the overstuffed sofa without bothering to remove his boots.

In the darkness DeWitt felt time slip. He might have been a teenager again on a high school camp-out. They'd be sharing a can of beer Foster had filched from his daddy. Curtis would be talking about girls. Simpler times, smaller worries, even though Janet would be at school the next day, Foster's letter jacket around her shoulders, his class ring around her neck.

From the dark sofa, Foster whispered, "Listen, Wittie. I'm not having an affair with Janet and I didn't kill Loretta."

DeWitt lifted his wrist. According to the glowing face of his digital, it was five till eleven. The rec center was silent. A Torku stood at the doorway as though asleep on his feet. "Don't be scared to confess, Hubert. I'll take care of everything."

27

GOD'S GRACE COMES to those who wait, and Schoen had become an expert at waiting.

He checked his watch. Eleven-thirty. Around him, on Main Street, the townspeople were climbing ladders, hurriedly painting the Sign above their doors. Schoen imagined the quiet tread of the Angel, pictured scythed Death searching doorposts for God's mark.

His congregation stood ready, clubs and sticks in hand.

Quick footsteps on asphalt drew his attention. Dee Dee was walking toward him, her hands on her hips. "Jimmy, honey, you've gotten everybody upset. Everybody's so *upset*. And, I'm sorry, this is just *my* opinion, but that red paint looks tacky. It's dripping all down the doors. Can't you tell the men to be careful, and take their time? It's enamel paint, Jimmy. They'll never get that off."

"Don't embarrass me, Dee Dee," he warned. "Don't dare question me in front of my congregation."

As she turned to study the smears of red, he noticed her hair.

"Did I or did I not tell you to put a rinse on that?"

Her hand flew to her curls. "The frosting? I'm fixing to, honey. I just haven't had time, what with the revolution and all. I've made lemonade and coffee and gallons of iced tea. Sweetened and unsweetened. And I've helped the bake sale ladies put their sandwiches out. Tuna fish with pecans is what we voted on. I wanted watercress, but the girls didn't think the men would eat them. I cut the crusts off, anyway. Don't you think that's the most sophisticated thing, Jimmy? When you cut the sandwich crusts off?"

Everything else was going according to plan: everyone was under control but his wife. That night, when he asked, hadn't his flock embraced the sinners? Hadn't they forgiven the sins with streaming eyes?

"It's getting cold," she complained. "My fingers are freezing making all that tea. Everybody's overheated. The whole congregation's going to catch their death in this wind. When are you going to let us go home?"

"When it is finished." As punctuation, he turned his back on her.

Schoen wouldn't strike tonight. God's metronome ticked to a different rhythm than man's. The Master of Timelessness tarried; through millennia He abided. When the Signs were painted and the unrepentant culled, that's when the reaping would begin.

28

DEWITT AWOKE to find Seresen leaning over him. He sat up fast. The neighboring sofa was vacant. "What's the matter? What is it? We being attacked?"

"Everything is peaceful. And no one would wish to attack us. It is time to make deliveries."

Addled by a pounding headache, DeWitt followed Seresen outside. The morning was damp, the parking lot hushed, only the soft-footed Torku moving in it.

"Where's Hubert? I need to get some things straight with him."

"We will go in your car." Seresen opened the passenger door and got in.

DeWitt relinquished his questions to the dreamy, somnolent morning. Different times of the day brought the past back. Night reminded him of childhood friends; dawn, of fishing trips and early-morning café breakfasts with his father.

Yawning, he dug the keys out of his pocket. As he drove off, he pictured Denny sitting next to him: the fishing poles in back;

the tackle boxes with their brightly feathered lures stacked neat, each lure in its own narrow house.

When they arrived at Curtis's, Seresen led his workers into the convenience store; and while they restocked, DeWitt made himself a pot of coffee on the commercial machine. Curtis appeared, dressed in a ratty pair of sweats and a bathrobe.

"Jesus," he said. "What happened to you?"

"Nothing."

"Want a toke?"

"Shit, Curtis. Is that your idea of hospitality? Most people offer a beer. Every time we get together all you want to do is smoke."

"How do you know? You ain't been by." The little mayor sounded hurt.

"I've been busy. I got a murder to solve and your revolution to put down single-handed, remember?"

Curtis asked, "My revolution?" like a man trying to comprehend that he'd locked his keys in his car. "When did I start a revolution?"

"Weren't you there? I thought everybody else was down at the church last night plotting to kill me and the Torku."

"You're kidding! I missed the whole thing. I was watching *Animal House* on the VCR."

DeWitt drained the last of his coffee and tossed the cup into a green trash barrel.

"Revolution, huh? Sure you don't want a little toke?"

The Torku seemed busy, and order in Coomey was going down the drain. "Hell. Why not."

The sun had topped the horizon, turning Curtis's collection of cars-on-blocks a regal blue and gold. The house was too brightly lit, too immediate, to contain the magic kingdom of dawn.

140

In the bathroom, Curtis flipped down the toilet lid and sat. DeWitt perched on the rim of the tub. "Had a run on lighter fluid and Bic lighters." The mayor lit a joint and, in a neighborly gesture, handed it to him.

DeWitt took a toke and gave it back. "Lighter fluid? I don't like the sound of that."

"Meeting at the church, huh? I bet they had a dinner on the ground. I bet Patti Dix brought some of her jalapeño German potato salad. God, I love that stuff."

"What else is missing out of the store, Curtis?"

"Crap, I don't know. Who cares? I bet Irene Mostler made one of her chocolate cakes. And I know Dee Dee Schoen was there." Curtis shook his head. "The way I want to die is by nipping Dee Dee Schoen on the butt, coming down with lockjaw, and being dragged to death."

DeWitt blinked in surprise. "Dee Dee?"

"Bet she's a wild woman in bed. Bet her husband ain't man enough for her. I look into her eyes and can see there's a whole world of excitement. Lord knows there ain't enough to do around here. Already memorized my taped movies. What do you think, Wittie? Should I send her flowers or maybe a card or something?"

"You have the hots for *Dee Dee?*"

"Oh, yeah," Curtis said meaningfully, raising an eyebrow. "Dee Dee."

It was too warm in the little bathroom, and the space heater stank of propane. DeWitt got up and rummaged until he found Curtis's Dry Idea. Unbuttoning his shirt, he spread some in his armpits.

Curtis asked, "Why are they revolting, anyway?"

"People are stupid. You give them something, they tear it up. That's why they paint the graffiti. That's why they want to get to the other side of the Line."

Curtis handed him the joint.

DeWitt declined. The dope was hitting him wrong, making him maudlin instead of jolly. "The way I see it, whatever's outside that Line isn't the United States we remember. I imagine we're a whole lot better off with the Torku. What do you think?"

Curtis shrugged. "I got *Mad Max* on video, so I'm with you."

The mayor flushed the rest of the joint and they went outside. Seresen was already back in the car, waiting.

During the drive to town, DeWitt felt trapped behind a cottony bottleneck of sleepiness and old memories. He didn't bother to speak. When the van stopped on Main, DeWitt parked behind it. Seresen got out, and DeWitt got out with him.

The Torku workers began pulling boxes from the van. The few people who had been outside melted quickly into the shadows. The graffiti artists had been busy, DeWitt noticed. There was red paint above most of the shop doors: a sloppy upside-down V so incongruous that it made his scalp crawl.

When DeWitt and the aliens walked into The Fashion Plate, Darnelle looked up from sorting blouses.

Seresen put a bill of lading down on a pile of brassieres. "We have come to bring supplies. Do you want them?"

Darnelle ambled over to one of the boxes and, before the Torku worker could put it down, began examining the merchandise. "Good heavens, pastels. Spring and Summer colors. Nothing makes a statement here." As the Torku tried to steady the box, Darnelle pawed through it. "Nothing for our Autumns or Winters. These are just the wrong resonant essences."

DeWitt wandered to the window. At the curb, two pieces of white paper, caught in an eddy of air, tumbled and chased themselves like kittens.

"Come here, Mr. Kol," Darnelle said. "I'll show you what colors I mean." And she steered Seresen to the back.

142

The Torku workers had put down the boxes and were standing motionless in their Banana Republic shirts, a photo grouping of preposterous explorers.

"You got those sticks with you?" DeWitt asked.

The nearest Torku regarded him.

"You have weapons under those shirts? We may have some trouble."

They didn't answer, but one crossed to the window and looked out. DeWitt walked through the store, past the dressing rooms to the exit. He pushed on the steel bar and opened the back door.

The alley smelled of mold and rotting oranges. As he made his way toward Houston Street, Bo stepped into a square of golden sunlight at the corner. His eyes traced DeWitt's wound.

Bo asked softly, "You all right?"

"I'm fine."

"Where's Seresen?"

"Inside. Why?"

"I'm going in there. I'm taking Seresen into custody."

Suddenly the alley was blurred, Bo's face indistinct. Nothing was real, not even the garbage cans gathered like onlookers in a doorway.

DeWitt sucked in a breath. *"You're* going in there? *You're* taking him into custody? Aren't you forgetting who's police chief and who's the officer?"

"Forget who's police chief? Wittie, you never let me forget. You order me around. And the Torku. And your wife. And Hattie."

The bruised lump on DeWitt's head began to pound. "Hattie? Is she talking behind my back? Damn her! And you think you have the right to judge me? What would you know about relationships? It looks like you never had anyone in your house.

Everything so nitpicking clean. Everything in its place. You keep house like a girl, like a—"

DeWitt swallowed his next word. The unthinkable stuck in his throat.

Bo's eyes narrowed. "You don't know what I do after hours."

"You watch six-year-old news reports. And I bet you haven't had three dates in the past nine years. Why, Bo? I've seen how women look at you. Maybe it's the motorcycle uniform, but, even so, you must know you're . . . I mean, even I know you're . . . What I mean to say is, okay, it's not like you have two heads or three eyes or something . . ."

You looked so good in that uniform, Wittie.

"Come with me." Bo stepped forward, holding out his hand.

DeWitt remembered Bo groping Curtis's inseam. The surprised Curtis going tiptoe.

Kiss me first.

DeWitt pulled back. If Bo touched him, he'd knock him down. "Don't."

Bo halted, hand outstretched.

"Damn it, Bo. You could have told me. I wouldn't have fired you." It didn't matter that Bo was gay. It didn't. It was the lies that hurt.

The rigid officialness dropped from Bo's face. He looked young, sad, and frightened.

"It's just . . . when it interferes with your job, you see? It shouldn't interfere with your job."

"DeWitt." Bo's voice was weary. "You don't understand."

"I'm not totally insensitive. I mean, sure, there's been times I've done things I shouldn't. I've let a good-looking woman off with a warning when I would have ticketed someone else. You know how guys . . . well, I've never thought about it, but I guess for you . . . But Christ. Foster? You're in love with Foster?"

144

Bo stood ramrod straight, his cheeks aflame. "You're full of shit!"

"Take it easy, okay? I mean, big deal. You still in the closet? It's no good running from it. Building up all that rage. Is that why you killed that boy in Dallas?"

"Get out of my way, DeWitt."

DeWitt grabbed for his baton, but saw the futility of it. Bo was four inches taller, eleven years younger, and adversity had made him strong.

From Main Street came a bang, like the report of a large-caliber gun. Black smoke rose over the rooftops.

DeWitt whirled and ran for Darnelle's.

The Torku and Seresen had left The Fashion Plate. The boxes of clothes lay in a bright jumble. DeWitt burst through the front door. The bank, the police station were burning. Beyond the parked squad car, the UPS van was in flames.

A dark form with a ski mask darted from the drugstore, a sixteen-ounce Coke bottle in his hand. The bottle had a burning wick in it.

The wind-up. The pitch. Too stunned to run for cover, DeWitt saw burning sparks fly from the wick, watched the bottle hit the street and burst into flame.

The Torku workers began unbuttoning the pockets of their safari shirts. They pulled out their sticks. Through the inferno came the gigantic form of another UPS van. The truck squealed to a halt, its doors flew open, and more armed Torku piled out.

"Seresen!" DeWitt's shout was lost in the noise. "Stop! Don't do this! If you hurt anybody, I'll . . ."

What? What could he do? Events had been set in motion. Now the aliens would destroy what they had gone to such pains to save.

A startling Code Three wail. Bo's motorcycle sped around

the van and skidded to a stop between the Torku and the revolutionaries. Without haste, Bo turned off his siren and his lights. Sun glinted off his helmet, off the mirrored shades he wore. He set the kickstand, dismounted from his bike, and strode to the street's double yellow line.

"You are under arrest for suspicion of arson!" Bo stood, uniform pressed, boots spit-shined. "Destruction of private property. Assault with intent. Reckless endangerment. And littering."

The street fell silent but for the roar and crackle of the fires. Not even the Torku moved.

Bo spun to DeWitt. "Is your Polaroid in your trunk? I want to gather evidence. And I need flares for traffic. Don't touch that Coke bottle!" he warned the Torku who, accustomed to cleaning up after humans, were bending to pick up the garbage. "I'll want fingerprints."

The townspeople, some with masks and some without, had eased out of the shops and were standing, caught between exhilarating rebellion and Bo's daunting law.

"Give me your keys."

DeWitt put the keys in Bo's palm. Bo walked away. Alone, DeWitt surveyed the crowd: a hundred familiar faces. Smoke boiled from the police station. Flames tongued from the windows and licked at the walls. The sound of the fire was an airy rumble, like the noise of a passing jet.

Bo was still bent over the trunk, searching for something. What was taking him so long? Suddenly he called, "DeWitt?"

DeWitt walked toward the car, thinking that it didn't matter if Bo was gay. Nothing between them had changed. When he reached him, he saw Bo was empty-handed. Where were the flares, the camera?

Bo lunged, rattlesnake-quick, and pain drove DeWitt to his

146

knees. Bo had DeWitt's wrist in a bone-cracking grip and was twisting it behind his back.

"Don't try to fight me," Bo cautioned him.

Doc came running across the street. He looked in the trunk and shrank back as though what he saw there had cut him. "Wittie! How could you?"

"What are you talking about?" DeWitt struggled against the handcuffs. Bo seized the back of DeWitt's jacket, wrenched him to his feet, slammed him against the rear of the squad car.

And DeWitt saw the reason for his arrest. The answer lay less than six inches from his face. The trash bag of dope had been pushed off the wheel well, and there inside the dusty trunk lay blood-splattered pink cardboard containers and strands of bleached blond hair.

DeWitt would have fallen if Bo hadn't grabbed him.

Bo said calmly, "It's all over now, DeWitt. I've got you on conspiracy. Tell the people how the Torku murdered Loretta and how you covered for them."

The enraged crowd surged forward. A Torku grabbed the hem of DeWitt's jacket and pulled him off his feet. Bo's fingernails, seeking purchase, raked DeWitt's arm.

Above him and around him, shrieks. Bo's angry shout, like a call to order. Someone lifted DeWitt, flung him into the rear of the UPS van, and shut the doors with a clang.

His right arm was numb; his wrist ached. Fighting for breath, he sat up. Seresen was across from him. The walls of the truck muffled the townspeople's angry screams.

29

THE TORKU DRIVER peeled rubber down Main Street.

"My pocket." DeWitt rolled over on his side. "I have handcuff keys in my pocket."

Seresen reached into DeWitt's trouser pocket, his pliable hand molding to the contour of DeWitt's hip. The alien's touch reminded him uncomfortably of adolescent gropings in darkened theaters.

After an awkward moment, Seresen brought the key out, turned DeWitt over, and opened the lock. DeWitt sat up and moved away from the Kol.

"Don't hurt them," he said.

Seresen's eyes were mostly blue in the van's light. An inexpressive, blank blue.

"What have you told your workers to do, Seresen?"

"We will take the gas."

The back of the van was cold. DeWitt felt a chill as the sweat on his arms began to dry. "Is that all?"

"We will not give it back, either."

The van hit a bump and nearly knocked DeWitt over. Sere-sen, with his lower center of gravity, didn't budge.

"If you hurt anyone, I'll turn against you."

"Don't say that."

"It's wrong to beat people into doing what you want."

DeWitt pictured his father in that same downtown street, billy-club swinging, teaching uppity blacks the difficult lesson the city council wanted them to learn.

"Kill one of them, and you'll have to kill them all. Down to every last teenager, every last baby. They'll never forgive you. You'll never be able to turn your back on them again."

"You are stupid to say this. So stupid."

"And that goes for me, too. I won't be a traitor."

"Traitor?" There was an unfamiliar edge to Seresen's voice. "Traitor means nothing. I wish you would not talk about these things. It makes the world ugly."

"But . . ."

"Be quiet." The alien hunched into a shapeless lump of disgust.

The van stopped. Seresen, as though anxious to get away from DeWitt, opened the back doors and jumped down.

Cautiously, DeWitt followed, and found himself in the brightly lit Torku garage. One last, poignant glimpse of the parking lot and the trees, and the wall slammed to with an end-of-the-world clunk.

The garage stank of exhaust and old oil. Loretta's Buick was parked at the end of the long row of delivery vehicles. In testimony to how the revolution was faring, his own squad car was there, too.

Squinting in the cold glare of the fluorescents, DeWitt walked to it. The car had been messily hot-wired. He got out his keys.

In the trunk lay a flat, pink box marked BLUSH. A smaller box that had to be lipstick. With a fingernail he scraped some of the crusted blood off the cardboard. A lock of bleached blond hair was snagged in the spare's balance weight. DeWitt had pushed Foster too far. He should have never given him the keys.

Exhausted, DeWitt crawled into the back seat, made himself a pillow of his jacket, and closed his eyes.

He dreamed he was climbing the Line again, only the energy was sticky as candy. His arm sunk into the glow, and when he pulled his hand out, he saw with horror that his flesh had been stripped to the bone.

A knock by his ear startled him awake. Seresen was staring in the squad car window. "Lunch," he said.

Mouth filmy with sleep, DeWitt got up and followed the alien down the row of parked vehicles. The Torku had made him an apartment of sorts in an empty bay. A single bed squatted near a wall of graduated hoses. A round Formica table and two chairs stood in a corner festooned with fan belts.

"You will be hungry," Seresen told him. "You will need a place to sleep since you cannot go home. A phone is on the nightstand. You can call your wife later."

"Is the town all right?"

"Eat and call your wife." With that, Seresen walked through the door to the Torku living quarters, locking the door behind him.

DeWitt rummaged through a box on the table. Inside were chilled cans of Coke, assorted sandwiches, chocolate, and six family-sized bags of chips. Fishing out a pimento cheese sandwich, DeWitt tore off the plastic wrap, sat down on the bed, and called Janet.

No one answered.

30

DeWitt's bladder was painfully full by the time he got up from the cot. He walked to the door and knocked, but there was no response. After pacing a while, he picked up the phone and dialed 911.

A Torku answered. "Yes?"

"I need to go to the bathroom."

"Come in the door," the alien said and hung up.

The door? DeWitt looked at the garage door, but knew that wasn't the one the alien meant. Then he turned and stared at the door to the center.

He was both drawn to and repelled by the center, the same sort of ambivalence he felt toward the Line. *Things change*, Foster had said. Staring at the very ordinary green steel door, DeWitt wondered what extraordinary things he would find behind it.

Timidly he knocked. When no one answered, he put his ear against the painted metal and listened, hearing only the rush of his own blood in his ears.

The knob was chilly. "Coming in," he warned breathlessly as he pulled the door open.

It was a bathroom. A white commode sat in one corner; a plastic shower curtain stamped with fish and seahorses was hung in the other. On the tile floor lay a fluffy blue rug. And on the opposite wall was a connecting door of green-painted steel.

He pulled up the fake-fur-covered commode lid, and with a groan of relief urinated into the blue water. On top of the tank, he noted, a Torku decorator had placed a yellow ceramic carp.

When he was done, DeWitt tried the connecting door and found that it was locked. He searched the cabinets. Towels and washcloths were in one, sheets in another. In a closet next to the sink he found six sets of uniforms, all his size.

There was a click as a bolt was shot. Seresen walked in.

DeWitt said, "Don't you know how to knock?"

The alien tightened his pliant hand into a fist and tapped on the rim of the sink. "I want to talk to you."

DeWitt turned and went back to the garage. "How's the town?"

"It is fine."

"I don't believe it." DeWitt sat on the bed next to the phone and tried his home number again. The phone rang fifteen times before he hung up. "I want to talk to my wife."

Seresen walked out.

After a few minutes' wait the phone rang. DeWitt snatched up the receiver. "Hello?"

"DeWitt?" The furious voice belonged to Janet.

Out of the corner of his eye DeWitt saw Seresen coming back.

"Janet, listen to me. Listen to me, honey. I know everything."

A beat of silence, like the startled pause of a heart.

"I know about your affair. I know what you helped him do. God," he whispered, "you left tire tracks, Janet."

DeWitt suddenly understood the helplessness of mothers

152

who begged the police not to take their sons; who fretted that the cuffs were too tight; who asked if there were blankets enough in jail to keep their children warm.

He tried to picture Janet's arrest. Her trial. Her execution. He knew that if the law took her from him, it wouldn't seem that she had ceased to exist, but that she had simply gone missing, like his father.

"DeWitt, what are you talking about? Are you trying to blame me for the murder? God! You find out I'm having an affair and this is the way you get back at me? Nobody will believe you, DeWitt. Nobody. The evidence was found in *your* trunk."

"Janet, you know your boyfriend put those things in my car."

"My boyfriend. My *boy*friend? You make me sound like a teenager sneaking out of the house."

Quietly, "Is that how it feels?"

"He'd never plant evidence. He'd never do that."

"Stop protecting him. Think what he got you into. You may think you're in love, but goddamn, look what the man did. Go to Bo. Tell him — please, won't you do what's right? Foster was in my trunk last night. I gave him my keys —"

"What?"

"Foster got into my trunk. He uses Mary Kay. He must have had some extra boxes. I was bleeding all over myself last night, and he had the bloody towels in his hands. He knows I suspect him, and he had to get rid of me." Hadn't she figured it out? But maybe she didn't help Foster get rid of the body.

"Listen, Janet. Bo's an honest cop —"

"I know that. Don't you think . . ."

"Once he starts questioning Foster's alibi, once he asks himself why Foster lied to me, once he thinks about those tire tracks, he's going to put it together. And then nothing will stop him. Not friendship, not pity. If you don't have any knowledge of the murder, tell Bo. Janet, I know you love Foster. You probably always have. But if you feel anything for me at all, at least let me try to help. There were stones from Sparrow Point caught in the tire treads, and no telling what's in the carpet of that Suburban. Fibers, hairs, traces of blood. I tried to get Foster to say that I loaned him the car, but—"

"Bo told me he found the evidence in your trunk!"

"Janet, think! The squad car was in the driveway all weekend, so low on gas, I took the horse. There's no way I could have driven to Sparrow Point. Besides, I have Goodyears, not Dunlops."

She was weeping now, huge gulps of misery. "I can't believe this. I can't . . ." She hung up.

DeWitt put down the phone, lay back in bed, and stared at the ceiling.

Seresen said, "They are well, your people. We will not hurt them. I want you to tell me that the revolt will end. Tell me that your people will be friends with us again, and that everything will be the way it was."

"I want you to change the Suburban's tires. Put Michelins on. You go to Bo if you have to. Tell him about Foster getting into my trunk . . ."

Foster in exchange for DeWitt. Would Seresen be able to choose?

"And if worse comes to worse, I want you to protect my wife and kids. Promise me."

Seresen made a small, odd noise. "This is not the right attitude. All things will go back to normal. Your wife loves you. I want you to say this."

DeWitt closed his eyes. "Saying things doesn't make them happen."

"Yes it does." A squeak as the alien sat down on a chair. "Saying makes things so. What occurs is of no importance. What is

154

important is perception. It is belief, not the act, that creates resonant patterns. You don't have the right attitude. I try to make happy policemen. I don't know why you insist on making unhappy ones."

There was a screech of metal as Seresen pulled his chair to the side of the bed.

"We worship universes, and universes leak. They leak thought. They leak dream. The pattern of the tree is in the leaf. All things affect the spin of the electron."

DeWitt pulled the covers around him.

"What appears to be random is pattern: flights of birds, schools of fish, dust floating in sunlight. We worship everything. Your attitude is wrong. I tell you that somewhere a happy policeman with a happy family understands this. And somewhere that policeman explains to his friends. This is important to us."

"Seresen, the town's falling apart. People are going to get hurt. Just do what I tell you."

When no response came, DeWitt opened his eyes. The alien was looming over him, shapeless hands clenched as though they wanted to throttle. His skin had turned color: not pale but amber, the hue of a warning light.

Gradually Seresen mastered his frustration. His fists relaxed. Amber turned to brown. "I will be back when you see things better."

Rapid footsteps as the alien stalked away, a bang as he shut the door behind him.

31

SERESEN DIDN'T RETURN. Under the ceaseless noon of the garage's fluorescents, hours blurred into days. Days into weeks. DeWitt paced back and forth before the garage door, feeling for air leaks and not finding any.

In the Buick's trunk he found a pink basket labeled in Loretta's rounded, exacting script: *Kol Seresen*. The basket was filled with Mary Kay samples: face cleanser, hand lotion, a mask for oily skin.

That was why she had wanted to see Seresen. The meeting hadn't been about Foster at all.

The news didn't cheer him.

DeWitt ate all the sandwiches in the cardboard box. The Torku didn't bring him more. When he dialed 911, no one answered. No one answered at his house, either.

He tried to think happy thoughts, but knew that outside, war continued. That Seresen never changed Janet's tires and never talked to Bo. He pictured the Kol's body lying half-in and half-out of the center, flies enjoying an exotic feast.

And down Main, the bodies of humans would be stiffening, eyes open to the watery sun. Stray dogs, gone feral, would be gorging themselves on the soft parts first: the anus, the belly.

Nobody would come get him.

He found a ballpeen hammer and used it against the wall, but the alien material neither chipped nor dented. The shock of the blows, after a few minutes' work, made his body ache.

It was in the bathroom, sitting on the toilet, elbows on thighs, door closed to the illumination of the garage, that he witnessed Torku change.

The strip of light on the floor was not to his right where it should have been, but in front, where light was impossible. Frightened, he got up from the toilet, not taking the time to wipe, pulling his pants up with him. He fumbled for the light switch and flicked on the overhead fluorescents.

Flamingos. The shower stall now had glass doors instead of a curtain. And on the doors were pink flamingos.

DeWitt fled. He waited, and peeked inside again. The flamingos were still there. He stayed in the garage, going into the bathroom only when he absolutely had to, and quickly.

In the garage, he paced.

One day, in the middle of a step, there was Seresen standing in the open doorway of the bathroom.

"Everything is quiet. We will make deliveries now."

Six other Torku walked into the garage and loaded boxes into a UPS van. Seresen approached. "And you will come with us."

The wall of the garage rose, letting in a cold breeze. Slowly, as though any sudden move might bring back his solitary confinement, DeWitt turned. In the parking lot it was snowing.

The Kol pressed a sandwich and a root beer into his hands. "I hope you have thought about what I said."

Things change. That was the lesson DeWitt had learned. The universe was unreliable. Blink, and the world is transformed. He tore open the package. The sandwich was chicken salad and it nearly came apart in his frantic hands.

With a motherly gesture the alien drew a blanket around DeWitt's shoulders. Seresen himself was dressed head-to-toe in what looked like a poncho. His huge, shapeless feet were stuffed into fuzzy boots.

DeWitt's hands shook so much that he spilled half of the root beer, opening it. He downed the rest in three swallows.

"There is more food and drink inside." Seresen walked to the truck, DeWitt at his heels.

There were blankets on the floorboard, and a cooler filled with canned drinks and fruit. Grabbing an orange, DeWitt tore a hole through the peel and sucked the sweetness out. Juice dribbled down his chin.

"You understand the nature of the universe now?" Seresen asked.

"Yes." DeWitt tossed the orange away and picked up an apple. There was no order. Bathrooms changed from blue to pink, and fish became flamingos.

Seresen started the van and drove out of the garage. The tires fought for traction in the calf-deep snow. DeWitt devoured the apple and opened a Dr Pepper. "What day is it?"

"If you understand me, then you know time is arbitrary."

"Arbitrarily, then, what's the day?"

"Wednesday."

"The date?"

"December twenty-eighth."

DeWitt had been locked up sixteen days, and had missed Christmas. It didn't matter. Time was arbitrary. Bathrooms sailed through mutable truth. DeWitt leaned his cheek against the chill door until his face grew numb. In another universe, he supposed, a happy policeman had opened presents.

The van slid to a stop, and everyone climbed out. Curtis's bait house was wrapped in swirling white.

DeWitt followed the aliens inside the convenience store. The heat was off. The store was stocked but for the spots where flammables once stood. There was no lighter fluid by the charcoal, no scented lamp oil next to the candles.

Pulling the blanket around him, DeWitt slogged through foot-deep snow to Curtis's house. He knocked and got no answer. After a while he opened the door.

"Curtis?"

His breath emerged in ghostly wisps of fog. Stepping quietly, he made his way to the kitchen. Dishes jutted from the sink's opaque ice like fruit in dishwater Jell-O. Pipes behind the cabinets had burst, and ice made a glistening rink over the scarred linoleum. Hunched in his blanket, DeWitt stood, afraid to explore farther. At last Seresen came and led him away.

His legs were weak; his feet tripped over themselves. In the yard the Kol had to pause so DeWitt could regain his balance.

"What did you do with Curtis?" DeWitt asked.

"Nothing. We did nothing. He is at a neighbor's."

"Where's my wife? My kids?"

"At a friend's home." Seresen patted his arm.

Three Torku came to help DeWitt into the truck.

"Please. I want to see my family," DeWitt asked uncertainly.

"Yes, yes." Seresen started the truck and drove out of the frozen yard. "I know."

The van moved slowly down the broad white river that was Guadalupe Street. In a yard to the right was a black lump. As

DeWitt stared, it moved. Irma Jenkins was boiling a pot over a charcoal grill. She looked up as they passed, her face set into lines of hatred.

DeWitt watched her until they were out of sight. "Why?"

"Why what?" Seresen was concentrating on the road.

"Why is Irma Jenkins outside? What is she doing?"

"Cooking. I told you we would take the gas."

Comprehension hit, as blinding as the light from an arc welder. "No propane? None at all?"

"As I said, no gas. Those with electric heat are taking their neighbors in."

"You can make electric heaters," DeWitt said.

"We have made some."

"But not for everybody. Why?"

"We make them for those who ask. Electric stoves also. Not many ask. Perhaps they do not feel the cold."

"How cold has it been?"

"Very." Seresen steered carefully toward Main. "What can we do if your people do not want heat?"

"You're letting them die."

"No one is dying. I ask you not to say such things. We do not allow anyone to die. If they want heat, we give it. You and I both know there is a universe where humans have warmth, and, given time, that universe will share its pattern."

DeWitt pulled Seresen's hands off the wheel and held the alien hard by the wrists. "Explain why you're doing this."

The van wandered like an unleashed and curious dog from side to side until it slewed to the right and softly nosed into a pyracantha bush.

The Torku's skin turned greasy in an instant. DeWitt recoiled. "The leaf is the —"

DeWitt closed his eyes. "Oh, give me a break."

The van stalled. Seresen started it again and backed away from the bush. "You understand what I tell you. It is your choice to reject it."

DeWitt watched the snowbound, lightless houses pass. "Everything you want just for the asking? It's too damned easy, Seresen. Like a belief in reincarnation or something."

"Yes. And I suppose you are most comfortable in making life difficult." On Main, the alien turned. Except for a few burned buildings, all evidence of the rebellion had been cleared. The street was a blank white field. A few people standing on the sidewalk hastily made snowballs, threw them at the truck, then ran.

Farther down DeWitt saw two bundled figures standing by a horse.

"Stop!" DeWitt said.

Seresen slowed and stopped. "Yes?"

"I know that horse." DeWitt jumped out and baby-stepped across the ice to the pair.

They turned. DeWitt recognized Hattie only by the brown eyes above the muffler.

"Hey. How are you?" he asked.

She stared through him. The horse snorted, sending twin plumes of steam into the gray air.

DeWitt stomped his feet. The wet chill was already numbing his toes. "Hattie? I've missed you."

She didn't speak. He turned to the other swaddled figure and a greeting died in his throat.

Bo.

"Did Janet come see you?" DeWitt asked him. "Did Seresen? Did they tell you Foster planted the evidence in my car?" He searched Bo hard for understanding. "Just say something, damn it! Won't you talk to me? I need to know if everyone's okay."

Hattie backed the horse. DeWitt watched the pair walk across the snowy yard, the animal picking its way carefully with its delicate legs. The two had their heads down. In their bundled dark clothing they could have been any big city's bums.

"Does everybody still think I killed Loretta?" DeWitt cried. "Has Foster confessed?"

They didn't pause. After a while DeWitt returned to the warmth of the van.

32

"I WANT TO SEE MY FAMILY NOW," DeWitt said.

"Yes," Seresen replied, but stopped at the drugstore instead.

It had been damaged by fire. The back wall was scorched, and through a hole in the roof snow was falling, making a drift on the magazine rack. Hip-deep in snow, a swim-suited model on a six-year-old *Cosmopolitan* smiled glossily up at DeWitt.

He realized that Seresen was standing quietly at his shoulder. "There was more fighting while I was locked up."

Seresen turned to watch his workers set electric appliances on the sooted linoleum: Mr. Coffees, woks, space heaters. "Things are better, now. I think the gasoline may be gone."

"Look at me."

Seresen turned those shrimp-pink eyes to him.

"Tell me the truth. Did you kill anybody?"

A worker stopped what he was doing to watch them with alarm.

"Yes," the Kol said.

DeWitt touched the snow near the *Cosmopolitan* model's bare thigh. The paper had gone wavy with moisture, as if the woman were crinkling in on herself with cold; or with shame.

"Who? Curtis?"

"Yes. Because you believe it, it has come to be. Curtis is dead. Now that I have said it, it becomes true, so I am guilty as well."

The corner stank of old damp smoke. DeWitt's eyes stung. "My family?"

"Because you believe it and now I say it, your family is dead. In other worlds Torku kill humans and humans kill Torku with no reason other than your belief."

"Seresen, are you lying again?"

"There are no lies. Not ever. In deciding what to have for breakfast, you alter existence. I tell you humans and Torku live in peace. Can't you believe that?"

"I want to see."

"Yes, yes." Abruptly Seresen walked out of the store.

Someone had painted an erect penis on the crosswalk sign's stick figure, DeWitt saw as he climbed into the truck. And up the street, The Fashion Plate, like the bank and the police station, was gutted. The windows were shattered. Sweaters hung like thick, black liquid from distorted racks.

"Darnelle?" DeWitt asked.

"Dead, dead. Yes, all dead," the Kol said in exasperation.

They drove by the Biblical Truth Church, where a small crowd had gathered. DeWitt caught sight of a short, bulky figure standing with the rest.

"Stop the van."

"No."

"That's Curtis back there. Stop the van!"

"No."

DeWitt grabbed for the door handle, but the Torku worker stationed beside him was quicker, pinning him against the wall until the church was out of sight.

"Some people sleep there now. They gather to visit and share food. The church has electric central heating."

DeWitt stopped struggling, and the Torku let him go. "Why didn't you want me to speak to Curtis? What are you afraid he'll say?"

"I think you will kill more people in other places, and I am tired of it. It is why we came here, to teach at least one of your people the truth, so resonance may be sustained. You are a perturbation in the universe. Those people at the church can't help what they do, but you have been told the difference."

"Did you ever wonder if there are people in those other places thinking bad things about us? I don't see the point."

"Responsibility is the point." Seresen geared down. "Reciprocity is the point. The borders of existence are permeable. Who knows what we will decide for breakfast and in doing so change a world? We must treat each universe as gently as we treat our own."

Ahead was a black kid in a blue snowsuit, his gloved hand raised like a crossing guard in an elementary school poster. The van crunched to a halt a good twenty feet from the boy.

The snow had stopped. Sun shone though a thin blanket of cloud, casting crystalline light over the day. DeWitt noticed how the light picked out the citrus-peel texture of the Torku's dappled skin. The boy lowered his hand and stood, looking up the hill to his right.

DeWitt wondered what the kid was waiting for.

"Maybe we shouldn't stop here," he said.

Seresen ignored him. The van's engine rumbled like a contented tiger. The vibration made the dashboard buzz.

"It's dangerous stopping like this."

The kid looked back at the van, then up the hill again. DeWitt wished he could see what the kid was seeing. The black child's face was wrapped in a muffler; a hood was over his head.

Shrill screams, as sharp as rifle shots. DeWitt flinched, accidently pushing the Torku worker hard against the door.

Down the hill came a flash of red and yellow and black. A little girl was riding the snowy incline on an inner tube, her blond hair flying. Two more kids came sledding after, one riding on his stomach backward.

The kid in the blue snowsuit took a last look up the hill, then waved the van through.

As they drove past, DeWitt saw Denny standing with Linda. Linda was blowing up their old air mattress. Tammy was with a teenage boy DeWitt didn't recognize.

"We are dead," Seresen said. "Caught in an ambush by humans with gasoline bombs. Are you happy now?"

The Kol goosed the accelerator, jerking the van forward, making it fishtail. The Torku worker turned an anguished orange and his shapeless face crumpled into an expression of despair.

33

SIN WASN'T A STENCH, it was cockroaches. Jimmy Schoen knew that now. He could hear scuttling in the walls. When he walked the church floor, he felt the crunch of carapaces. Brown bodies crawled over the food on the table, food that the sinners had brought.

The church had the air of a tawdry winter festival. There was gaiety and laughing, but Schoen didn't smile.

Couldn't they see that the sinners dirtied things? That they left disease where they swarmed? But his parishioners talked proudly of Christian charity. They murmured God's grace as they passed out sandwiches and punch.

Schoen frowned, a shepherd displeased with his sheep. The faithful had lost their conviction somewhere between the burning of Darnelle's store and the holy conflagration of the pharmacy. In the end, his own congregation had put out the fires.

Schoen was cold despite the crowd. He pushed by Granger, avoiding the touch of his chitinous back.

"Dee Dee?" Schoen called.

Dee Dee and one of the bake-sale ladies bracketed Hubert Foster. His wife had still not fixed her hair.

"Dee Dee?" he said sharply. "We'll go to the parsonage now."

"Just a minute, hon. I was going to get Hubie a Coke. Sharon, wouldn't you like a Coke, too? And maybe another smidgen of Martha Johnson's apple pie?"

"Do you think I should?" Sharon asked worriedly. "I feel bloated. What do you think?"

"Well," Foster said after a moment's study. "Just around the eyes."

The woman squealed in dismay, and covered her face with her hands. "I knew it! I bet I've gained ten pounds—"

"Dee Dee?" Schoen asked.

Without turning, his wife waved a hand in his direction. "Now Sharon, you look just fine. I bet Hubie wouldn't have noticed at all if you hadn't called it to his attention. Maybe you're just tired. Don't you think that's it, Hubie?" Dee Dee asked pointedly. "She just looks a little peaked."

"Oh. Yeah."

"Dee Dee?" Schoen raised his voice.

She patted Sharon's knee. "See? That's it. Just a little tired."

"Maybe I will have that Coke, then," Sharon said. She sounded uncertain. But when Dee Dee got to her feet, she added, "And half of a sour-cream brownie."

Schoen caught his wife's arm. "We're leaving."

"I would, honey. Believe me, I would. But there's so much to take care of. Hubie wants a Coke. Sharon wants a Coke. I have to keep an eye on the coffee maker." She pulled her arm from his grasp and went to the refreshment table.

Schoen stalked to the door, hearing whispers soft as six-legged feet in his wake. From the back of the church a shout of contemptuous laughter. Schoen's face burned. He shouldered his way though the double doors and into a blast of icy wind.

Outside, adults had gathered to help children make a snowman. Children who came to Sunday school toiled alongside those who did not.

"Morning, preacher," the dope-dealing mayor said. "I been looking for Dee Dee. Where'd she run off to?"

Schoen didn't stop. Head down, he shoved against the contrary wind, his coat flapping around him.

34

ON THE EIGHTH DAY of DeWitt's second imprisonment, Seresen woke him up. "We are going. You will drive."

Seresen got into the squad car. DeWitt plucked the keys from the trunk and climbed behind the wheel. As the garage wall slid open to darkness, DeWitt checked his watch. Five-thirty in the morning.

"Deliveries?"

"No."

DeWitt backed into the lot. The snow had melted, except for patches under the trees.

Seresen pointed. "This way."

DeWitt turned right. "Where we going?"

"To Hell," the Kol replied grumpily. "Isn't that where Pastor Jimmy says you humans go if you do incorrect things?"

DeWitt followed Seresen's gestured direction, left. They were heading away from town.

"To Hell. You and I together. Isn't that what you want?"

"Not really."

"Then what is it you want?"

"Look, Seresen, I'm not going to get into an argument with you."

"Yes, yes. I might kill you or something. You and I, we've killed before. Turn here."

DeWitt nearly missed the turn. The entrance to the overgrown dirt trail was slick with muddy ice. The car skidded. DeWitt spun out of it with a dull patter of mud in the wheel wells.

Brush tickled the car doors. "We need a four-wheel drive for this, Seresen. We're going to get stuck."

After a mile or so of obdurate silence, Seresen ordered DeWitt to stop. "And turn off the engine, please. There is no need to waste gas."

DeWitt obeyed. Wind chattered in the ice-coated branches.

"Extinguish the headlights also. You will deplete the battery."

DeWitt's ears picked out the liquid sound of a stream to his right.

"Get out of the car," Seresen said.

"Why? What are you going to do?"

"I will get out of the car as well."

To their left the sun was rising, turning the sky a delicate pink. The alien made his way through the damp shadows and stopped under a pine. DeWitt slogged after.

"Stay here," Seresen said.

DeWitt's puzzled gaze followed him back down the incline to the car. When the alien opened the door, he startled a flock of grackles. Framed in the car's interior glow, he turned to watch the birds' raucous flight, as if reading pattern in it.

DeWitt hugged himself. The cold air held the crisp scent of evergreens and the mellow odor of sylvan decay. Down the hill he heard the car door slam. He waited for the sound of a hotwired starter. There was only more stirring of birds. A solitary bat flitted across the sky, its flight like a scrap of black paper.

The tip of DeWitt's nose was cold. His nose ran. He snuffled and pulled his face lower into his beaver collar. A rising sun, still behind the hill to the east, was forcing the sky to choose between pink and apricot.

He glanced down the hill again. Seresen was a dark, motionless shape framed by the car window. DeWitt was tired, sleepy, and not in the best of moods. He wanted to give up, walk down the hill, and tell Seresen that he had won. Order, as DeWitt knew it, sucked. It had taken his wife, turned the town against him, made him a murder suspect. Law and order certainly hadn't brought him peace. He looked down at his blue uniform and wondered why he ever wanted to be a policeman.

Then he noticed something orange by the trees. He walked toward it curiously. A piece of colored construction paper. No, a flagman's signal somehow forgotten there in the forest debris.

He jumped back, slipped, and went down on one knee. The orange was a sleeve. In the sleeve was part of a hand, two of its fingers missing.

Scrabbling in the mud and leaves, DeWitt retreated, his pulse a kettledrum. "Oh," he said in the small voice of a man who has walked in on a woman dressing.

Now that he knew what was lying in the shallow, rocky grave, he could see the patterned sole of a dirty Nike and a gourd shape that wore a patch of brown hair.

He sat down hard on a log. The red, bloated sun had climbed the hill and was peering at him through the trees by the time he decided that he could stand. Then he did what he knew he had to do. What order required. He walked over and studied the bodies.

The boys were on their stomachs, the older slightly over the younger, as though even now he was trying to protect him. Rain and wind had uncovered the backs of their heads, and patches of scalp showed in a parody of male pattern balding.

Even before DeWitt knelt, he knew what had caused their deaths. Holes had been punched through the yellowing craniums, as if beaked creatures inside had fought their way to birth. The murder weapon, a jagged piece of concrete, had been buried with the bodies.

He heard the *sluck-sluck* of footsteps in the mud. Seresen was coming up the hill.

DeWitt said sadly, "Look what you've done."

A breeze rustled the pines. "Nothing has happened. You must say that."

DeWitt got to his feet and dusted off his hands, a useless gesture. His pants were muddy from belt to cuff. "Fuck!" Picking up a clod of dirt, he threw it at a tree. "The problem with you people is that nothing's real!"

"Everything is real. Belief the most real thing of all. I know that someplace the children are well and happy."

"Why'd you do it? Because the boys hurt one of the Torku?"

Seresen turned on his flat heel and walked down to the car. "I will not play your ignorant game anymore."

It was a long while before DeWitt came down and opened the trunk. He rummaged behind the trash bag of dope, around the evidence Foster—for mere survival—had planted against him. There he found the small camping shovel he kept for highway emergencies. He picked up the tire iron.

Walking around to the passenger side, he tapped the tire iron against the glass. "Get out."

After a hesitation, the alien obeyed.

DeWitt pushed the camping shovel into the Kol's hand. "Damn you. We're going to bury the kids right this time."

35

THEY RODE TO THE CENTER IN SILENCE. In the parking lot, Seresen got out. DeWitt waited for the garage door to slide back. It didn't.

"Hey!" He shoved the gear lever into Park.

The alien paused at the door.

"Where do you think you're going?"

"I am going home. You may go home as well."

DeWitt approached the Kol, thinking that now was the time. Now. He would take out the cuffs, read Seresen his rights.

But order could give birth to chaos. Arrest Seresen, and the town would hold a lynching. Lynch Seresen, and the Torku would kill them all. "You're not worried I'll talk?"

"No. Talk if you must."

"Look. You and I both know that it's better if nobody finds out about this."

"Good. Perhaps you are finally learning something." Seresen opened the door.

DeWitt pushed it closed. "But I want some concessions."

Seresen turned his pink eyes toward him, and DeWitt couldn't tell if what he saw there was irritation or amusement. "I don't know why you killed Loretta and her boys. It's convenient for me to believe that there was cholera in that well, and that you were trying to save the rest of us. Do you understand?"

"Of course I understand. That is precisely why I am here. I create my universe in brightness, and you create yours in dark. You drag us down with you. But if this is what you want, it becomes so."

"I know you're lying. And I won't be the fall guy. Understand that."

Seresen nodded in resignation. "All right."

"Can't I come in for a quick shower? People will ask why I'm so muddy."

"Then tell them. Tell them the truth as you believe it."

DeWitt parked his hands above his belt as Seresen opened the door and walked in, leaving him alone in the bright mid-morning sun.

The world was not the way DeWitt had left it. He no longer knew his place. Was he cop or fugitive? It took an odd sort of courage for him to climb into his squad car and drive home.

To hide the car from prying eyes, he pulled as far into his carport as possible. Sometime during the revolt, his family must have returned. The kids' bikes were parked at careless angles under the fiberglass overhang. A molting Christmas tree, stripped of all ornament but stray tinsel, had been tossed in a corner.

He walked to the door, took a breath, and turned the knob.

The house was the same: the almond refrigerator, the yellow no-wax floor. Janet and the kids were seated around the familiar glass-and-rattan table, having lunch.

He found haven where he least expected it: not in the present but in the past. The kitchen was a saga of Thanksgivings with cornbread dressing, a child-free morning making love to Janet against the Formica counter, a frustrating afternoon spent installing the dishwasher.

Denny's eyes went round with astonished envy. "Daddy's *dirty!*"

Linda jumped up and ran to him, Denny and Tammy at her heels. He knelt and pulled his children close, thinking of the small bodies he had buried and how deflated they had looked, as if the insides of children were air.

His own children's bodies were round and firm. Against his left ear he could hear the prosaic pump of Tammy's heart; on his right cheek he felt the warm, milk-scented tickle of Linda's breath.

Loretta's boys, what was left of them, were dressed in jeans, and the younger had been wearing one of those bright, plastic raincoats mothers buy so drivers can see the kids on rainy days. That was the orange that first caught DeWitt's eye, the orange of the dead Loretta saying, *Careful, careful, that's my child.*

"Kids." Janet herded the children up. "Go back and finish your lunch."

"Daddy wants to eat, too." Denny craned his neck and shone his bright face at her.

She ignored the purity there. DeWitt wondered how she could. Suddenly he was kneeling alone.

"You're filthy. Get cleaned up."

He got to his feet and faced his wife. Odd. He had always seen her through the gauzed lens of memory. Now, in the jut of the chin and the lines around the eyes, he caught a glimpse not of the girl she had been but of the middle-aged woman she was becoming.

The kitchen changed. The dishwasher, the kitchen table, the Denny-made dent in the refrigerator door seemed an enclosed, self-balanced system. DeWitt was an interloper there.

Perhaps this was how divorce felt. Perhaps it wasn't a thing of shouts but of quiet estrangement. *Do you love me at all?* he wanted to ask. *Did you ever?* He wondered if those twenty years had been a fraud. As it was in the Torku center, light was out of place, and he was lost.

"Take a shower. Change your clothes."

He obeyed. While he was showering, Janet came in the bathroom. Through the curtain she was more Torku-shape than human. "When you're dressed, I want you to leave."

DeWitt put the washcloth down. "Is he moving in with you? Has he already?"

"I don't need him. I don't need you. Things have been fine here, without a man around."

"Janet? There's no place for me to go."

"Go back to your friends." The shadow at the curtain went away, leaving a bright vacancy.

The door slammed.

"But they're not my friends," he whispered.

36

When Janet told the children their daddy was leaving, Tammy lurched up from the table and ran to her room, leaving the other children staring in perplexity at her chair.

"When are you coming home, Daddy?" Denny asked.

DeWitt felt time slip, arbitrary and fluid, through his fingers: the Denny-stain of grape juice on a chair cushion; the scar on the linoleum where Tammy once dropped a hot pan. "I don't know."

Linda put down her sandwich. "Your presents."

The two children darted from the dining room and came back with three foil-wrapped gifts. The largest and most poorly wrapped was from Denny. Odd bits of Scotch tape made a second grimy ribbon around the package.

"Merry Christmas, Daddy," Denny said.

Balancing the gifts, DeWitt walked out to his squad car. He took the time to brush the dried mud from the vinyl before sitting down.

He drove through the small subdivision, turned down the straight shot of Ledbetter Road. When spots of color in the winter-blasted lawn of the cemetery caught his eye, he drove though the brick gates and parked.

He made himself an extra large joint for courage, then headed across the dun grass toward the small patchwork quilt of pink and white.

The carnations around the gold ribbon that read REST IN PEACE were wilted; the hothouse rosebuds were dropping petals. He smoked awhile before daring to look at the bronze marker. LORETTA JEAN HARPER, the plaque read.

Loretta would never rest in peace, not with her children buried in the hasty mud, not with the love she'd put into that orange raincoat.

He went back to the car and smoked another joint. By the time he left the cemetery, he was high. Disgusted with himself, he opened the window, but the cold air failed to sober him. He looked at the speedometer: eighteen miles an hour. He pressed the accelerator. The car pounced. Startled, he hit the brakes. Tires squealed. From their pasture an Angus heifer and her calf eyed him.

The car had stalled. He started it again. And, as though the destination was inevitable, he ended up at Billy's.

He parked behind a tree and studied Billy's Ford truck in the front yard. But he didn't realize he planned to face Billy until he found himself halfway down the hill.

He stopped. From the back of the house he could hear the racheting sounds of a pump. What would he say? *Buried your kids, Billy. Seresen and me. Made that alien finish what he started.* Then they'd dig up the bodies and bury them right, with Pastor Jimmy to talk over them, and with flowers to sweeten the air.

He took a step forward.

Am I crazy? I can't tell anyone about this. Yet he kept going until his palm pressed the rough surface of the bricks.

Inching around the corner, DeWitt saw that the garage door was open. The sound of machinery was louder, and water was pushing bits of construction detritus down the concrete drive.

He walked a step farther. *I'm sorry*, he'd begin. And then what? Odd, that the words wouldn't come. It wasn't as though he hadn't any experience in bad news.

Parents, wives, husbands would open the door to his knock, little confused smiles on their faces. When he told them of the death, they would stare as if they hadn't heard. But sometimes the words sank in at once, as if the survivors had been expecting tragedy all their lives.

The garage door gaped; the sound of the compressor was almost deafening. Taking a breath, DeWitt walked around the jamb.

"Billy?"

Billy, about three feet into the garage, flinched in surprise. Something laid a burning track across DeWitt's leg. He stepped back and saw that his twill pants were cut open. Across his drenched skin was a bleeding, angry welt.

His puzzled gaze rose. Billy's cheeks were pasty with shock. Then Billy lunged, the nozzle of the sprayer held before him like a knife.

DeWitt caught the jellyfish sting on his raised forearms. In his blundering, backward flight he knocked over an empty paint can and sent it rolling down the drive. Wet uniform flapping, he ran to his car. There he stopped and looked back. The yard was empty, Billy nowhere in sight.

Odd. As if Billy had tried to kill him.

DeWitt scowled as his brain struggled to process information. If the commercial spray rig had bruised him from a foot or so away, it could gouge out flesh if held closer. It only misted rain the night of the murder, yet Billy's yard had been sloppy with mud. Had Billy been cleaning out his paint sprayer again?

DeWitt dug into the glove box, took out his small set of binoculars, and focused on the Ford pickup. Dunlops. Of course, Dunlops.

He keyed his mike. "Come in."

"Here," a Torku answered.

"This is DeWitt Dawson, and I'm at—"

"We know where you are."

Of course. The Torku knew where everyone was. They'd probably watched Billy bury his kids.

"Get Bo out here quick. Tell Seresen to bring my gun, understand?"

But the Torku was already off the line.

From the hill DeWitt had a clear view of the house and the yard around it. Billy still hadn't emerged. The compressor was chugging away, from here as faint as the hum of a mosquito.

Something he should do. Something . . . He couldn't think. *Stay straight,* he warned himself, and took a few deep sobering breaths.

On the wall facing him were three windows, one the smaller, higher square of a bathroom window. An electric meter bulged like a transparent pimple from the bricks, installed, DeWitt supposed, more from tradition than for need. Below it sat the dull metal of the main breaker switch.

Oh. Cut off the juice to the house.

He crept back down the hill, wondering if Billy was watching. He grabbed the steel bar of the main breaker and pulled. The clatter of the compressor hushed.

In the silence, a noise of engines. Two UPS vans were coming down the hill. The first braked beside DeWitt. Seresen stepped out and handed him a bill of lading. On the pink slip was printed DR. BERNARD CULPEPPER AND OFFICER BODEEN WOODRUFF. Doc must have been with Bo when the Torku grabbed him. DeWitt

181

initialed the page, and workers shoved the two men from the van.

"Goddamn it." Doc brushed angrily at his sleeves. He looked at DeWitt and snapped, as if the uniform were his own and the rips DeWitt's fault, "What'd you do to yourself?"

"Billy just tried to kill me with an airless spray painter. And he has Dunlops on his truck. And a Tommy Lift. He murdered Loretta."

Doc's mouth quirked as if he was considering a laugh. Didn't they understand? DeWitt's words tumbled like puppies. "You see, Foster and Janet are having an affair . . ."

DeWitt caught Bo's look of surprise and realized the embarrassment his words were causing. "Foster—maybe he thought he could get rid of me for good—or maybe I just scared him when I accused him of the murder—but he was the one who put that evidence in my squad car."

Bo took DeWitt's injured arm. For a moment DeWitt thought he was going to go for his cuffs. Instead, Bo studied the welt.

Suddenly he stood back, cupping his hands around his mouth. "Billy! Billy Harper! It's Bo Woodruff. I want to talk to you."

The house was silent. In the nearby woods, one grackle called tunelessly to another.

Bo turned to Seresen. "You brought our guns?"

"No guns."

"He's got saws in there," Bo said. "Screwdrivers and God knows what else. We're unarmed. If he's guilty, he's going to fight."

"No guns."

Bo nodded. "Wittie? You want to take the back?"

"Uh . . ." Before Bomb Day, DeWitt had put his life in Bo's hands more than once. The man was still a good cop. Nothing between them had changed, really.

182

Bo walked DeWitt beyond the earshot of the others. "You been smoking dope again?"

"I'm high, Bo, but I'll be okay."

Bo's cheeks puffed, and he let out a long sigh. "We'll have to go in there anyway. You'll take the back?"

"Sure."

Bo sprinted toward the front door. Hitching his belt, DeWitt went to the back and peered into the damp recesses of the garage. It was empty. The door to the kitchen was closed. He tiptoed to it, wondering how fast he was moving. Stoned as he was, he couldn't tell. The door opened without a hitch, without a squeal. Billy had always done fine work.

The kitchen smelled of newly hewn pine. Cabinets of pale, raw wood had been hung. *Stay straight*, DeWitt cautioned himself when he realized he was standing stock-still in the kitchen, watching the whorls of the woodgrain. He went forward and turned right at the dining room.

A buzz. Something punched DeWitt hard in the stomach. The buzz rose in pitch, then choked off.

Billy stumbled back, staring in surprise at the thing he held. "Goddamned worthless piece of shit," the man hissed, annoyed that he had chosen the wrong tool for the job. On the side of the charcoal-colored metal was a Black and Decker logo. The head of the cordless drill was wet, and there was red on Billy's hand and on his shirt.

DeWitt screamed. "Bo!"

Billy lunged again, the drill once more humming dutifully. DeWitt seized Billy's wrist. Warmth was running down his leg. There was a sick lethargy in his right thigh.

"Bo!"

Where was he? Why didn't he come? DeWitt couldn't run, the wall was at his back. Billy had located a soft spot for entrance:

the drill was eye-level. DeWitt knew he wasn't strong enough to stop it.

Suddenly Billy was gone.

DeWitt slid down the wall into a sitting position. The Black and Decker drill was lying next to his foot, and on the other side of the room Bo had Billy in a hammerlock. With his free hand the officer was beating Billy in the face with a brick. Billy's nose was at a crazy angle, his mouth open, his teeth bloody. The brick fell.

Then Bo was there, bending over him. "DeWitt?"

DeWitt couldn't move, couldn't speak.

"Christ," Bo said in a squeezed voice, and he ran from the room.

A stomach cramp hit. Then Doc, Bo, and the Torku were looking down at him. DeWitt lay doubled up, feeling insignificant, weak, and embarrassed. Any moment there would be a load of muddy warmth in his shorts, and everybody would laugh.

"I'll need a scrub nurse," Doc said. "Call in Delsey Mc-Gowen, tell her to meet us at my office. She needs to look up his blood type and find somebody to match."

The Torku bent to lift him. DeWitt would have screamed, but didn't have the breath.

"No, no. He's going into shock. Get something to carry him on."

The Torku left and came back with a door. They put DeWitt on it and straightened his legs. And pain sucked him down into dark.

He opened his eyes to the brown metal of the van's ceiling; saw Billy lying unmoving, his face slick with blood.

Bo's voice came from a distance. ". . . drinking?"

And Doc: "None of your fucking business."

"Are your hands going to shake, Doc? Will he die on the operating table because you're boozed up?"

"Don't start. I've doctored you since you were a baby. I can handle myself just fine."

"Handle yourself? I was raised by a drunk. I know all about just fine."

"There's no anesthesiologist and Delsey's no scrub nurse. The last time I saw major surgery was in residency. So don't blame it on my drinking. If he doesn't die on the table, he'll die later of peritonitis."

"Shhhh. He's awake."

DeWitt reached out. Bo came into focus, his features blurred, as if DeWitt were seeing him through murky water. Frightened, DeWitt struggled to swim to the light.

Then Bo took his hand and it didn't matter. Nothing between them had changed. DeWitt's fingers tightened, as if Bo could pull him from the undertow.

"Oh Christ, Wittie. I'm sorry," Bo said.

37

DEWITT WAS CHOKING. He fumbled at the thing shoved down his throat. Doc's face came into view.

"Check that monitor."

The room was gray fog, shot here and there with incoherent light.

A woman: "Stopped throwing PVCs . . ."

Doc: "This vein's collapsing."

Don't leave me, DeWitt thought, but the voices were moving away.

"BP?"

"Eighty nine over . . ."

". . . more whole blood. Tell Seresen."

Doc's face emerged from the mist, close enough to touch. "Sinus rhythm?"

"Steady. His wife's outside. Wants to know if she can see him."

"Not now."

"She wants to know how he is. What do you want me to tell her?"

"Not now!"

DeWitt let the fog close.

A radio was on in a far room, and from it came a woman's familiar voice. Eyes shut, he lay pinned by pain and exhaustion.

". . . not myself anymore," the voice said.

He wasn't himself anymore—his mind too light, his body too heavy.

". . . woke up one day and started wondering how Janet Raeburn had gotten lost."

Janet, voice apologetic, was speaking to him from the radio. Someone held his hand.

"I was always a good girl. A good girl, my mama said. I did what Daddy expected of me. Then what you expected. And then the kids."

I love you, he wanted to tell her, but his mouth was numb.

"DeWitt? It sucks being a good girl. Did you know that? Did you know that nice guys come in last and good girls always lose? I love you. But, God, I was so tired of being good. And he wanted me so bad that he would have done anything. My fault. I saw how he—I could see it in his eyes. And it was like power, Wittie. You know how he is. How he would never have— But I can't say I'm sorry. You don't know what it felt like. Wittie? A little power. A chance to say no once in a while."

DeWitt didn't understand: Janet had all the power. Couldn't she see that in his eyes? He would do anything for her.

"Please. God. Don't die on me, Wittie."

Anything. . .

Her hand in his, he sank like a lead sinker into cloudy water.

The sheets were damp and sticky. He was lashed to the bed. Under bracelets of cloth his skin was chafed.

He must have groaned, because Delsey leaped to her feet, spilling loose pages from her much-read paperback. Doc came in from the hall.

Delsey glanced at her watch.

"Don't bother checking the time. Orders are morphine PRN."

DeWitt felt a tug at his arm. Delsey, nut-brown face lined in concentration, stuck a needle in his IV shunt.

"Might as well make him comfortable, Delsey. No sense worrying about addiction. No sense worrying about anything if we can't get his fever down."

DeWitt wanted to ask where he was, but the effort was too great. Then suddenly he knew: he was lying in Doc's examining room. In a corner were piled blood-stained sheets. A trash can overflowed with crimson-dotted gauze.

"If he seizes again, call me." Doc's hair was mussed, his white coat awry. "And keep the ice . . ."

DeWitt slept.

A heavy, dark silence. Nighttime. His bonds had been taken away; the bed was cool and dry, the sheets crisp. Next to the bed was a lamp. It cast a spotlight over a table piled with the refuse of illness: a jar of water, an open Kleenex box, a sagging blue ice pack.

The room reminded DeWitt of an airplane cabin after a long flight; of a darkened schoolroom at the end of the day.

"You awake?" Delsey asked, looming out of the shadows. There was a blue plastic box in her hand. "Let's take your temperature." From the plastic box she took what looked like a bank pen, with its attendant coil of cord.

DeWitt tried his voice. "Water."

"Temperature first," she said, putting the pen under his tongue.

He looked behind her broad form. Across the room was a

188

counter filled with cards and flowers. And three wrapped packages: the children's Christmas gifts.

Delsey removed the thermometer from his mouth, picked up
a water glass, and slipped the straw between his lips. The water
was cool, its touch strange to his throat.

As he drank, she followed the direction of his eyes. "People
brought you things." She took the water away. "You want to
rest now?"

He shook his head.

"Want me to show you what you got?"

"Please."

She picked up the cards and read them one by one. She read
the names from the notes on the flowers. Etta Wilson. Purdy
Phifer. B.J. and his family sent their best wishes. Granger left a
wooden dog that wagged its tail.

"Your wife brought the Christmas presents. You want me to
open them?"

From Denny, a green-painted ceramic mass that was either
an airplane or a fish. From Linda, a popsicle-stick birdhouse
made with exacting care.

Delsey dug her hands into the tissue lining the third box and
held up a slip of paper. "Tammy says she'll mow the lawn this
spring. There's a PS. It says to remind her a little."

Nothing from Janet. Nothing made from haphazard love, no
painstaking appreciation built piece by piece, no promises.

"There's something else," Delsey said, going to the counter.
She came back with a small stuffed tiger dressed in police blue.
A plush toy no bigger than a kitten.

Hattie had been to visit.

"She says you know what this meant."

DeWitt took the tiger. The toy was heavier than it looked:
stuffed not with batting but tiny pellets.

Their affair had begun in the café over coffee. It had insinuated itself past an argument—Hattie indignant that control of the town had passed to the Torku and DeWitt. During a lull in the fight, she sat back and hooked her fingers in the loops of her jeans. *Don't look at me that way, Wittie. I'm a pushover for a uniform.*

Astonishment at first. He laughed.

She laughed, too. *Really. Uniforms are turn-ons. Naval uniforms, Russians in their long coats, SS officers in old movies. Christ, I get weak-kneed over mailmen. Don't smile like that. Are you making fun?*

No, I—it's just that I always thought of you—

As a controller? Then embarrassed: *Nothing personal, okay, DeWitt? But I like the fitted shirts you wear. How they hug your waist. I watch you sometimes when you have your back to me. How your pants fit.*

Two years of Janet turning away from him in bed. Just when DeWitt had accustomed himself to abstinence, lust came like an illness. He sat in the café, high-fevered and trembling.

He said, *You never showed me your show barn. I'd like to see your horses, Hattie.*

She looked at him. He hoped she was seeing the uniform, the fitted shirt, the tighter-than-regulation pants, and not the man.

Humble, groveling. *Hattie? I'd like to see your horses very much.*

"You rest now," Delsey said.

He closed his eyes.

"Your wife's coming to visit tomorrow."

Janet. A counter full of cards, and nothing at all from Janet. "No."

"What?"

"Don't let her in."

190

A sigh. Delsey tried to pry the tiger from his grip, but he held on.

"You awake?"

Bo was standing nervously at the side of the bed.

"Can you talk? Can you understand me?"

DeWitt said, "Yes."

"The police station's burned to the ground, and the Torku haven't gotten around to rebuilding it. Billy's locked up in a room at Granger's house, but we can't keep him there forever. Everyone's pushing for a trial. The charge will be capital murder. I tried to get the Torku to send Billy across the Line, but they refuse. Explain to Seresen that an execution would be grotesque. The damned alien won't listen to me."

"Yes."

"You promise."

"Yes." DeWitt closed his eyes in what he thought would be a blink, but was slumber after all.

He awoke to daylight streaming in the window. A cardinal was perched on the sill: a blood spot in the blue of the sky. Someone, probably Delsey, had moved a television and VCR into the room. *Star Trek, The Movie* was playing to an empty chair.

Light from the window made a glare on the screen. DeWitt closed his eyes and listened to the voice of William Shatner.

A door opened in the background.

"Are you awake?"

Seresen. The alien waddled across the room, stopping to give the TV screen an incredulous glance. He took the chair, dragged it to DeWitt's side, sat, and leaned over confidentially. "You must tell the Bo that we do not want the man."

DeWitt licked his lips. He couldn't feel his tongue, his mouth. He wondered if he was drooling. "Okay."

"It is entirely your affair. The acts you do are unimportant. Besides, we are the observers only, and we are allowed to affect the outcome only so much. You should have the trial this Bo talks about, if that is the way you do things."

"Okay."

"Good." Seresen patted his arm. The alien's touch felt spongy.

Doc was weaning him off the morphine. DeWitt was awake more often; and being awake involved pain. On the third day of the dosage reduction, while he and Delsey were watching *The Exorcist*, Bo and Curtis came in.

"I have to talk to you," Bo said.

Delsey turned down the volume right at the good part and made her rubber-soled way out of the room.

"Okay," Bo began heatedly. "So we're going to have a god-damned trial. But when the town votes Curtis as judge—"

"But I'm Justice of the Peace," Curtis said.

"Listen, DeWitt. You know and I know there's a difference between a JP and a real judge. This man can't preside. He doesn't know criminal law, and this isn't some sort of game. If Billy is found guilty—if he's executed—Jesus! Curtis is so consistently flaky, people don't even know he's a hophead. They can't tell Curtis stoned from Curtis sober. I wanted to tell—"

"Motion denied," Curtis said. "See? I know some stuff."

Bo gave Curtis a dark look, then said to DeWitt, "He doesn't understand what this *means!* I tried to explain. You know what he said? He said that if the people of Coomey found out about his dope, they'd find out about you. You see what he's doing? To shut me up, he's using you as a shield."

192

"Objection," Curtis said.

"Out of the room, Curtis." Pain made DeWitt's voice no louder than a whisper.

Curtis stared as though he hadn't heard.

"Go on."

Lips pursed, Curtis left.

"Don't expose him," DeWitt told Bo.

"But—"

"Not for me, for him." DeWitt was running out of energy. "I know Curtis."

"If you're afraid for yourself . . ."

"No." DeWitt let his hand drop to the bed. "Don't spoil. Rise to the occasion. Maybe."

"You okay?"

DeWitt nodded, but the cramps were back.

"I didn't want to bother you . . . "

DeWitt waved a hand to show it was all right.

"They're picking a prosecuting attorney and a defense counsel. A lot of people want prosecution, but nobody's come forward to defend the poor bastard. Looks like it will be a court-appointed thing."

"You."

"Huh?"

"You be defense."

Bo didn't speak. DeWitt had closed his eyes against the pain, but curiosity coaxed them open. The officer looked crushed. "I can't be defense."

"You be . . ." DeWitt groaned, shifting his body.

"How can I defend him adequately, DeWitt? I know he's guilty."

"Confessed?"

"Doesn't need to. I found Loretta's clothes and purse buried right next to Billy's house. He burned them, but there was enough there—" Bo stopped when DeWitt reached out and grabbed his sleeve.

"Best person," DeWitt wheezed. "Needs to defend him. Do it right."

"But—"

"Please. Promise. Do it right." DeWitt's fingers slid from Bo's jacket. "Ask Seresen. Show you kids."

"He knows where the kids are buried?"

"Ask Seresen."

"If the aliens saw it, I could get depositions . . ."

"No."

"Why not?"

"Lie," DeWitt gasped. "Can't help it."

"Listen, you okay? God, Wittie, it looks—"

"Call Doc."

"Right away."

Bo left. The doctor came into the room and gave DeWitt a shot. He missed the end of the movie.

Three days later, Doc came into DeWitt's room with Granger. "Okay, Chief. Let's get you on your feet."

DeWitt stared at the two incredulously.

"More you lay around on your butt, the longer the recuperation's going to be. You're going to start walking a little every day now."

"No, no." DeWitt waved his arms in panic.

"Granger?" Doc said.

The big man came forward, put a beefy arm under DeWitt's shoulder, and lifted him like a sack of meal.

"No, no," DeWitt said.

"It don't hurt as much as he's letting on, believe me," said Doc.

Granger pulled DeWitt up. When DeWitt's bare feet hit the linoleum floor, he bent double at the waist and stayed there.

"Walk," Doc commanded.

DeWitt took a sliding step.

"Stand up straight."

"No."

"Suit yourself." He made DeWitt shuffle three doors down and three doors back.

The next day, Doc and Granger came in and made him do four doors.

The next day, Bo came to visit. "How are you?"

DeWitt stared at the ceiling. "Um," he said.

"I found the kids' bodies."

"Joy."

A pause. "Doc said you were in a bad mood. He said that's how he can tell when people start feeling better. Isn't that funny?"

"Ha, ha," DeWitt said.

"There was a tire iron thrown in the brush. It had fingerprints on it."

DeWitt looked down. Bo was standing by the bed, tired and grim, sunglasses in his shirt pocket, vulnerable eyes exposed.

"They mine?" DeWitt asked quietly.

Bo looked at his motorcycle helmet, turning it over and over in his hands. "I don't think so. You put your tire iron back into your trunk."

"Seresen told you what I made him do?"

"Yes."

"He upset with me?"

"It's hard to tell."

With a grunt DeWitt turned on his side, face to Bo's belt

buckle. He'd been able to do the turning-on-the-side trick for three days. "Do me a favor."

"Sure."

"When you see Seresen next, you tell him the policeman's happy, will you?"

Bo didn't answer.

"The policeman's happy, you got it?"

"Okay."

DeWitt rolled over on his back. Bo was staring at him—a distinctly unhappy policeman. Silence settled between them like a fine winter rain. He studied Bo's tall shadow on the wall.

When Bo spoke, his voice was pained, as though speaking was a burden. "Anyway, since I'm defense counsel, I can't lift the prints off that tire iron. I'm teaching Purdy how."

Bo's shadow moved. He was playing with his helmet again.

"Thank you," DeWitt said.

"Hum?"

"You saved my life. Thank you."

The shadow went still. "Janet wants you home."

DeWitt forgot for a moment to breathe.

"You hear me?" Bo's voice had a waver in it. Sympathy or something else?

Maybe he had loved Foster the way DeWitt in high school loved Janet. Maybe Bo sat in front of the TV at night, fantasizing Foster sitting beside him. A solitary house; an imaginary playmate.

Bo's voice was stiff. "Are you going home to Janet, DeWitt?"

Old hurt, older than the pain in his belly, welled from DeWitt like blood from a wound. His eyes searched the counter for Hattie's tiger, but someone, maybe Janet, had taken it away.

"I don't know," he said.

38

SOMETIME DURING THE DRUGSTORE FIRE Jimmy Schoen's fingers had set loose his parishioners' hearts.

Now, down the table Foster and Tyler were smiling: Lucifers with pleasing faces. When Schoen looked at his plate, he thought for a queasy instant that his eggs had moved, that his brown, slick-backed sausages had begun to crawl.

He closed his eyes, a weary Job. God was testing him, not with boils, but with his people's pestilent disregard.

He should have been jury foreman, yet a Papist had been elected. Worse was the presence of Foster, false prophet, evangelist of nihilism. Schoen opened his eyes in time to see the jury nod in agreement and laugh at something witty Foster said.

A Torku came into the room, filling coffee cups from a Pyrex pot. The jury members seemed easy with the demon, too, laughing and joking with it.

As though life itself were a prank.

Schoen's hand clenched on his glass so hard that it shook, spilling juice in sticky, orange waves.

"Will you wish some more?" the demon asked politely.

What else should Satan be but courteous? The world the devil had created was an easy place. Hell, Schoen had discovered, was not made of flame but of an obliging, seductive anarchy.

"No," Schoen said without looking up. His voice was hard, his words clipped. There was, he congratulated himself, an unwavering discipline in his tone. "I think I have had quite enough."

39

DEWITT WAS IN BED through the selection of principals. He missed the *voir dire*. The trial preparations went on without him as the sun rose and set outside the windows and the stars at night slowly careened. On a Tuesday, Doc came in, helped him dress, and sent him into the world.

They drove to the center in silence. Leaning on Doc's arm, DeWitt limped into the familiar green-and-cream rec hall. Rows of folding chairs had been set up in two sections and the room was packed.

Seclusion had become such a habit that he nearly fled when people jumped up, chattering, to shake his hand. Miz Wilson tore him away from the well-wishers and, like leading a prize bull into the auctioneer's ring, took him to the front row and sat him down behind the defense table. Billy's hands were folded before him. Bo sat at his shoulder, dressed in a three-piece suit. Hattie was at the prosecution table by her oldest boy.

DeWitt's gaze rested on Hattie. She didn't look his way. Like Billy, like Bo, she was staring straight ahead—in expectation or nervousness.

Is the whole town watching me watch my lover? he wondered. *And later on the telephone, or over dinner, what will they make of that?*

DeWitt looked to the right. In the double line of folding chairs that served as jury box, Pastor Jimmy plumped like a disgruntled pigeon. Tyler was leaning back, his fingers laced across his belly. Foster was there, too.

There were dangerous places in the center, like doors that shouldn't be opened. DeWitt looked left.

Down the row, Seresen was sitting with two other Torku, and fidgeting in the chair next to the alien was Denny. The child caught his father's eye and waved. At the very end of the row Janet turned to stare.

"All rise!" Granger bellowed.

With a rustle of clothing and clanks from the folding chairs, the crowd came to their feet.

Directly in front of DeWitt, Bo stood, hands in his pockets, awaiting sacrifice. He would go where DeWitt had sent him — into the dark basement of the town's resentment. No one else would have had the courage to tread there; no one else would have gone with such a dutiful stride.

Curtis walked in, surveyed the standing spectators, and glanced over his shoulder as if expecting to see the President of the United States at his heels. Mounting the podium, the mayor sat down. A look of awe crossed his face when everyone took their seats.

In his arms were Perry Mason paperbacks, porcupined with yellow markers. He arranged the books on the desk.

"Your Honor?" Granger stage-whispered.

Curtis looked up, startled. "So, is the prosecution ready?"

"Ready, Your Honor!" Hattie shot back in a crisp voice that made the jury jump.

"Defense?"

Bo uncrossed his long legs and stood. "Your Honor? Defense requests . . ." His voice trailed to a nervous stop. "A change of venue."

Gasps peppered the room.

Curtis rubbed his cheeks. "Far out."

"If it please the court," Bo went on, "my client can't get a fair trial here. After the alleged attack on Chief Dawson . . ." The officer swung his hand to point out DeWitt. "In which my client was simply defending himself—"

Hattie lurched to DeWitt's rescue. "Objection!"

With a negligent wave, Curtis motioned her down.

Bo stammered, as though his train of thought had been derailed. "Anyway, it was p-prejudicial."

Curtis's round face grew pensive. "Approach the bench?"

It was a moment before the two lawyers rose, as if they thought Curtis had been asking their opinion.

"Better get you up here, too, Seresen," Curtis added.

The alien pulled himself out of the folding chair, and in whispers the principals began a heated discussion at the bench. Curtis leaned over the table, buttocks in the air. Granger inched his way in from the side and was listening. The jury strained forward, frustration in their faces.

The huddle broke up. The two lawyers went back to their respective tables, and Seresen waddled to his chair.

"Motion denied," Curtis said, banging a red-handled Sears hammer on the tabletop.

"Then if it please the court," Bo said, "I move to delay the trial for a competency hearing."

"We been through that, Bo," said Curtis, who sounded not pleased at all. "We don't have no psychiatrist. Billy done killed everyone who knew him well enough to testify to competency . . ."

DeWitt winced.

Bo threw a Manila folder onto the table with a sharp, angry slap. "Objection, Your Honor. Move to strike. When the judge himself—"

"Okay, okay. I'm sorry." Curtis's face turned red. "Forget I said that. Let's have opening arguments."

Hattie stood. In her dark suit and white blouse, she looked like a gangly adolescent playing grownup. Her very awkwardness brought a lump to DeWitt's throat. It reminded him of the first time he saw Tammy on a bicycle.

And yet she embarrassed him. The same tired suit she wore to each city council meeting; the same wine stain on the blouse she'd never had the time or patience to remove. A run laddered one leg of her hose. Why couldn't she dress herself better? Even now the town's eyes must be swinging from attractive wife to plain lover, wondering what charm had made DeWitt stray.

In a monotone that barely carried to the front row, Hattie read, "We're going to prove that Billy killed Loretta in a fit of anger. That's second-degree murder. But that by the time he went back to the car and beat his own kids to death with a rock, that was premeditated." Abruptly she offered a wavering, sick smile to the jury, said, "Thank you," and sat down.

"Is that it?" Curtis asked.

She nodded. Bo stood, pulling at the hem of his vest. "First-degree murder," he said in a tone even softer than Hattie's. "That means with malice aforethought. What we're going to prove . . ." He paused, swallowing hard, throttled by stage fright.

The jury peered at him, confused. Quickly, DeWitt looked down at his lap.

"We're going to prove," Bo said in a hoarse but stronger voice, "that Billy, after striking out at his wife in anger, then going around the edge of the house to his kids, was so furious, he stepped into the realm of temporary insanity." A fluttering sound: the paper Bo was reading from was trembling. "That's all," Bo said.

"All right," Curtis said doubtfully. "First witness."

Hattie stood. "I call Purdy Emmanuel Phifer to the stand."

A single spectator's giggle proved contagious and an epidemic of hilarity spread. DeWitt turned and saw Purdy making his way down the aisle. He had on a police uniform and looked ridiculous in it.

"You were there when the boys' bodies were found?" Hattie asked when Purdy took his seat.

Purdy was round-eyed. "Yeah. Bo and me —"

"Answer the question yes or no!"

Fishing in his pocket, DeWitt found his notebook and a pencil. "Don't badger your own witnesses," he wrote and passed the note to her son. The boy read it without interest and set it on the table.

"Yes," Purdy said.

"And tell us what you found."

Purdy seemed desperately trying to choose between negative and positive. "Bodies?"

"The bodies of . . ."

"Loretta's kids?"

Hattie spun away. Placing her hands behind her back, she said, "All right. Tell the court in your own words about the scene."

Purdy turned to the jury. "They was lying in a shallow grave. We found a tire iron back in some bushes where it'd been throwed . . ."

This part of the questioning went so smoothly that DeWitt

guessed Purdy had been coached. His pity for Hattie began to fade.

"This tire iron?" Hattie grabbed a red-tagged tire tool from the floor near her table, walked forward, and shoved it into Purdy's face.

Purdy examined it. "Yeah."

Hattie dropped the tire iron on Curtis's table, where it clanged satisfyingly. "I enter in evidence State's Exhibit A." Returning to her table, she got a thick square of plaster and set that on the desk as well. "And State's Exhibit B. So," she turned to Purdy, "what did you find on the tire iron?"

"Dried paint."

"And in the paint you found?"

A self-satisfied smirk worked its way across Purdy's face. "Fingerprints."

"Whose?"

Purdy's chubby arm pointed across the room to Billy. "The defendant's."

"Objection," Bo said with what sounded like boredom. "Witness is not an expert."

Hattie swiveled to Bo so fast, she nearly tripped. "He taught him, Your Honor. That man is an expert and he taught him how to lift those prints."

Bo sat quietly in the firing line of her accusing finger.

"Did you teach him how?" Curtis asked Bo.

"Yes."

"Then you certified him. Overruled."

Hattie sat. "No further questions."

Purdy was halfway to his feet when Curtis asked, "Cross?"

A hound fearing punishment for an indiscretion, Purdy cringed back into his seat.

"No questions," Bo said.

Purdy slunk away.

DeWitt noticed the hurt, questioning look that the photographer cast at Bo; and that Bo, writing something on a blank page, did not meet Purdy's eyes. Peering over Bo's shoulder, DeWitt saw that he was doodling: a frowny face, then a smiley face. The pyramid of heads was grotesque, a cartoon version of the Cambodian killing fields.

A bang from the hammer as Curtis broke for lunch. Janet was making her way down the row. DeWitt started to turn to her, but collided bellies with Seresen.

"Come with me," the alien said and started off across the makeshift courtroom.

DeWitt gladly followed. On the way, Curtis grabbed him. "How am I doing?"

"Fine, Curtis. Just fine." DeWitt watched, alarmed, as the alien made for the green steel door.

"I read them books, you know? With those criminal cases and all. Them Perry Mason judges got it all down."

"Uh-huh."

Seresen paused and turned, surprised not to see DeWitt behind him.

"So you think I done okay?"

"Yeah." DeWitt caught the alien's eye.

Curtis leaned up to whisper, "Staying off the dope for a while, Wittie. Trying to, anyway. If I need some help . . ."

Absently DeWitt said, "Sure. Anytime." He hurried toward the Kol.

"You must have lunch." Seresen ushered him through the door. The room in which DeWitt found himself must have been the Torku dining hall. A long black table, fuchsia chairs huddled to it like pigs at a trough. Behind the table a windowed wall which broke the laws of physics and engineering: from a perch

205

high on Griffin Hill, it looked down a cedar brake and into town. With a quiet clunk the door closed behind him.

"Sit down," the alien said.

DeWitt pulled out a low, wide-seated chair. In the windows a white bird darted from a dark-green cedar and soared toward Main. The pigeon, a spark in the glowering sky, banked over the beige modular walls of the center. DeWitt raised his head, as though he might catch sight of it through the ceiling.

Another Torku emerged from a door, an aluminum plate in his hands. The worker set a Banquet fried-chicken dinner in front of DeWitt, a plastic knife and fork beside it.

"Aren't you hungry?" DeWitt asked Seresen when the worker left.

"I will talk. You will eat lunch."

Obediently DeWitt picked up his fork.

"So you are the happy policeman?" the Kol asked, his brown skin turning an obviously delighted pearl.

DeWitt nearly gagged on his potatoes. The cook hadn't microwaved the dinner long enough, and the gravy was cold. "Yeah. Listen. I'm sorry about making you—"

"The trial is interesting."

DeWitt dropped his fork.

"Too orderly for my tastes, but then you cannot help yourselves, I suppose. Still, there is this: When he is arrested, you all say the Billy is guilty; just before the trial, you speak in terms of alleged. And now, even though you keep to your silly rules, everyone pretends not to know anything. Have you taught your people this trial?"

With his fork DeWitt poked skeptically at the chicken breast. "Not really. It—"

"I have very great hopes for you."

206

"Seresen, listen . . ." DeWitt wondered how the alien would react when the jury found Billy guilty. When the town executed him.

"Eat. I will come to get you when they are ready." The alien got to his feet.

"Seresen—"

"Later." The Kol walked away.

DeWitt didn't finish his lunch.

40

DEWITT WAS GAZING OUT THE WINDOW when Seresen returned and led him to the human side of the center. Curtis walked into the courtroom and gaveled for quiet. The trial started again.

Hattie entered the burned purse and clothes into evidence, then called Doc to the stand to testify that the indentations in the boys' skulls matched the shape of the rock found in the grave.

When Hattie held up poster-sized photographs, the ones that Purdy had taken, a hush fell over the room.

"Objection," Bo said. "Inflammatory."

But the photos weren't inflammatory at all. They were, despite the subject matter, beautiful. The three black-and-white stills of the boys had been taken during the exhumation. The photographer's eye had caught the spill of light on a maimed hand, the drift of leaf mold on bare ribs. The lack of color made the scene timeless, as if it had filtered through a membrane between universes. The photos had less to do with death than with composition, perspective, and light. There was no color to expose the tawdriness of rain-battered, loamy clothes, the gaudiness of bloated blue flesh. There was no stench, no orange accusation of that raincoat.

The jury sat on the edges of their seats. Only Hubert Foster's eyes wandered. Expression sad, he studied his hands.

Are they clean? DeWitt wondered. When Foster looked down, did he see DeWitt's misery on his fingers?

Bo objected; Curtis overruled. With a sigh, a small shake of his head, Foster returned his attention to the trial.

Hattie propped the stills on the desk. "Prosecution rests."

Everyone, the jury, the spectators, the Torku, was staring at Billy. Everyone but his counsel. Bo was tidying up his papers, putting the collection of cartoon heads into his briefcase.

Curtis, too, had been watching Billy. Now he jerked himself out of his reverie and tapped the hammer against the table once. "It's four-thirty. Let's adjourn and convene tomorrow at nine sharp."

Bo turned to DeWitt, opened his mouth as if to speak, but then his eyes drifted left. Instantly, Bo became occupied with his briefcase.

"Wittie?" Janet said at DeWitt's shoulder.

As he turned, Denny grasped his fingers. "Hi, Daddy. We came to visit you, but you were asleep. Did you see my dead soldier?"

"What?"

"The dead soldier I made for you in Sunday School, Daddy. I'm gonna make a lot more. Soldiers with guns like I see in the movies. And tanks and things. We can play war."

They had played war. Now Janet and Foster lay wounded; DeWitt shot through the heart. He looked for Hattie and saw her by the table. She was putting her notes away, her eyes downcast.

"Daddy." A tug on his hand. DeWitt's gaze returned to his son, where he knew it belonged. "We're going home now, okay?"

And DeWitt said, "Okay."

Outside the center, blue-gray clouds advanced across the horizon. The icy breeze of a norther hit DeWitt's back. He was tired; his incision ached. He followed Janet as if all decisions had been taken from his hands.

The Suburban was a steel-walled, sheltered prison. On the way home, the children chattered. He didn't speak. At the house, Janet heated a twelve-count package of tamales in the microwave.

When they were all seated at the table, she passed the serving dish. He picked up a tamale, then put it down.

"Aren't you hungry?" she asked.

He couldn't look at her. His reply was sour. "Doc told me no spicy foods."

The two girls exchanged worried glances. Janet prodded a chicken tamale with her fork as though it were a creature she wanted to awaken.

Denny was bouncing in his chair. "Daddy's a hero," he announced to the silence around the table.

"I know," Janet said.

DeWitt left his lunch uneaten and went to take a shower. While he was shampooing his hair, Janet entered the bathroom and stood in the gap of the curtain. She had put on her robe. Her cornsilk hair was down.

"I missed you," she said. "In the hospital when you wouldn't see me, I wondered whether freedom was worth that."

"I don't know what you're talking about." But he did. What he had thought a happy marriage she had seen as an armistice: between her as the occupied territory and him as the invading force. He put his head under the shower and picked up the soap. Water beat him with tiny, angry fists.

Without warning Janet slipped the bathrobe from her shoulders and stepped naked into the shower. He saw the splay of her toes on the porcelain, then looked up at her bare breasts.

Time compressed—past the affairs, past the marriage. He remembered sweaty college fumblings in his old Pontiac, and how her breasts had dropped into his hands like ripe fruit from the discipline of her bra.

Gently she took the soap away. "Here. Let me do that."

DeWitt leaned his forehead against the cool tile. Her hand slipped down his back. "It's over. I told him I never wanted to see him again."

She left room for his reply; he didn't use it. She kissed his shoulder, pressed her face against his back. His penis stirred to life.

"Why Hattie? I thought you wanted someone who would agree with you. All those years I thought . . ." In the rush of water he felt the quieter, slower wet of her tears.

Because Hattie was simple. She wanted a policeman, DeWitt thought. *And you wanted more.*

Janet slid her hand between his legs and fondled him. "Tell me I'm better. Please tell me I'm better than she is."

"Harder," he told her instead.

Soon he turned, pressed her against the wall of the shower, and they made slippery, dangerous love. Just before he came, he was more excited than he had ever been with Hattie, nearly as excited as those frustrating evenings in the Pontiac.

When he came, the urgency left softly, sadly. The wound in his belly began to ache. She stepped away, leaving him braced in the corner, water rolling down his chest.

She toweled and put her bathrobe back on. "Why did you let Hattie be herself? Why did you want me to change?"

211

"God, Janet. Come on. Not once—not once in the time I've known you did I ask you to change."

"But you *do*," she said, as if DeWitt were a dimwitted god she longed to please. "You do it all the time. You organize my life as if I hired on as your maid." She made her "funny face," a private after-the-party grimace used to ridicule people they didn't like. "If you'd get the housework *organized*, dear, you could get finished faster. *I* could get it all done in the morning, and have the rest of the afternoon off."

"I just wanted to be helpful."

"Did you ever wash a dish? Did you? Did you ever change a diaper? What makes you the damned resident expert on housework? On raising kids? For twenty years I kept my mouth shut. Maybe I was right: maybe keeping the peace *was* better than speaking my mind."

Keeping the peace was his job. "You talk about me like I was some sort of monster. Did I ever hit you? Did I ever yell at you? Janet, did I ever once raise my voice?"

"Only because I never raised mine."

"I don't want to talk about this."

"Right. Whenever I want to talk about anything important, your face shuts like a door."

"I'm sorry." But if what she said wasn't true, he had no need to apologize. And if it was, no apology would be enough.

The water turned cold, and he shivered. A small, irritating pain in his midsection—the drawing ache of something that would never quite be healed.

"Oh, Wittie," she sighed. "Twenty years of you playing deaf. And now I have to wonder. Do you want someone who will stand up to you? Is that what you want? I could be loud and overbearing like Hattie. I could—"

"Don't drag Hattie into this. She was the only thing . . ." His throat swelled with unshed tears. He remembered Hattie standing in the courtroom, dressed in her wrinkled blue suit. Even now, with the ruin of his marriage around him, loyal Hattie meant less than his unfaithful wife. "Hattie loves me."

"I love you, too."

Chilled, he bent to turn the shower off.

"Do you hear me, DeWitt? I love you. But I won't be your damned 'little woman' anymore."

She left the bathroom. He watched her go, wondering how he could set right the twenty years of harm she imagined he had done her.

41

WHEN COURT CONVENED the next morning, Bo stood, clasped his hands behind his back, and in a loud, self-assured voice called William James Harper to the stand.

"Tell us about the murder, Billy," Bo said in a patient, tolerant way, as if to remind the jury to be forgiving, too.

"She was making the kids sick again," Billy said.

A murmur went through the courtroom.

Bo raised his hand before Curtis could reach for the hammer. "Making the kids sick? How did Loretta make the kids sick?"

"Kept food out till it spoiled. Then she'd feed it to 'em. Sometimes she just got tired of fooling with the boys, and that was the way she'd calm 'em down. They'd be in bed a couple of days with the fever and all. Have her some rest, she'd say." Billy looked around the courtroom, blinking slow. "But that time she got 'em too sick. Had to call Doc out."

DeWitt saw Doc in the third row from the door. His face was stricken.

"So what happened then?"

Billy scratched his knee. "Sunday evening she brings the boys over. She was out of gas and wanted me to give her some. Loretta was always thoughtless that way. Never planned for nothing. Always wanted a free ride. Anyway, that Sunday, them boys was feeling better, and they was messing up her kitchen. Gotta get out from under, she says. Wanted me to take care of 'em." Incredibly, his lips parted and he laughed, exposing the pink of his gums. "Wanted gas to get home and wanted me to take care of her kids."

"You didn't feel you could care for the boys?"

"Construction site's no place for babysitting. Boys get under foot all the time. So," he said, leaning back in the chair and hooking his thumbs in his belt, "she come around the side of the house. I was cleaning up my spray painter —"

"Exhibit E?"

"Right. Had just sprayed with latex, and needed to get the paint out. So all the time she's yelling over the noise of that spray painter, and she just got louder and louder until I reached out to hit her and shut her up, only my hand's holding that nozzle . . ." His voice trailed off, and he shrugged. A small grin tugged at his mouth, as if he was still amused by the joke that fate had played on Loretta.

"You knew the spray painter was dangerous."

"That's a commercial rig. Spray comes out at seventy-five hundred p.s.i. Blow a hole right through your hand."

"Were you aware of what you were doing when you struck her?"

"Naw." He shrugged again, just one shoulder. "Wanted to clip her a little so's she'd shut up."

"So the first blow was an accident."

"Yes, sir. It was accidental."

"Then what?" Bo asked.

Billy took a deep breath, leaning back farther, as if he were

215

sitting back from the dinner table after a good meal. "She fell down. She was still moving around a little and trying to scream. So I hit her again. There was a lot of blood that time."

"How did you feel?"

"Hell, feel? I felt like I couldn't think straight. I was mad at her for what she'd made me do. Loretta was always like that, pushing me and pushing until I lost control."

"And then?"

"I come around the house to where them boys was and I seen 'em playing Superman. Jason had that raincoat Loretta bought him, and they was running around the yard chunking concrete at a bandsaw I set up. I took that rock out of the boy's hands, asked him what he thought he was doing."

"What did he say?"

"Nothing, but his face was sassy, you know? Loretta never taught them boys to mind. She was a who-re," he said, making two bouncing syllables out of the word. Billy stopped and looked speculatively around the courtroom, as if judging how the aliens had set their joints and laid their baseboards.

"So you . . ."

"I hit him."

"With the chunk of concrete."

"Yes, sir."

"What happened then?"

"He dropped. That other boy, he just took to his heels." Billy shot straight up in his seat. His eyes narrowed as though even now he could see the child fleeing. "I yelled, 'Commere!'" The command cracked like thunder through the courtroom, leaving an awed hush in its wake. Billy's face was taut: the veins in his neck bulged. "'Goddamn it! Commere!' But he just kept going, and I went after him because nobody, nobody runs away from me like that!" Gradually Billy sat back, his face relaxing, the boy in his mind fading.

"And did you catch him?"

"Goddamned right I did. Taught him something about running away from his daddy."

"With the chunk of concrete?"

"Right. The one that run was Billy Junior."

DeWitt closed his eyes. When he opened them, he saw Billy picking at a hangnail.

"Tell me about your relationship with your wife," Bo said as he turned to face the stunned jury.

"What about it?"

"You said she was a whore. Why?"

"When we was living together, she was always on the phone. Said she was talking to them church biddies. Said it was them Mary Kay customers, but I knew better. Laughing and joking with 'em and then shutting up when I came by."

"An affair. Then she threw you out. But no one, no one runs away from you like that. Did you often go by Loretta's house? To see if her lover was there?"

"Damned right. Didn't want her hiding from me. Thought she could do whatever the hell she had a mind to. Well, that ain't the way a marriage works."

"But you never saw anyone."

Billy looked bewildered. "No."

"Another man. How did you feel about that?"

"How do you think? Made me goddamned crazy."

"Crazy." Bo let the word sink into the courtroom. The jury studied Billy as if he were a stranger. As if he might just be insane.

"And is that why you left Loretta's body the way you did, and buried the boys?"

"Right. Wanted the man she was playing around with to see her up real good."

DeWitt noticed Hattie's frown. There was paper in front of her, but she had stopped taking notes.

"So you sat around your house and thought about your wife in the arms of her lover. You'd drive over, stand in her yard, and yell things. You were lonely. You were obsessed. Obsessed enough to make—"

"Objection! This isn't a dime-store romance novel, Your Honor."

"Sustained."

Bo sighed. "How about other women? Did you get along with them?"

A sharp, mirthless laugh from Billy. "You know how women is. Always wanting more. Always hot for it. A man can get satisfied, but them women," he said, shaking his head. "Nothing you ever do's enough. They's all who-res. Know what I mean?"

The courtroom was quiet. Bo stood, notes apparently forgotten. "All of them," he said. "Every woman you've known. All of them whores. Tell me, Billy, did you ever hear the term *premature ejaculation?*"

Billy's eyebrows twitched.

"You're afraid of women, aren't you? All your life they seem to be running away. They have control over you. Over your desires. You want to stop them. You want to—"

"No!" Billy half-rose from his seat.

"Did you ever seek help for a sexual problem?"

"Ain't nothing wrong with me! It's them. It's all of them."

Bo's head sank. Billy, still rattled, eased back into his chair. "No further questions at this time, Your Honor. Defense reserves the right to recall."

"Your witness," Curtis said to Hattie.

She stood, her face full of fury. "When you killed the boys, you were so mad you couldn't think straight?"

"Right, and—"

"But you could think straight enough to hide the car where the Torku would find it. You could think straight enough to bury the boys. But the boys were small, and a foot under the loam is all white rock. So you just left Loretta where you thought nobody would find her, hoping the coyotes would finish the job. That's why you burned the clothes and left the body out to rot. You were just too goddamned lazy to dig her a grave, weren't you?"

"Objection!"

"Overruled."

Bo pounded the table. "Damn it, Curtis! She's not even giving him time to answer! You can't allow—"

Curtis screamed, "Sit down!" Then to Hattie: "Get on with it, prosecutor, make your point!"

And Hattie did. "That stuff about wanting her so-called boyfriend to find her is a lie, isn't it? She never had a boyfriend, did she? You killed her because you don't like anyone to run away from you, isn't that right?"

"Objection," Bo said wearily. The wind had shifted. DeWitt could feel it. Bo had to know it, too. Indignation gathered in the room; hung silent, ominous, like an approaching storm.

Hattie turned away. "No further questions."

Bo stood. "Defense calls Marvin Howell Murphy."

"No," Hattie said, momentarily forgetting her role.

"Overruled," Curtis told her, not forgetting his.

Hattie's son slouched to the stand.

"Has your mother ever hit you?" Bo asked as soon as the boy was sworn in.

Marv paled. He glanced to Hattie.

"Did she ever whip you?"

The boy flinched. "Yes, sir. But only when—"

"She ever threaten to kill you?"

"She . . ."

Bo shoved his face into the boy's and shouted, "Answer the question!"

Miserable, Marv looked at his mother. Hattie was covering the bottom of her face with her hand as though to still her son's mouth.

Curtis leaned across the table and said gently, "It's all right, son. It'll be all right. Just answer the question."

A lone tear worked its way from the boy's eye and slid down his cheek. "She'd say stuff like she was going to duck my head in the toilet and flush it." His eyes searched the crowd. "And she'd say she was going to pull my arm out of its socket and beat me over the head with it, stuff like that." His wandering gaze snagged on Bo's frown.

"No more questions."

"Cross?" Curtis asked.

Hattie was already on her feet. "I ever beat your head in with a rock and kill you?"

"No, ma'am."

"No more questions." Hattie turned her back on her son and let him walk to the prosecution's table alone.

"DeWitt Earl Dawson," Bo said.

DeWitt was so surprised by the call that he didn't move until the man next to him elbowed him in the side. He got to his feet and went to the witness stand.

There were sharp edges to the morning light. From the eastern windows, sun struck Bo's watch a glancing blow. He turned, and the light fell full on his face. Bo's cheeks glowed like a candle in the dim room.

He gave DeWitt an apologetic look. "I called you up here as an expert witness in temporary insanity."

"I don't think—"

"Temporary insanity."

DeWitt watched Bo pace.

"You're an officer of the law, correct?"

DeWitt cleared his throat. "Yes."

"And you take your job seriously."

"That's right."

Bo's charcoal-gray form eclipsed Seresen's moon-round, pink eyes.

"Would you say you're a controlled man?"

Crossing his legs, DeWitt said, "Yes. I'd say I was controlled. It's part of my job."

"You're forced to take abuse?"

"Sometimes." DeWitt glanced around the room, picking out the traffic offenders: the drinkers, the speeders, the runners of red lights. Often, when he stopped them, they forgot to be polite. DeWitt could not afford to.

"Have you ever, during an arrest, let's say, hit an unarmed person in the performance of your duty?"

"Never." It was warm in the room. DeWitt pulled at his collar.

"Never. And you've never hit a suspect when he or she was subdued?"

"No." DeWitt shot an angry glance at the officer. "We've worked together for over nine years. We've talked a lot about excessive force, remember? You know I believe it's legally and morally wrong."

It was Bo who went to the dangerous edge of control.

For DeWitt it was always yes sir and no sir to people who were too drunk to get out of the front seat. May I see your driver's license, sir?

"Legally and morally." Bo's head was down, and it seemed he was pondering DeWitt's answer. Then he lifted his gaze. "Edward Theodore Wilkins."

DeWitt blinked, trying to place the name.

Then, like a stray shaft of wheat in a mown field, a lanky teenaged boy rose from the seated crowd.

Eddie.

"You remember this boy, Chief Dawson?"

"Yes."

"What?" Bo inclined his head, cupped his ear. "Please speak up, or I'll have to get the boy himself up on the stand."

Where the light hit the side of Bo's cheek, the skin was smooth and almost translucent. Just under the jaw was a spot the razor had missed.

"No, I remember."

"Did you ever hit this boy?"

"Yes."

"Speak up, please."

"Yes!"

"Was the boy unarmed?"

DeWitt looked down at his own lap. "Yes."

"Was he fighting you?"

"No."

"And didn't you, without the boy's provocation, hit him hard enough in the stomach to knock him down?"

DeWitt nodded.

"Wasn't the blow strong enough that it could have easily caused his death?"

"Objection!" Hattie's voice. "Speculation!"

"Sustained."

A whisper of feet on carpet. Bo was pacing again. "Did you ever hit anyone else?"

DeWitt started to shake his head, but stopped.

"Your daughter?" Bo asked. His face was pinched, his blue eyes anguished. "Please. Answer the question."

DeWitt's throat constricted. He glanced at Janet and wished he hadn't. "Yes."

"Did you hurt her?"

"Yes."

"And if you had had a rock in your hand at that moment, it's possible you might have killed her."

"Objection!" Hattie shouted. "Calls for—"

"Sustained."

"Your Honor, who are we trying here, anyway?" There were twin spots of color on Hattie's cheeks, and her curly brown hair had escaped its bun. Her indignation made her look frightening and clownish, all at the same time.

"I told you, sustained. You won your point, prosecutor."

Bo walked to the defense table. DeWitt, thinking his testimony was finished, began to rise. Bo froze him with a stare.

"On or about December third of this year, did you enter the defendant's house, and did you do so without a search warrant?"

Anger pulled DeWitt the rest of the way from his seat. When he realized he was standing, he quickly sat down, avoiding Curtis's questioning look. "That's correct."

Bo nodded. "And could you tell the court what you found?"

DeWitt cautiously relaxed. "Pornographic magazines. Women's underclothes."

The whispers in the courtroom became a babble. Curtis

hammered the table so hard, he chipped it. He looked down at what he had done, as if he were a child whose careless play had broken something of his mother's.

"From the evidence," Bo said slowly, darting a meaningful glance at Hattie as though to forestall an objection, "could you tell if the underclothes had been used for cross-dressing or something else?"

"From the evidence, I'd say he was a fetishist."

"In your professional opinion."

"In my professional opinion, yes."

"And in the house did you find a red bra with white hearts?"

DeWitt slowly opened his mouth. His lips felt gummy.

"Please answer the question." Bo tapped the point of his pencil against the defense table, the measured beat of a dirge.

"Yes."

"Whose bra was it? I remind you that you're under oath." DeWitt saw Bo turn to Janet.

"My wife's," DeWitt muttered into the dead silence of the courtroom.

"No more questions," Bo said so abruptly that he caught Hattie on her feet, ready to object.

"Your witness."

"No questions."

Bo said, "I recall William James Harper."

DeWitt's legs were shaking. As he walked past Bo, he tried to catch his eye, but Bo was concentrating on the paper he held. The paper was blank.

"When did you come into the possession of the red-and-white bra, Mr. Harper?" Bo asked.

Billy was slumped in the witness chair. "'Bout six years ago, near as I can recall."

"And how did you come into possession of it?"

Billy looked startled.

A bang, sudden as a gunshot. Foster had risen, his metal chair fallen behind him. "Stop it!"

Bo turned fearfully toward the jury box, as though he had heard footsteps in a nighttime alley.

"Bo! Don't do this!" Foster's hands were in fists. Tyler was trying to right the chair and pull him down into it at the same time.

"Bailiff, sit that jury member down!" Curtis commanded. "Order, goddamn it! Come to order!"

To DeWitt's left was the sound of hurried movement. Janet was gathering coats. Head lowered, silken hair curtaining her face, she herded the kids from the room. It would happen. It would happen now. DeWitt had sent Bo into that basement, and he had come back with a knife.

A moan from Foster, "Oh, God, don't do this." Tyler and Granger wrestled him down, and Curtis gaveled for quiet.

Bo watched Janet leave, his mouth in a razor line. He turned to Billy. "How'd you get the bra?"

"Found it."

"Where?"

The courtroom was catacomb-silent.

"In the woods near the lake."

DeWitt knew he should scream for Bo to stop, but it was too late. Arbitrary time was running too fast for him to catch it. Running as Janet had run from the hall.

"What was it doing there?"

"You sure you want me to tell this?" Billy searched Bo's face for clues.

"Just answer the question."

"Was with some other clothes."

"Whose clothes?"

225

Billy motioned with his shoulder at the door through which Janet had just disappeared. "Miz Dawson's clothes. She was naked."

A curious frost started in DeWitt's feet and spread through his body. There were rules he must follow: he would look straight ahead. Not at Foster. Not let his feelings show.

"Was she with anyone?"

Billy looked into Bo's eyes. A pause, and he said, "She was with you."

Odd how still and quiet it was, and how distant the witness stand suddenly seemed. Yet, miles away, Bo was pacing, Billy speaking. "You and her was down by the water. She was on top, as I recall. And—"

DeWitt's world lurched. Assumptions toppled. He lunged to his feet. Bo turned, his face bathed in sunlight.

DeWitt hit him, drove him into the bench. The table up-ended, and Curtis fell with it. Blood sprayed from Bo's mouth.

As Granger pulled him away, DeWitt heard the screams of spectators, his own inarticulate roar. Bo's hands were cupped to his face, and blood streamed between his long fingers.

Granger lifted DeWitt under the arms and carried him from the ruins.

42

DeWitt put his hand on the squad car's door, leaned his head back, and looked at the sky until its cloudless depths made him dizzy. If he could reach high enough, his hand would plunge into that wet, cold blue. If he could fall upward, he would fall forever.

He opened the door, sat in the front seat, and put his hands on the wheel. In front of him was Bo's motorcycle, a pale pebble caught in the tire's treads. Bo's driveway was white rock gravel. Why hadn't he remembered that? Had the clues been there all the time?

A while later Hattie came around the stucco corner of the center and stood, watching. At last she approached and got in the squad car with him.

"We had the summation. Jury's out," she said.

If he could go high enough, he could swim out of Coomey. And on the other side of the Line, where the air was sweet, there would be a happy policeman.

"You okay?"

He clenched his hands on the wheel so hard that his knuckles stung.

"Bo used you in the summation. He said you proved what a good man, a law-abiding man, was capable of. What we're all capable of. He was still bleeding pretty bad, and had to stop every once in a while, but I guess he made his point."

Bo had used him the whole time, through the investigation. And before. *You have control, Wittie,* he had said, his blue eyes wide. But underneath the water's surface tension, the deep swift current was Bo.

"After the jury went out, we talked, Bo and me," Hattie said. "He told me he hadn't wanted to make you testify, to bring up Janet, but the trial started to get away from him. Temporary insanity was the only defense he had. He said it was important that Billy got justice, that he had to get as good a defense as possible. He didn't want to have Billy's execution on his conscience."

There must have been a lot on Bo's conscience. Enough to make him realize that he had taken his night stick to DeWitt not in defense of the past but in a desperate struggle for the future. Enough jealousy—yes, enough of that—to make him plant the evidence in the squad car's trunk.

"He's going to lose," Hattie said. "And nobody will ever forgive him. But he did a fine job. A damned fine job. You can move in with me until you decide what you want to do." She put a hand on his arm.

He leaned against her, closed his eyes, and breathed her scent: a blend of perfume and horses. For an instant he felt the pull of the sky, and it seemed, to his delight, that he was floating.

43

"Let's poll again." Tyler rubbed his eyelids as if the stalemate had given him a headache. "An oral poll."

Foster didn't hesitate: "Guilty."

"Guilty," Irma Roberts whispered as she stared at her hands.

Gene Arbuster nodded, a hangman's glower on his beefy face. "Guilty."

Next in line, Jimmy Schoen shook his head. "We are all of us guilty of sin. The prosecution is an adulteress; the defense counsel an adulterer. The man who sits as judge grows illegal drugs behind his privacy fence." He looked up into eleven pairs of angry eyes. "I have seen what each of you do in your solitude. God hears your clandestine thoughts. You are, each of you, guilty."

Foster had been subuded since the end of the trial. Now, his voice had an uncharacteristic edge. "Get real, you fundamentalist prick."

Irma Roberts, one of Pastor Jimmy's own sheep, lifted a private hand to her mouth and tittered.

"Guilty or not guilty?" Tyler insisted.

"Guilty!" Arbuster shouted. "For Christ's sake, admit that he's guilty! I'm tired of sitting here on my ass with you as the single holdout!"

"God will damn you all," Schoen said.

Foster laughed. And Jimmy Schoen, God's prophet, last defender of the faith, pointed a finger at him. "You, Hubert Foster. Fornicator, anarchist, and blasphemer. Admit to your sins."

Foster said, "Bo was my friend. And nobody but me understands what he did in there. What it cost."

"It will cost him his soul. That's what it will—"

"You know when Bo and I became friends? Do you, preacher?" There was something in Foster's gaze: a sad victory. "It was two years ago. Your wife and I were in my Corvette when Bo found us. It's no place for what we were doing. I thought he'd arrest us or something. He asked me to get out of the car. We talked. When I told him how things stood between me and Dee Dee, he said he understood. He offered us the use of his house."

Schoen sat dumbstruck. Comprehension should have come easy. The words were simple, they were words he had used all his life. But somehow, spoken together, they made no sense.

"Dee Dee?" Gene Arbuster asked. "For Christ's sake, Hubert. You're screwing *Dee Dee Schoen?*"

Foster ignored him. "Hey, preacher? You realize where Bo's house is located? Surrounded by cedar trees. In a little dip in the hills. Just out of range of your damned telescope. You listening to me, Schoen? Don't you get it yet? Bo offered me his house so you couldn't spy on us like you did everybody else. I'm in love with Dee Dee. Have been for three years. From the first time I slept with her, I've been begging her to marry me. And after the revolt she says she's had enough. She doesn't feel sorry for you anymore. She's at your house today, packing. She and the kids are moving in."

Irma Roberts cooed, "That's so sweet." Then she caught Tyler's shocked look. "Well, of course it's *wrong*. But still . . ."

Schoen knew he should speak, or reach out and smite Foster the way DeWitt had smitten Bo. But he sat, frozen by surprise.

"Well." Tyler recovered quickly. "Judy? Guilty or not guilty?" He skipped Schoen as though the preacher were a bit of shame hidden behind a fence.

"Dee Dee *Schoen?*" she said.

44

HATTIE SAID, "Jury must be back."

DeWitt lifted his head. Hattie's son Marvin was staring at them from the corner.

"I can't go in there," he said.

Hattie climbed out of the car, pulled DeWitt from his seat. "You have to."

They walked in together. People looked at him, then quickly looked away. When DeWitt sat, Bo turned around once, but went back to his papers. His cheek was purple, his eye nearly swollen shut.

Curtis walked in and asked Tyler, "Have you reached a verdict?"

"We have, Your Honor."

Granger took the piece of paper Tyler offered and walked it to Curtis. Curtis read for what seemed a long time, his thumb and finger worrying the page.

"Will the defendant please rise?"

Bo got to his feet, and Billy stood with him.

"William James Harper," Curtis said with extraordinary gravity, "the court finds you, in the murder of Loretta Jean Harper, guilty in the second degree." He looked down at the sheet again. "In the matter of William James Harper, Junior, the court finds you guilty of murder in the first degree. In the matter of Jason Eddings Harper, the court finds you guilty of murder in the first degree."

Curtis set the paper on the desk and put his hands over it, as though to prevent its escape. He turned to the jury. "And the sentence?"

Tyler shook his head. "*You're* supposed to give the sentence."

"No, goddamn it, that's your job."

"Nobody told us—"

Curtis's voice shrilled. "You get back in that jury room and don't come out until you have a sentence for me to read. Shit!" he shouted into the quiet. "Do I have to do everything for you people?"

When Tyler hesitated, Curtis snapped, "Bailiff, take the jury into the other room and don't let them out until they've come up with a sentence." With a clang of his folding chair, he got to his feet and hurried into a doorway to the left. Granger led the jury away.

Granger came over, asked Billy to rise, and handcuffed his hands behind him. Bo and Billy sat.

Granger disappeared into the jury room. Soon he emerged and walked across to the makeshift judge's chambers. Then Curtis came out, his eyes heavy-lidded from marijuana.

The jury filed in. Tyler handed a folded slip of paper to Granger. Granger accepted it like a thing stamped FRAGILE, and delivered it to Curtis.

"Will the defendant please rise?"

Bo and Billy rose together, as though both had been found guilty of murder.

"Do you have anything to say before sentence is passed?"

"*I do*," Bo said. "May I?"

Curtis nodded.

"What we're doing here is wrong." Through his split lip, Bo's voice was muddy. "We should have had a competency hearing. I should have asked for a change of venue before jury selection, but I didn't get the chance. You didn't ask if there were any pretrial motions."

A stony calm settled on Curtis. He sat back in his chair.

"Billy should have been tried for one murder at a time, but everybody wanted it over with quick. Now that the verdict's in and the sentence is about to be read, there's no higher court to appeal to, and for justice to be served, we need that option. Just because people call you Your Honor doesn't mean you have any. Damn it, Curtis, you're no criminal court judge."

Curtis brought his eyes down to the folded bit of paper. He sucked in his bottom lip.

"And God help us, I'm no defense counsel."

At the back of the courtroom a child started crying, "Ma-ma-ma." A crooning *sh-h-h-h* from the mother. Bo waited until mother and child were quiet, then said, "When the sentence is carried out, we'll all be guilty of murder." He sat down.

Curtis asked, "Is that it?"

"Read the goddamned sentence."

"Death," Curtis said without consulting the paper.

45

FOLLOWING GRANGER'S ORDER TO LEAVE, most of the spectators went home — reluctantly, looking over their shoulders. Seresen stayed with the small group of principals; and Curtis tried to get him to take Billy. "You keep the man," Seresen said and walked away.

Curtis followed on the Kol's heels, a large dog after a small child. "We'll have to kill him, and we don't really want to do that."

At the defense table Billy sat handcuffed, watching the scene so calmly that DeWitt wondered if Bo had slipped his client a joint. A few feet away, Bo sat in a bubble of solitude, staring into space.

"Acts are unimportant," Seresen said.

"Well, okay," Curtis said. "Forget what the sentence was. Just take him, hide him someplace and tell us you done killed him. Fly him into space or something."

"The policeman will explain." Seresen gestured at DeWitt. DeWitt shook his head.

Curtis's voice broke. "Then at least give us the guns back. We'll shoot him."

Seresen sat next to Bo. "Guns make you think of violence. I don't like guns."

"Okay, all right, if that's the way you want it. Doc, get the injection ready."

Doc's arms unhinged and fell to his sides. "No."

"Death by injection. That's state law."

"I don't give a shit about state law. I never killed nothing in my life, Curtis. Don't even go hunting. I ain't going to be no executioner for you."

"It's for him!" Curtis pointed at the expressionless, motionless Billy. "Don't you understand? I want somebody who knows what they're doing, so it don't get all fucked up! It'd be horrible if it was fucked up!"

Doc stalked angrily out of the room.

They waited. Bo cradled his bruised cheek. Seresen, hands in his lap, swung his short legs back and forth like a kid in church. Billy looked at the wall.

A few minutes later Doc was back, carrying his bag. Bo saw and slowly got to his feet.

"Let's take him to the judge's chambers," Doc said.

Granger pulled Billy upright. The condemned man's face, under the fluorescent lights, was a ghastly gray. "Come on, son," Granger said.

Billy put his foot out as though he wanted to comply, but the knees seemed to go soft on him.

A low voice from the doorway: "I have come to pray with the prisoner." Pastor Jimmy was standing among the rows of folding chairs, a Bible in his hands. "He needs to make his peace."

"Get out! You don't have any right to be here! You don't have any goddamned right!" Doc grabbed the condemned man's other

236

arm and, expression furious, pivoted, forcing Billy and Granger with him into the chambers. After a hesitation, the others followed. As DeWitt left the courtroom, he saw in Pastor Jimmy's eyes such a pathetic confusion that it made his throat constrict.

In the small chambers it was standing room only. Doc looked around distractedly. "Need a glass of water or a Coke or something."

Seresen left. He came back with a can of Diet 7-Up. Doc pulled a bottle of pills from his bag and shook some out into his palm. The pills were tiny and white, like saccharin tablets.

"Atropine. Take them all at once. It'll be quick, understand, son? There won't be much time to think about it."

Doc upended his palm and spilled the tablets with a dull rattle onto the polished wood. Granger unlocked the cuffs, and everyone but Billy quit the room.

The courtroom was empty, Pastor Jimmy gone. Bo took a seat on a folding chair and looked at his hands.

"Clouding up out there," Doc said.

Granger regarded the doctor with amazement, as though he had just heard a potted plant speak. Doc checked his watch, took a quick, shallow breath, and looked out the window.

"Another norther. One right after the other." Doc almost turned to look at the closed door but caught himself in time.

Granger said in a hollow voice, "Lot of snow this year. Strange weather."

Doc looked at his watch again, ran unsteady fingers through his beard, and went and opened the door.

DeWitt pushed through the small crowd frozen at the jamb. Under the glare of the lights Billy sat, the can of 7-Up and the pile of tablets untouched.

Curtis squeezed his eyes closed, as if struck by a toothache. "Get a rope," he said.

46

SCHOEN TOOK AN UNSTEADY STEP, and then another, wondering where his feet were taking him now that his family was gone. He found himself at his car. Somewhere during his journey, the Bible had dropped from his hand. "Lord?"

No one answered.

"Lord?" he breathed.

"Jimmy? That you?"

Startled, he turned. Dee Dee was standing a few feet away, near Foster's empty Corvette. Schoen chided himself. He shouldn't be surprised—righteousness always conquered sin. It irked him that he was so glad to see her.

"Get in the car, Dee Dee, and I'll take you home. I'll explain to the children what has happened. Then you will get on your knees, and together we'll pray for your forgiveness."

"Oh well, honey, I *would*," she said, looking at her watch, "but I promised Hubie I wouldn't be more than an hour. I came to remind you to change the furnace filter, and rinse the dishes before you put them in the dishwasher. Otherwise you get these little specks. I put instructions on each of the plants. The Peter's

Plant Food is on the sill in the kitchen window. If the water looks blue—like the toilet bowl blue—you've put in too much and you'll burn the leaves. And don't forget the lint trap when you use the dryer. Goodness, there's a lot to remember."

"Dee Dee . . ." Schoen's eyes filled.

"But don't you worry. I left you all kind of notes. And I put up a lot of my lasagna—I know how you love that. It's in the freezer, in these little single-serving Tupperware containers? Microwave them on medium for fifteen minutes, not on high, because the cheese will bubble and get all over the—"

"Dee Dee!" He wanted to tell her that he loved her. "It's my fault," he said instead. "I should have spent more time with you and the children. I should have been a more forceful shepherd."

"Oh Jimmy, really. All I wanted was ranch salad dressing once in a while." She walked to Foster's Corvette and drove away.

When she was gone, he climbed into his Pontiac and folded his hands prayerfully on the wheel. The velour upholstery had trapped the scent of his wife's perfume. And the milky odors of his children. But he, an aromaless man, had left no trace.

47

THEY PUT ON THEIR COATS and went outside. Granger took a rope from his pickup. The center's automatic floodlights winked on, casting tree-latticed shadows across the parking lot.

Putting the finishing touches to his hangman's noose, Granger gave DeWitt an embarrassed shrug. "Haven't tied one of these things since I was a kid."

Doc was kneeling, taking a stethoscope and blood-pressure cuff from his bag.

Granger lowered his head, and his voice grew faint. "But then, I was always sort of handy with things." He threw the end of the rope over an oak limb. The noose swung, its long shadow spanning the grass. Hattie came out with a chair.

Granger called, "Curtis?"

Curtis emerged from the dark, hands in his pockets.

"Who'll do it?" Granger asked.

Curtis looked at the bench where Bo sat with Billy. Then at a button on his coat.

Hattie spoke up. "And we need a sheet to wrap him in, and some kind of coffin." She cleared her throat. "And a grave."

Granger nodded. "Seresen can find us a box. I'll call Tyler. He can meet us later at the cemetery with his backhoe."

First Doc and Granger, then Seresen and Hattie walked away. DeWitt could hear their footsteps long after the shadows swallowed them. The freshening wind beguiled the noose into a dance. Bo rose and went to Curtis. The breeze plucked and snatched at their conversation.

". . . what you're getting into."

Curtis shrugged. ". . . matter now."

". . . killed like this!" Bo urgent, gesturing. "Curtis, listen to me, you don't have any idea how horrible . . ."

Curtis put his hand on Bo's arm. The officer flung it away. More words, too low to distinguish. Curtis handed Bo a joint. DeWitt watched the officer light it, take it to the bench, and tuck it in Billy's mouth.

Seresen reappeared with four Torku and a packing crate. The workers set the box on the ground and went back into the center.

Hattie returned, not with a sheet but with an old quilt. At the bench, she paused. Billy, dressed only in jeans and a flannel shirt, was shivering. Hattie arranged the quilt around Billy's shoulders, as if tucking in one of her boys. He lay down, making himself as comfortable as he could with the handcuffs. His eyes closed.

Bo came to DeWitt. "You have to stop this. No matter what you think of me, you have to stop it now."

"It's the law."

"It's *not* the law! Hanging's not the law. I've seen a man strangle to death. Three minutes of convulsing on the sidewalk like he was trying to tear himself apart. DeWitt! Don't turn away like that. If you go through with this, you'll never forgive yourself."

DeWitt faced him. "Don't act all of a sudden like you're concerned."

"I didn't mean . . ."

"You destroyed my wife. You told everyone what she did, don't you see? Now when she's in the supermarket, when she's walking down the street, she'll wonder what people around her are saying. Every goddamned whisper, every look. Did she really deserve that?"

"There wasn't any choice. The trial—"

"Janet was going to leave you, wasn't she?"

A flash of anger. "What happened in that courtroom wasn't about Janet. The law's the law."

DeWitt swiped at his eyes. "Well, isn't justice a blind old bitch."

Granger and Doc came back, carrying a jug of moonshine. Bo helped Billy sit up and drink. The jug was passed around. Curtis took a long swallow. DeWitt took a sweet, cloying pull. Snow began to fall.

Billy raised his head, caught the flakes on his face. "I like snow."

DeWitt glanced Billy's way.

"It's nice it's snowing, don't you think?"

Half-formed patterns of snow moved about the parking lot. Drifts settled around the curb. DeWitt took another pull and felt the first amusement-ride lift of inebriation.

Granger asked the time.

"Near midnight," Curtis said.

Granger took the quilt from Billy's shoulders. Without conscious choice, DeWitt stepped forward. When he touched Billy, the man fell to his knees.

Billy was a small man. DeWitt had never realized how small. It didn't take much effort to lift him, to drag him to the chair.

Billy's feet plowed furrows in the snow. "No, Granger! De-Witt, wait!" He looked up at the noose and whimpered, "Wait."

Twin clangs as his boots hit the top of the metal seat. They were scuffed boots, workman's cheap lace-ups, their soles caked with ice. He started to sink; the boots slid, drawing lines of brown mud on the chair.

DeWitt grabbed him, and the incision in his belly stung. He didn't want to be angry with Billy. He knew it wasn't right. Yet it was so hard to hold him up.

"Just a little while more. Please." Billy's tiny voice.

"Get something Wittie and I can stand on." Granger's quiet baritone.

"Get up." Hattie poked DeWitt in the ribs. "Get up. You can't get him positioned any other way."

Something bumped his leg: another folding chair.

"Hurry," Hattie said. "Let's get it over with."

DeWitt and Granger pulled Billy erect between them. Billy's breaths made steam-engine puffs in the cold air. His eyes were wide, as if, hands cuffed behind him, he wanted to grasp the world with sight. "Wait! I ain't ready."

Granger's kindly voice: "Don't draw it out, son. Don't make it harder on yourself."

Billy's teeth chattered. "I ain't drunk yet, Granger. Oh, please. I ain't drunk yet."

DeWitt's side ached. "Let him have another drink."

Hattie handed the jug to Granger, who lifted it to Billy's mouth. With a sputter and glistening drool, the liquor came back up.

Granger returned the jug to Hattie. "Stand up straight, Billy. Let me get the noose on you now. Don't give yourself time to think about it."

Billy looked at DeWitt from the dark, cramped place of his terror, and suddenly it was just the two of them: DeWitt and Billy, alone with what they were to do.

DeWitt said, "Everything's going to be all right, Billy. I won't do it till you're ready. And when it comes, it'll be fast, over before you know it. Granger? The noose. No, don't fight it, let him put it around you. I won't do anything until you say. Look at me. That's right. Now lift your head a little."

When the rope went under his jaw, Billy stood tip-toe, his boots skidding on the metal.

DeWitt held him, one arm around his neck, the other under his chest. "I got you. Step away now, Granger. I got him."

Granger walking away; the grass, everyone receding.

"Close your eyes." DeWitt could stand all night if need be, holding Billy from the waiting earth. "I want you to count to ten."

Billy's eyelids twitched.

"Count, Billy. Can you do that for me?"

"One . . ." Breathy, unsure.

"Count as slow as you want to. It's all right."

"Two."

A shudder through Billy's frame. Not fear, exhaustion. His shoulders slumped.

"Go on."

"Three."

"Close your eyes."

"Four."

DeWitt held Billy as he might have held Janet during the last dance of the prom. They swayed there alone, fatigued, held up by unheard music and the press of the dark.

"Five."

It was late, past midnight of a long, long day, and Billy was ready for sleep. His chin rested, trusting, on DeWitt's shoulder. DeWitt held him tight. And kicked the chairs down.

They fell hard. The rope snapped taut with a jarring twang. Billy flopped and twitched like a fish at the end of a gaff. From his throat came gagging, airless grunts, as though he was trying to utter some last words. He butted DeWitt groin to groin, in a mockery of fucking.

DeWitt wasn't strong enough. His grip, his will weakened, and he fell, taking Billy's shirt with him.

Above, the tree limb bowed like a fishing pole whose line had hooked a tarpon.

Bo screamed, "God!"

The rope stretched and creaked, and Billy twirled, his feet pumping the air as if trying to sprint to freedom.

"Stop it!" Hattie's hands clapped the sides of her head. "Cut him down!"

Granger fumbled with drunken, hysterical haste at the knot on the tree.

There are things, like trust, like promises, that once broken can never be mended. DeWitt took a running leap and landed on Billy's shoulders. Through his hand and chest he felt the wet, firm pop of separating bone.

Billy gave a last shudder before his body went slack. His fists, pressed against DeWitt's belly, opened. For a peaceful instant DeWitt was eight again, and the body nothing more than a tire swing rocking back and forth, back and forth.

DeWitt let him go.

"Are you happy now?" Bo shouted. "Nine years, and I still dream about Dallas. How will you sleep at night, DeWitt?" Without waiting for an answer, he rushed into the snow-driven darkness.

48

SERESEN WATCHED GRANGER ease the body into DeWitt's waiting hands. Curtis wandered off muttering; Hattie walked away.

DeWitt laid the body on the ground, then realized Billy was still cuffed. He decided to bury Billy with his arms locked behind him, but glanced at the narrow packing crate and saw that the body wouldn't fit that way. Kneeling in the snow, he pushed the corpse over on its stomach. The head stared balefully over the back. Peach brandy rushed up DeWitt's throat with a sting of candied bile. He swallowed, looked away, and fumbled the key into the lock.

A snap—like a small bone breaking. He freed one slack wrist and let the body drop back on the other.

"Will you close his eyes, Granger? Just for God's sake close his eyes."

Granger knelt. "I can't," he said. "They's pooched out too much, Wittie. They won't stay put."

"Okay. Get him on the quilt."

Granger laid the quilt out next to the body. They each

grabbed a wrist. At the count of three, they pinched Billy's jeans at the outside seam and lifted.

Billy's head disappeared. Startled, DeWitt let him go.

"Wait a minute."

I ain't ready yet.

Granger dropped the corpse. The body wasn't lying flat. Billy's face was pushed into the snow; the back of his skull was under his shoulder blades.

"Hold on." Granger spun awkwardly toward Seresen.

"You okay?" DeWitt asked.

Granger waved a hand. "Yeah. Just don't let his head do that no more."

With a silent apology DeWitt pushed the corpse onto the blanket with his boot. "You can look now."

Granger turned, ran a hand over his mouth. "Get the damned top off that box."

They shoved Billy in sideways. With hammer and nails they secured the lid. They had just begun to slide the heavy box into the pickup when a car door slammed. The poorly-balanced coffin took a nose dive from the tailgate.

Catching the crate with his shoulder, DeWitt glanced up. Seresen was sitting in the front seat of Granger's pickup.

Granger too had caught sight of the Kol. "Damn it, DeWitt. Where does he think he's going?"

"Shhh. Quiet."

"I don't care what he hears. Goddamned turd-faced alien." Granger shouted, "Hey! What're you looking at? You think this is funny?" He grabbed the edge of the box and pushed, sending the crate slamming into the back of the bed. "I just don't like it, Wittie. He shouldn't have watched what we done. Makes me feel dirty."

DeWitt's hands were soiled with Billy's urine, Billy's drool.

The skin of his palms tingled with the remembered crack of bone. He shoved his hands into the snow and scrubbed until his skin burned and his fingers paled. Until his knuckles ached.

"Come on." Granger pulled at him. "It's time."

They climbed into the cab with Seresen. It was nearly thirty minutes before they drove through the cemetery's iron and brick gates.

DeWitt and Granger got out and walked over the blank, snowy field to Tyler. Tyler was shivering on the backhoe, hugging himself, Stetson pulled down to his eyebrows.

Granger said, "Get in the truck, Tyler. Get that engine started and that heater going."

The only part that showed between Tyler's sheepskin collar and the hat were his eyes. "Y'all look done in."

Granger helped him to his feet. "We been working up a sweat while you been sitting here freezing your ass. You get on in the truck now, and get some of that heat on you."

Tyler staggered to the truck.

Huffing white, frozen breaths, Granger and DeWitt toted Billy's coffin from the tailgate. As Seresen watched, they settled the box into the ground.

Granger got on the backhoe. In jerky mechanical fits and starts he scooped up the first load. The bucket poised in indecision over the grave; then he hit a lever, and clumps of earth drummed the wood, a noise like jittery feet.

By the time DeWitt had tamped down the grave, his arms were twitching with exhaustion, and his entire belly was sore. Tyler came over from the pickup. He slipped off his right glove and solemnly shook hands with Granger. Both men walked to DeWitt.

"We'll say some words." Tyler took off his hat and twisted it in his hands. Clearing his throat, he looked up into the drifting flakes. "I am the resurrection, and the life . . ."

DeWitt listened to the benediction; but the only message he understood was that of Granger's sobs.

Tyler finished, crossing himself. He took Granger by the sleeve. "He ain't dead. Ain't nobody really dies. You know that."

Granger nodded glumly. "I know."

"And Billy's in a better place now. You know they're all of them happier. And where they are, Billy's asked for Loretta's forgiveness, and she's taken him back. The kids are playing, the sun's shining, and every flower, every green leaf, every one of God's butterflies are out. You know that. Say it, then. Say it loud, like you believe it."

A sound from Seresen caught DeWitt's attention. Something was wrong. For a terrifying instant it looked as if the alien was dissolving into snow. His skin turned the delicate hues of ivory and lily. As DeWitt stepped forward, he heard the Kol whisper, "Amen." Then the alien walked quickly from the glare of the backhoe's headlights and into the dark.

"Seresen!" DeWitt called.

The three started after him. Halfway across the cemetery the round flat footprints ended.

DeWitt cupped his hands to his mouth. "Seresen!"

Granger got a flashlight. He swept its beam across the silent graves. "Not here. Let's go on home."

DeWitt said, "It's cold. He'll get lost. Seresen!" He ran a few yards farther into the graveyard before he stopped, confused. Tyler took him by the arm and led him to the pickup.

"Seresen's all right," Granger said when DeWitt took his place on the truck's bench seat. "He probably went home."

Of course Seresen was all right. And Billy was dead. Yet in

some back alley of his brain, the part that fretted that the front door was unlocked and the iron left on, DeWitt was afraid that Billy might wake up and find himself alone.

"I'll drop you on by your house, DeWitt," Granger said.

The cab of the pickup stank of gasoline, wet coats, and the hot-metal reek of the heater. "Take me to my car. It's at the center."

Wordlessly, Granger drove to the parking lot. The squad car was a lump in the white expanse: a corpse in a morgue, a cat napping under a sheet. Tyler helped DeWitt from the truck.

"You need me, you just call," he said.

DeWitt nodded and high-stepped his way through the snow. Behind him the pickup's engine revved. Its wheels spun. He turned to see the twin red dots of its taillights disappear down the street.

"Wait!"

I ain't ready.

The truck vanished. He stood alone in the icy wind, wondering what he could do without his keys. Too ashamed to seek shelter at the center, he went to the car instead. His keys were dangling from the ignition. He dug his car out as best he could, then drove to Hattie's. There was a single light on in the house.

Entering the kitchen, he whispered, "Hattie?" There was an elongated rectangle of yellow light across the linoleum. He walked down the short hall. The bedroom was dark. In the bathroom Hattie knelt before the commode, an aging naiad pondering her reflection. Her hair stuck out at argumentative angles, and her face was weary.

"Hattie."

She bent over and vomited in the toilet.

He put his hand out to touch her; she flinched away.

"I tried to make it quick."

He waited for her to say something. When she didn't, he went back outside. Standing at the trunk of the car, he rolled himself three joints.

The wind died. On the crisp, clear air he could hear the bark of a neighbor's dog. The clouds were breaking up, and through a chink in the sky a full moon cast its light on vanilla fields. From the barn nearby came the warm, whuffling sounds of the horses.

He finished the first joint. When he returned to the house, the light in the bathroom was out. He sat in the Barcalounger, tipped it back, and smoked the second reefer. He was asleep before he got to the last.

Billy stares at him, eyes like a rabbit in a hole. I ain't ready, Wittie. Bodies pelvis-to-pelvis, cheap boots sliding on ice.

His mama at the sink, boning a chicken. See how the joints fit together, Wittie? Ball nestled in socket, chin on shoulder. She pulls at the flesh, and leg stretches from thigh. The ripping sound of tendon. And the sick, wet pop of separating bone.

You see? They dropped those bombs so sudden.

His mama's eyes are white and empty. The skin of her face oozes and peels.

The world changed, and I wasn't ready.

A klaxon jolted him from his dream. Flailing in the dark, he knocked the ashtray to the floor. When the phone rang again, he found it by the sound.

"Hello?" DeWitt noticed the stuffiness of the room. Heard the faint sound of water dripping.

"DeWitt?"

"Yeah?"

"This is Granger. I called over to your house, and Janet said you might be at Hattie's. I couldn't sleep."

DeWitt listened to the slight hiss of static over the phone line and the drip, drip, drip from the window.

"Got up to get a drink of water." DeWitt noticed a tremor in Granger's voice.

He sat up; the Barcalounger squealed.

"I can see a ways from my kitchen window, Wittie . . ."

DeWitt's heart was doing triple time to the metronome of the water.

"Wittie?" Granger's voice fluttered like a moth caught in a screen. "You need to go look . . ."

DeWitt didn't want to hear the next words. Didn't want to know what horror Granger had seen. *His mama's blind, white gaze. Billy staring up from the burrow of his terror.*

"The Line's down."

DeWitt slammed the receiver home and shot up from the chair. He flung open the door. On the porch, drifts were melting to worm-holed islands of white. The snow was disappearing in a hot, hellish southern wind. And the horizon was black, dead black, for the first time in six years.

49

DeWitt RAN TO HIS CAR. The air was hushed and sticky. Around Hattie's ranch, melting snow conjured from the cold earth a viscous, knee-deep fog. It trickled down the incline where her house stood and, seeking its level, pooled deep in the hollow near the road.

He started the engine, flicked on the headlights. Their glare danced across the top of the mist, as if his car were a plane riding a bank of cloud. Purblind, he inched down the gravel road toward the highway, driving by landmarks. To his right, the top rungs of Hattie's board fence; to his left, the leaves of her sapling magnolia. Then the road dipped, and he drowned in white.

The fog was blank, close, shimmering. As if, now freed, all the ghosts from behind the Line had gathered.

A looming form at the driver's side. A pale, haunted face in the glass. The sharp *rap-rap* of knuckles.

"DeWitt?"

Hattie. He braked and threw the car into Park.

She was crying helplessly. Soggy, chest-hitching sobs, her hands at her sides and her mouth a tortured, wailing O.

"I woke up and you were gone. You were gone, Wittie! And everything was so hot and quiet and strange. I ran everywhere looking for you. And then I saw your taillights leaving. You left me! How could you do that?"

She had slept in her navy-blue suit; but had run barefoot down the gravel drive. Her toes were stubbed and bleeding.

He got out, put his arms around her. "The Line's down," he said. "Don't cry. Please don't cry. Get in the car now, Hattie. We're going to Granger's."

He drove, her quivering hand in his.

Granger's porchlight was lit. The huge farmer was standing on the porch with his wife.

"Stay here," DeWitt told Hattie. "I'll be up there on the porch where you can see me. Let go of me, Hattie, please."

He waded through the mist. Halfway up the steps, he saw the butcher knife in Granger's hand.

"You seen it?" Granger's baritone squeaked falsetto. "You seen how hot it is?"

"Yeah, I know. Put down the knife."

"Pastor Jimmy was right, Wittie."

Granger's wife was statue-still. The vacancy DeWitt saw in her eyes unnerved him.

"We died six years ago in a nuclear war, and we never knew it," Granger said. "This is what death is."

Fog licked the edge of the porch. Sweat broke out on De-Witt's body; and where the hot wind touched, his skin burned.

"Granger, drop the knife."

Light glinted along the blade. "Them Torku was sent to judge us, and we been found wanting. Demons coming after us now. I'll be ready for them when they come, Chief. And they're coming, you can bet on that."

In the small voice of sanity, DeWitt said, "You're scaring your wife."

"She needs to know how the cow ate the corn. Everyone needs to know. Oh God, Wittie." A deep inhuman sound, like the groan of floorboards. "We should've forgive Billy Harper."

DeWitt stared at the knife, afraid to move.

A beep from a car horn. Granger's wife gave a sharp little cry. DeWitt turned and saw headlights puncturing the fog. A Bronco, engine rumbling, stopped in the yard. The driver's door opened and a dark figure materialized in the gloom.

Doc's familiar bray. "Hi, Granger. Seen your lights on. DeWitt, you got to come with me. Pastor Jimmy's congregating people down on Main. Everybody's scared, Wittie. They're plumb ape-shit with panic, and there's no telling what they'll do."

50

On Main Street the people of Coomey stood disheveled and disoriented in the ankle-deep fog, like people awakened by a house fire. Under the glow of street lights women clutched robes shut over nightgowns, and men wore jeans pulled up over pajamas. Pastor Jimmy was in the bed of a pickup, preaching.

DeWitt freed his hand from Hattie's. Easing from behind the wheel of his squad car, he caught a heart-stopping cameo of Janet before the milling mob swallowed her.

Foster broke from the crowd and ran to them. "Did you see? The Torku are gone! I can't believe it! I just can't believe that Seresen gave up on us like that! Where *are* we, anyway?" he wailed. "Why is it so dark out there?"

Doc ambled up. "Hubert? Stop bitching and go talk some sense into these people. You, too, Hattie." He watched as the pair reluctantly left. "DeWitt? You go down to where the Line used to be."

"What?" *Wait.*

"That's your job."

But I'm not ready. Anything could be waiting. The ultimate nothing: a crack between universes.

"That's what we pay you for," Doc said.

"I haven't been paid in six years!" DeWitt's shout was so loud that Pastor Jimmy, arms still upraised, stopped preaching. "That's the goddamned definition of a job, when you get paid for it, right? Why do you expect me to do all your dirty work? Jesus, I even killed a man for you people. What more do you want?"

"If you're scared . . ." Doc began.

"If you're not scared, why don't *you* go see? Tell you what. I'll wait here, and if you're not back in thirty minutes, I'll go looking for you. Okay? Let's check our watches." DeWitt looked down at his digital. 10:15 A.M., his watch blinked, and it was still pitch-dark.

"I could call Bo . . ." Doc said.

"No, forget it. I'll go." DeWitt had to. Or he would go crazy. He couldn't stand with the crowd on Main, listening to Pastor Jimmy's terrified sermon and waiting for a dawn that might not come.

Doc nodded. "I'll get up on that pickup and see if I can prepare everybody for a possible attack, just in case you run into survivors. I got some of Purdy's unexposed film. When you get back, we'll see if it's fogged, and then we'll know for sure."

"Know what for sure?"

He shoved an envelope into DeWitt's breast pocket. "If there's radiation."

51

Jimmy Schoen gazed into the upturned faces, faces as pallid and unreachable as moons. The street lights were distant galaxies. Coaxed by fluctuating, eternal entropy, everything in the universe was moving away.

Dee Dee stood with Foster. Doc stood muttering with Purdy. Not even God stood at Schoen's side.

He was afraid. He'd preached so long of wrath that he'd overlooked mercy.

"Pray!" he screamed.

Surely God, even deafened by His rage, would hear the piteous entreaties of his children.

"Pray!" His own fear reflected in a hundred faces.

Some of the crowd were mumbling. Some were silent and bewildered.

Jimmy Schoen said, "Pray for mercy." And he tried his very best to imagine compassion falling like rain.

52

DeWitt wished that dawn would break—and just then the sky caught fire. He jerked his car to the shoulder and stopped. On the eastern horizon the sun popped up over the fog nonchalantly, as though it were accustomed to rising at eleven in the morning.

Heart lurching, DeWitt drove on. Ahead should be the Tucker house. And, just like the sun, there it was, its gap-toothed porch railing looming from the mist.

The closer he got to the Line, the slower he drove. He passed bare-limbed winter forest. A Mexican dove hooted from a deadfall.

What if the real test was starting now? Maybe Seresen had left a blank slate to be filled in by imagination. Maybe, if DeWitt thought hard enough, the war would have never happened.

But what if he found the place he saw in dreams: a star-shot, bottomless well? He pictured himself getting too close to the edge, pictured himself falling into . . .

No, not limbo. He mustn't create a limbo. Too much depended on him. He'd concentrate hard, because home had to be there.

He let the car coast around the last bend. The speed limit sign caught the pink from the rising sun. And then, where the Line used to be . . .

DeWitt gasped and stood on his brakes. The town's memorial trinkets lay in a forlorn row, bordering the place where the fog ended.

He hadn't been strong enough, had not held on tight. He'd let time slip: even in the dim light he could see that the foliage beyond lacked the hopeful glossiness of spring. Those leaves were dusty, beaten down by a long Texas summer and weeks of drought.

He shut off the motor. The hot engine ticked.

In the land of high summer, boys, bats in hand, would walk to the plate. People would be washing cars, watering lawns, sitting down to barbecue lunches.

And his father would be waiting.

DeWitt put his head in his hands. The Torku took them in March. He tried to imagine sudden thunderstorms and budding chartreuse leaves. But summer, chlorine-scented, hammock-indolent summer, called in a vacation-happy voice.

He opened his eyes: the trees hadn't changed. The sun was molten gold by the time he gave up the fight. He left the car to gather memories in his arms: a beer stein TO JERRY DEITZ, BEST FRIEND; a rain-worn lace tablecloth FOR AUNT RACHEL. He pocketed the police chief's badge. When the road was clear, he got behind the wheel.

What if the forest was an illusion? If he tried to drive through, he would tear that movie backdrop. The squad car's tires would spin on air. And he would be trapped between universes forever.

His hands clenched the wheel so hard, they cramped. He thought good thoughts so furiously that he poured sweat. He let the car take its time, and as it crawled, he hurriedly put a highway beneath it. He brought the forest ahead into being. Woods. More woods. The sun mounting the sky.

Beyond the crest of the next hill there should have been a logging road. And there it was, its barbed-wire and plank fence sagging. Around a curve, the mile marker, a blur in the pale light. For a terrifying instant he couldn't remember what lay around the next bend. And then he knew, and he built it there.

Beside the highway, a neat white frame building. A gravel parking lot. Warm light flooding from the windows. He parked and got out of the car. His hand moved to his breast pocket, to Doc's envelope. Radiation would be bouncing like popcorn from the trees, invading marrow, rending cells. He was already dying.

Christ, what was the matter with him? There was no nuclear war. There couldn't be. Couldn't be. He had to remember that.

He trudged the steps, put his hand to the knob, and froze. From beyond the curtain came the clink of silverware. Television sounds.

Zombies. Zombies were in there, having breakfast. The charred dead risen from their graves. *His mama's eyes, white and empty. Her burned face oozing.*

Oh, fuck. This is too hard. I'm just not ready.

But he took a breath and opened the door.

The walls of Olivia's Café were paneled. DeWitt remembered them as pale blue. His heart started to race. Not a big problem, though, not really. He just hadn't thought about the walls, that was all.

Except for Olivia, the diner was empty. For some reason he had made her thirty pounds heavier. Made her hair shorter and grayer. "Hey, DeWitt. Still got that cold?"

He stood stock-still in panic. Time was moving too fast, and he couldn't keep up. If he didn't focus his thoughts, the world would crumble. What would happen to him then? Not death. An eternal half-life.

"Summer colds are the worst kind of shit. Ain't that right, Hudson?"

A summer cold? Where had that come from?

Hudson poked his dark face through the slit between counter and kitchen. "Sure is. Hey, man, you losing weight. Want the usual?"

DeWitt's mind frantically leaped the six years. The usual. Eggs sunnyside up, a rasher of bacon, and hash browns.

"Sit down, honey." Olivia poured a cup of coffee and set it on the counter.

DeWitt shuffled across the room and sat. He watched himself pick up the cup. Watched Olivia light a cigarette. On the wall-mounted television a gray-suited W. C. Fields of a man preached from the top of a tank.

The Pearl Beer clock read 6:07. A beefcake calendar was taped to the wall. Mr. August's shirt was open, his pants unzipped. The pouty, muscular Mr. August of 1991.

"You look like shit." Olivia leaned close and put the back of her hand to his forehead. "You're so pale. Didn't I tell you yesterday you ought to get into bed?"

Yesterday. August 1991. The Torku had stolen six years; DeWitt had carelessly misplaced six months. In DeWitt's trembling fingers the cup shook, sloshing coffee.

"Why are you so damned quiet, Wittie? Something happen?" Olivia placed his breakfast in front of him. Dry whole-wheat toast. Oatmeal.

Everything was wrong. Time, the breakfast, the walls. The world was slipping. If he didn't work hard . . .

But up there, on the TV screen, Russians queued up at

McDonald's. Statues of Lenin toppled. A general of the Evil Empire made jokes and drank Pepsi Cola as he was interviewed by CNN. People laughed in Moscow streets and waved striped banners of red, white, and blue. DeWitt couldn't remember seeing Russians laugh before.

Time wasn't important; what DeWitt saw on the screen was. He sat back and smiled. Outside the curtained windows the diurnal Earth revolved and his newly minted sun climbed the sky.

53

HE DROVE BACK TO TOWN FAST. Success couldn't come that easily. He looked in his rearview mirror, afraid he would see his world rolling up like a poster freed from its frame.

Yet it stayed put. And on the Coomey side of the Line, the winter-blasted trees were budding.

The crowd on Main was singing hymns. The sun had topped the trees, the buildings. Blue shadows striated the ground.

When DeWitt got out of the car, Denny burst from the gathering and ran to him. "You was gone so long, Daddy. And Tammy kept asking if you was dead, and Pastor kept saying as how we was all going to Hell, and all the grownups was crying."

He lifted the child. "Daddy took care of it."

"I know." Denny nodded. "I wasn't scared."

For children faith was effortless. The world beyond the Line seemed misty now, like a land DeWitt had once visited in dreams. DeWitt pressed his son to him, that warm body where his adult belief was held in account: a blind trust.

He took a breath. Walked toward the pickup, saw Jimmy

Schoen turn. Heard the singing trail to silence. Noticed peripherally that the crowd had hushed.

DeWitt grabbed the fender and stepped onto the tailgate. His voice, when it emerged, was still and quiet. And very humble. Nothing like the voice of a world-builder.

"Why don't we turn on *Good Morning America?*" he said.

54

JIMMY SCHOEN'S EYES were glued to the television, where Russian Orthodox worshipers trod the splendor of a gilt-laden church.

"That's all real interesting about building new universes, DeWitt." Doc, hands in pockets, paced the restaurant. "And it's fun to think Tyler's praying in the cemetery convinced Seresen we'd been Torku-saved. But I'm a practical sort of man, and it's easier for me to believe that while we was behind the Line, life went on like it was supposed to. And that, weird or not, this Russian revolution would have happened anyway. Maybe there just wasn't no nuclear war."

Staring at the television, Schoen realized that God had turned from him. He didn't understand why. Perhaps God loved darkened churches, incense and candles, and the sonorous chanting of priests.

Then Doc said, "Maybe Jimmy lied about Bomb Day."

Schoen couldn't lie. He was God's anointed. When he opened his lips, what issued forth was divine truth.

Doc went to Schoen, peered into his face. "On Bomb Day,

when we lost the TV transmission and all the lights went out, did Civil Defense call you like you said?"

Schoen's gaze floated over the restaurant, over the sinners' angry scowls, over his parishioners, who averted their eyes. Somewhere, out beyond the summery hills, God's voice faltered to silence.

"You Bible-thumping bastard! Answer my question! You never got no call before the phones went dead, did you? You let us live six goddamned years thinking our world was gone just to prove your tight-assed, fundamentalist point!"

Schoen turned and walked out the door, hearing a rumble behind him, reverberations of secular judgment. Climbing into his car, he drove home, and at the front door fumbled numb-fingered with his keys.

The house was dirty. On the kitchen counter lay the refuse of lonely meals. Schoen thought to open his Bible, but didn't. Thought to turn on the television, but couldn't.

He glanced at the wall phone and had the overwhelming urge to talk to someone. But he knew that, like God, no one would accept the call.

55

DeWitt, stirring his coffee, ignored the gaiety around him, careful to guard his thoughts. Keeping the universe balanced was trickier than he had imagined. So much to remember. He even avoided Janet and Hattie, because he wasn't yet sure what he wanted to happen next.

Foster came up to the table. "Hey, Wittie."

"What's up?" Maybe if DeWitt could change the future, he could also change the past. Hell, he could make anything happen.

Foster tugged at an ear. "The whole town's running around like kids at Christmas."

"Uh-huh." He could get rid of Bo. That's what DeWitt could do. Or maybe not. There might be rules.

Foster picked up the salt shaker. Put it down. "Boy! You should see how things have changed. Everything's light now. Doritos light. Fat-free this. No cholesterol that. The town's tearing into bags of these new Keebler chips, and Stan's trying to tell them they have to pay. You might run over there later and just remind everybody about . . . well."

"Okay." A Ferrari? Too selfish. How do you top world peace?

Foster's gaze roamed the ceiling. "My house has new drapes. A new couch. There's an interesting message on my answering machine from a Gulf Breeze Travel. My suitcases are gone."

Oh. Feed the hungry. House the homeless. That was it.

Foster cleared his throat. "Bank's all redecorated. Mauve and gray. Nice. Very nice. Chic."

Protect the orphans. Heal the sick. DeWitt could—

"And . . ." Foster's voice broke. "And almost everything's normal. Almost everything's . . ."

DeWitt finally looked up. The banker's face was ashen. "What's wrong?"

Foster collapsed into a chair. "A little problem."

"What kind of—?"

"Just a little. Oh, just a *small*, I guess . . ."

DeWitt grabbed his arm.

The man's eyes were wide and frightened and empty. "Money."

"You mean nobody being used to paying—?"

"No." Foster squeezed his eyes shut. "Oh, Jesus, Willie. The money in the vault's missing."

"Oh." DeWitt sat back. "I can fix that easy. No, really, Hubert. Seresen taught me all about universes and creation and stuff. Come on."

They got up and walked across the street.

In the bank, he shut the front door, then pushed the vault closed. "Now calm down," he said. "And just picture the money in there."

Foster squeezed his eyes tight with what looked like a constipation of faith. DeWitt opened the vault: it was empty.

Foster wailed, "I knew it! I knew it couldn't be this easy!"

"You're ruining my concentration, Hubert. Go on outside."

269

Foster left. DeWitt closed the vault. Opened it. The shelves were still vacant. He tried to control his growing panic. He slammed the door shut. Jerked it open. He thought about the money so hard that in the un-airconditioned bank sweat rolled down his back.

Fifteen minutes later, his arm muscles aching, he walked outside. Foster was waiting on the steps.

"Did it work?"

DeWitt sat on the steps beside him. "No." Nothing made sense. He had learned Seresen's lesson, hadn't he? How could he have caused a Russian revolution, then fail at something so simple?

Foster sighed. "Maybe it's my fault, Wittie. I burned it."

"But you said the safe was fireproof."

"The money wasn't in the safe. I burned it in my barbecue pit over three years ago, to show Seresen that money wasn't important."

Fatigue dropped from DeWitt like an old coat. He sat up straight. Laughed and slapped his thigh. "So that's the reason! I was starting to worry. If the money didn't exist in our universe, it makes sense that—"

"Starting to worry? *You* were starting to worry? What do I tell the examiners? What can I say that they'll believe? The only proof something strange happened in Coomey is lying in Billy Harper's grave."

A gust of wind swept down the street, kicking up dust, making the telephone wires sing. The sweat on DeWitt's face chilled, and instantly he was sober. "Wait a minute, Hubert. You can't do that."

"I know I can't defend myself in court. I just wanted—whatever happens—to make you that promise. DeWitt? Are you listening? I said I won't talk. In a minute I'm going to go back over to the restaurant and tell all the rest of them they can't talk, either. Nobody outside Coomey will believe Torku; but they'll believe vigilante justice. They'll start to poke around. The Texas Rangers, the FBI, *60 Minutes.* Not only you but Granger and Hattie and Curtis. They'll order an exhumation, they'll arrest everybody. They'll . . ."

Shock nudged things into new alignments. Pitfalls opened and quandaries gaped. DeWitt ran to his squad car and drove off, tires squealing. Down Main stood the intact structures of the police station, The Fashion Plate.

He sped down Ledbetter and through the cemetery's brick entranceway. He parked and ran across the soft ground to the backhoe. The newly risen lawn on the south of the cemetery was undisturbed. No telltale bumps, no sinks.

Car wreck. Please. Billy died in a car wreck. DeWitt started the backhoe and began to dig. Two hours later he turned off the engine.

When he was sure his legs would support him, he got up and walked the long rows of graves. Loretta's tombstone had vanished, too.

Maybe universes weren't as parallel as DeWitt thought. Maybe Billy was still alive. Of course. That was it. He'd be a construction foreman. He'd have a chicken-fried-steak-and-mashed-potato belly. Billy would have gotten lazier, a little more mellow. He'd be in marriage counseling.

DeWitt drove to Loretta's house. The road was back—a clay trail from the highway through the trees. He inched the car down it. Rounding the corner, he saw the boxwoods, the redbud tree.

He got out of the car. The foundation of Loretta's house was weathered by winters of ice, summers of drought. Stubborn weeds pushed through cracks in the concrete.

The new world order collapsed, and DeWitt with it. He fell to his knees on the muddy earth and sobbed.

56

CURTIS'S TELEVISION WAS ON, the VCR blinking a message that the tape had played through and then reversed. Before Bomb Day, the set had been tuned to WFAA. *Jeopardy* was playing.

DeWitt backed out of the room and tiptoed to Curtis's study. He rummaged through a two-drawer cabinet; through a desk. He went through a stack of papers on a chair. It was there that he found it, stuffed in a Perry Mason novel: the execution order, written in Tyler's own hand. In an overflowing ashtray he found a Days Inn matchbook.

Only when the note was ashes did he go to the bedroom and shove at the blanketed mound on the bed. "Get up!"

Curtis groaned and tried to crawl lower into the stale covers.

DeWitt poked at him. "Get up, now!"

Curtis sat up, blinking. "What bug bit your butt? And why's it so hot?" Then his eyes fell on the television. "Christ, Wittie. That looks like *Jeopardy*."

DeWitt pulled Curtis from the room.

"What's going on? Goddamn it, Wittie, stop pushing. Get your hands off me, will you? Was that *Jeopardy*?"

In the backyard Curtis's marijuana stood bright green and lush, the unculled seeds having fallen haphazard and thick.

Abandoning the stunned Curtis on the back porch, DeWitt darted into the garage and came out with two hoes. "Start digging them up."

He shoved a hoe at him. Curtis backed away.

"The Line's down. The Torku are gone. You understand me? We've been living six years in a fucking dream world! Now dig these things the hell up!" He began hacking furiously at the plants. The heady odor of sap rose.

Curtis's fist connected with his side. DeWitt fell into a pile of marijuana. Curtis threw himself on DeWitt's back and hit him again.

Untangling himself, ducking blows, DeWitt grabbed Curtis's wrist and cuffed it.

"What's got into you?" Curtis asked. "You ain't acting like yourself at all! Jesus, Wittie, I thought we was friends! I thought . . ."

"Get real, Curtis. I'm still a cop."

Manhandling Curtis to the house, DeWitt locked the other cuff around the outside spigot. A silent heap of dejection, Curtis sat watching DeWitt level the rest of the plants and carry them to the compost heap.

DeWitt stood over the pile, wondering if he should burn it. He didn't dare. The sheriff's department would be cruising the town, the Department of Public Safety prowling the highway. DeWitt's own daddy might drop by. He would have to remember that life in this world continued without a blip, except for those six lost months. Time was so fucking arbitrary.

He went to the bait store and took four economy-size bottles

273

of Liquid-Plumr. He got the ginger jar out of the bathroom and his own trash bag from his trunk. By the time he had soaked and buried the evidence, the sun was low in the sky and his shirt was soggy with sweat.

He freed Curtis.

Curtis struggled to his feet, swaying. "You sorry son of a bitch," he said. "You're fired."

Half an hour later, DeWitt climbed Hattie's porch, weighed down by a dark loss of faith. The house was empty. He looked around the living room. A photograph of the young Hattie with Al Shieba and his blue ribbon; a photo of a girlish Hattie and two infant boys at the beach.

It was time. He walked out the back door and across the yard. Hattie looked up from grooming her bay mare. With the hand that was holding the currycomb she pushed an errant lock of hair back into place. It didn't stay.

"You okay? You look . . ."

Of course he was okay. His father was probably alive. Everyone safe on the other side of the Line. So what if he hadn't created the universe? There had been no war. Happy endings were still happy, weren't they?

Hattie turned her eyes to her work. "Are you going back to Janet?"

"Yes."

The currycomb made a teeth-on-edge sound through the mare's mane. More hair slipped from Hattie's bun; it hung about her face like spiderwebs. She would always be older than Janet, always plainer; she couldn't help that.

"You never were any good at changes." She dropped the currycomb into a bucket. "Do me a favor."

"Anything."

She looked up. "Don't ever feel sorry for me. Don't do that. You're the one who's the loser."

"Hattie, don't—"

"Damn it, DeWitt, don't make a face. Don't patronize me like that. And don't you walk away! Don't you dare walk away! You owe me enough to listen."

Facing her was so difficult.

"No one else understands how much Seresen took from you. Not Janet. Not Curtis. Not Bo. For six years you were an important man, running to Seresen, getting things done. Life was easy. Now it won't be. Not ever that easy again."

DeWitt closed his eyes.

"You'll look around town and you'll remember, because importance is something a person never forgets. You'll go back to your house and resume the payments on your mortgage. You'll scrimp to buy clothes for your kids, because we never paid you enough, did we, Willie? And every day from now on, you'll have to face the fact you're just the police chief of Bumfuck, Texas. But you'll remember and sometimes you'll want the Line back, even if it means people on the other side dead."

"Are you finished?"

"Yes."

"Curtis wants to fire me. When the City Council meets, will you support him?"

She turned away. "No. But if I wanted to be kind, I would."

57

WITH A BRUSH AND YELLOW PAINT DeWitt obliterated the penis. Doc hadn't been the author of this graffiti, although he had been guilty of the rest. No need for the physician's rebellion now that the Torku were gone.

The anonymous artist had given the crosswalk figure a parody of a young man's forty-five-degree erection, and one that was uniquely bowed. DeWitt thought that if he could put the town's male teenagers in a lineup, tumescent pricks exposed, he would be able to pick out the model of that self-portrait.

Dipping the brush into the can of paint, he paused and looked at the library windows. Although the holiday was three weeks away, Halloween fever was building. The children's drawings in the windows were play-scary, dominated by stick witches and green goblins and amoeba-shaped ghosts.

But there were other ghosts in the drawings. Here a pink-eyed Torku held a child's hand; there a Rocky Road–colored Torku delivered pints of chocolate ice cream.

Everywhere a Torku.

Two months gone, and DeWitt could barely remember Seresen's face. Two mind-numbing months of the speed trap and refencing cattle and ticketing runners of Coomey's single red light.

He squatted and tamped the top back on the can. Beside him he heard the hollow *tunk-tunk* of a basketball on the sidewalk.

"Chief," B.J. said, hugging the basketball to his stomach.

I got a warrant. Open up that fly and let me see your erection. But the artist couldn't have been the shy, diffident B.J. "How's it going, son?"

B.J. held the basketball like a stuffed toy. "I buh-buh-been muh-muh-meaning to . . ." he began, hampered by emotion.

DeWitt's eyes narrowed.

The boy's face worked. A blush spread across his cheeks, darkening his umber face. "It muh-muh-me, Chief. The Torku left buh-because of me."

DeWitt rose from his crouch. When B.J. stepped back, DeWitt realized how threatening he must look. He turned to the sign. A yellow drip was bisecting the stick figure's leg.

"I never muh-meant to hurt anybody."

The drip continued down; it sliced through the black border to hang, a yellow teat, on the bottom edge.

"You were part of the rebellion, weren't you, B.J."

"Yes, suh-suh-sir. You gonna arrest me?"

DeWitt leaned his back against the squad car and stared at the long blue shadows on the library lawn. "No."

He propped his hands on his wide belt, again surprised to feel the presence of his gun. Two aimless months and DeWitt had begun to wonder what it would feel like to put the muzzle of his new Glock 9mm into his mouth, and if he could pull the trigger. It wasn't that he wanted to. It wasn't even that he believed he'd do it. But time and again the thought rumbled in his mind like approaching thunder.

"Muh-mama afraid I get in trouble. She say she expect more out of me than throwing gasoline bombs at the chief of police."

DeWitt nodded.

"It just that everybuh-buh-body just got into the mood of it, you know? And we was all real sure them Torku was killing us and putting germs in the well and all. Felt real ashamed when I learned the truth. Kept thinking as how them Torku never done us no harm." His face crumpled like brown tissue paper. He hugged the basketball tighter. "They never duh-done us no harm."

After an awkward moment DeWitt put the paint can on the floorboard, got into the squad car, and drove off, leaving B.J. on the sidewalk with his basketball: the statue of a sad god with the world in his arms.

DeWitt stopped behind a Department of Public Safety car parked at the curb. Across the vacant lot where the rec center had once stood, grass was already wearing its autumn tassels. In the center of the field stood Bo, facing the woods expectantly, hands clasped, head slightly cocked, as if waiting for a bus.

If the bus should come rumbling and swaying across the grass, Seresen driving, Loretta and Billy and their two kids in front, and Pastor Jimmy in back, DeWitt wondered if Bo would get in.

The officer had returned for the funeral. He looked strange in his DPS uniform, his sunglasses in his pocket, his guileless eyes sad. When DeWitt had gone up to shake his hand, Bo whispered, "My fault. My fault."

But it was Seresen's fault. And it was Jimmy's. Pastor Jimmy and his terrible fear of freedom.

Of all the bodies, his had been the most peaceful. DeWitt found him dressed in his Sunday best, the bottle of tranquilizers beside him, Doc's name printed on the label.

A mutter in DeWitt's mind, a gun-oil taste on his tongue. He lit a Marlboro and rolled down the window. Nothing moved but the heavy-headed, wind-tossed grass. A few blocks away he could hear the piercing shrieks of children's laughter. To the east a big dog gave a thick-chested bark.

Bo turned, started back to his car, but halted when he caught sight of DeWitt.

"Surprised to see you," DeWitt said, getting out. He dropped the butt of his cigarette to the asphalt and ground it out with his boot. They watched each over the hood.

"Came in to meet the Realtor. Wanted to see Hubert. A shame that the bank failed, anyway. He was the only friend I ever had." Bo's melancholy gaze wandered. "So. How are the reserve officers working out?"

"Fine. Don't need more than a couple of reserves. Not much happening anymore."

"Hubert told me it was your recommendation that got me the job with DPS. I suppose I should thank you for that." When DeWitt didn't respond, Bo went on: "He hasn't forgiven me for what I did to you. To Janet. Maybe it was senseless to come."

I forgive you, DeWitt wanted to tell him, but couldn't.

Bo's little-boy eyes returned to DeWitt's face. *I wish I could forgive myself*, they said.

"DeWitt? That bank robbery. Strange how it happened, the night after the Line went down. No fingerprints, no suspects. I read your report. I talked to Hubert, and . . ."

"Don't ask."

A pause, and then, like a promise, "No. I won't."

Bo walked away, tall, straight, and solitary. DeWitt got back in his car and drove home in the dwindling light.

The house was cluttered, the kids watching TV. DeWitt—a new habit—picked up some of the jumble and set it aright. He walked to the kitchen. It was empty. A pan of squash sat atop an extinguished burner. He got a spoon from the cabinet drawer and took a taste.

The powdery smell of Janet reached him before her arms did. As she hugged his waist, he stiffened. Her hands dropped. He turned in time to see the hurt in her face.

"Scared me." Simple answers had been better for Hattie, who liked her truth straight. But for Janet the lies went down easier, like oil.

She moved away. "Your daddy's here, out back with the barbecue. Your mama's sorting through the kids' school clothes."

He took a beer from the refrigerator and opened it, his back to her. His back was always to her now. Asleep, they kept their distance. Awake, they watched their tongues.

Outside, evening advanced. Lights began to come on in the neighboring houses. Beer in hand, DeWitt trudged across the yard toward the flickering orange glow of the fieldstone pit.

"Daddy?"

His father turned, and again DeWitt was surprised how much the man had aged. The plumb line of his back was bent now, the stick-wielding hands gnarled.

"How you doing, son?"

"Fine."

In the dying light, his daddy's eyes searched his. Then his daddy picked up the long fork and turned his attentions to the brisket. "Since you lost that weight back toward the end of summer, you seem different. Are things all right between you and Janet?"

DeWitt rubbed the tight muscles in the back of his neck. "She's tired of being tied down with the house. She wants to do things she's interested in. She doesn't keep the place as neat, but that's all right with me. It's okay, really." And he meant it.

The meat sizzled. His daddy prodded the brisket, nudged it this way and that. "You two seemed closer before. I wondered what went wrong."

"Just . . . some things happened."

"Bad things?"

"Pretty bad."

"Oh."

DeWitt gazed down into the red embers. Smoke rose: the fumey odor of charcoal, the sweet tang of barbecue sauce.

"Your ma and I had our ups and downs, too, Wittie. But we worked it out." His daddy's voice was stiff. Eyes locked on the coals, he fussed with the meat.

Certainly the other DeWitt and his daddy had joked together. In that other universe, they had laughed. Where was that happy policeman now? Where did he go? DeWitt had searched the cemetery a second time, and had finally found the tombstone marked WILLIAM HARPER. But he hadn't read the station records; hadn't the heart to disturb the grave of the DeWitt he'd replaced.

"Daddy? What would you think of a cop who had done something illegal?"

His daddy didn't look up, but the fork paused. "What kind of illegal we talking about?"

"Murder." The confession was out before he knew it, dropped like a lead weight from his tongue. He followed the law when he had done it, but in some other world he had murdered Billy. In this world, he had murdered Bo, and with each cold and angry look, he was killing a little more of Janet.

The gray head jerked up. "Cut it out, Wittie. Billy's hanging wasn't your fault."

In DeWitt's grip the beer can trembled, spouting foam. Curtis—maybe Hattie—had talked. His daddy's eyes were kind, but they were disenchanted, too, like a Jesus who has lost His faith.

DeWitt swayed, looked down. The grass needed mowing, he noticed.

Just a second, he'd say as his daddy handcuffed him. *Just a second and let me mow my yard. Let me paint my trim. Please let me fix the lock on the screen door like I've been meaning to.* So much needed finishing.

"I know it happened in your jail. I know you should have took his belt away; but you didn't. We all make mistakes."

The leaf can't escape the pattern of the tree. DeWitt would be the cause of Billy's death, always.

"Come on, son. His wife and kids killed in that house fire. Her folks taking the bodies up north so he couldn't even visit their graves. Then him arrested with a collection of women's underclothes. Billy didn't want to go through a trial for burglary. Sometimes a man knows when he's ready."

DeWitt sucked night air into his lungs. In his mind the thunder stilled. He lifted his head, his eyes misting. Patterns coalesced in the sky's spangled chaos: Orion, the Big Dipper. He saw the ruddy dot of Mars, where canals once existed because an astronomer believed.

Truth was so easy, really. It was order's lie that was hard. Flights of birds and stars and lives had patterns, if you stood back and looked at them right.

"Brisket's done," his daddy said. "You ready to go in?"

In the light of the kitchen doorway Janet waited, as she always had. As she always would. Because in the world DeWitt just this instant created, he placed her and renewed her there.

"I'm ready."

Ready. A satisfying word. It made the world feel as if life were a bag of groceries that had just been put away, and everything was in place.